# Soul-lights

# Soul-lights

Fiona Angwin

Priory Press

Published by Priory Press Ltd
The Priory, Abbots Way, Abbotswood,
Ballasalla, Isle of Man IM9 3EQ
www.priory-press.co.uk

First published 2012

ISBN 978 0 9551510 9 5

Edited and typeset by
Frances Hackeson Freelance Publishing Services,
Brinscall, Lancs
Printed in Great Britain by
Bell and Bain Ltd, Glasgow

# Acknowledgements

Nobody writes in a vacuum, and this book would not exist without the help of a number of people. First of all, my heartfelt thanks to my friend, Jeff Foster for his assistance in developing the students' characters, for having faith in the book and, of course, for the 'Sweariness Dictionary'. Also to the 'zoo gang' for their support while I was writing it ... have a read, TZ team ... you're in there! And to our wonderful god-daughter, Becky, for letting me borrow her name.

Thanks also to Linda Mann, my lovely publisher, Frances Hackeson, my brilliant editor, and Tina Betts, my patient literary agent. Also to Lucy Mann, our helpful reader come guinea pig ... I've always had a soft spot for guinea pigs! Last of all, eternal thanks to my patient husband and closest friend, Richard Angwin, for putting up with me when I get so caught up with writing that nothing else gets done!

# Chapter 1

Thren leaned over the side of the cathedral, looking down on the city with disgust. 'Major waste of time,' he thought. 'What on earth am I doing here – or, to be more precise – what am I doing here on earth? I mean, this is seriously not cool.'

He leaned further out, adjusting his position until only the tips of his toes rested on top of the battlements. The rest of his body was suspended in thin air, balanced at right angles to the building. He wondered what it would be like to fall. FALL ... now there was a word with a bit of meaning to it. He fluttered his wings softly to maintain his position.

'Like what did I do that was so bad? Cracked a couple of lousy jokes about the sheep is all, and *zap* – guardian duty. I don't know why He's so obsessed with them anyway. I mean, talk about being on a lower plane.'

Thren suddenly back-flipped, landing on both feet on the parapet wall. He tried to survey the city with something approaching interest, and failed. He supposed it was pretty, in a dull sort of way, with all the fancy buildings and flashing lights, but it wasn't a patch on Home.

'I guess it's time I got to work,' he thought gloomily. He stared downwards and started to look through the city; through the thick stone walls and the electric lights, through the noise and the colour – to see a different kind of light, a different kind of colour.

Glow-worm lights – that was how he thought of them, but given the mess that kind of thinking had just got him into, perhaps it was time to be a bit more positive.

The trouble was, being positive just wasn't Thren's thing. It wasn't in his nature. Even his name, Threnody, meant lament. He was just a downbeat sort of angel. Always had been. And now he was supposed to get all excited about helping these glow-worms, these sheep, these humans. Ugh!

The little lights he was watching weren't powered by electricity. They were soul-lights, very soft and fuzzy and all the colours of the rainbow. Just by looking at them Thren was supposed to be able to tell what state their owners were in, and who might be in need of his help. *'Like I care!'* But he was still struggling with the idea of these maggots having souls at all. 'I mean, they're so primitive they make ants look cultured, and at least insects know how to work together.'

He tried to remember what he'd learned about soul-lights and what the different colours meant, but he hadn't really paid attention at the time. 'Humans are *not* on my list of priorities,' he thought. Still, he'd have to make a bit of an effort now, or he'd be stuck here for good.

*Decisions, decisions.* He picked a light at random, it was small and golden and seemed to be flickering erratically. It was as good a place to start as any.

Next decision, to fly or to walk? He was supposed to draw as little attention to himself as possible, so flying was meant to be kept to a minimum, emergency use only, but that didn't make much sense when he was invisible anyway. Besides, he'd walked up all those steps to get onto the cathedral roof and his legs were tired. He hadn't got the hang of using his body in this heavy atmosphere yet – let's face it, he wasn't used to having a physical body at all. 'So who's going to know if I fly, right?'

Thren dived off the cathedral roof and flew steadily

towards the golden light he'd chosen. *Wham*. He hit the side of the building that housed that particular soul-light and thudded to the ground with a yelp of pain. He would have to learn. Just because he could see through buildings it didn't mean they weren't there, and he couldn't fly through walls. Open windows *yes,* brick walls *no.* Thren lay on the ground shaking with shock. The fall had hurt, the ankle he'd twisted on landing hurt and angels didn't do pain. He'd never experienced it before in his entire existence. "Are you okay?" It was a girl's voice, sounding concerned, and a bit nervous. "I saw you … fall."

Ouch, that word again. Thren plastered a weak smile on his face and stared up at the girl. This was *really* embarrassing. His first real encounter with a human, and here was he – a guardian angel – writhing on the floor while the maggot was doing the concerned, caring stuff. This was *totally* not right.

"Shall I help you up?" She reached out a hand, then had second thoughts about the offer. After all, this was someone she didn't know from Adam. Thren was just about to tell her that he *did* know Adam – personally – and it was no big deal, when he realised that he'd just read her mind. Was that supposed to happen?

"Do you want me to call an ambulance?" asked the girl. She was getting nervous. He could sense it. For a moment he saw the situation through her eyes. She'd just seen a guy with big, white, feathery wings try to fly through a wall, and fail, and now he was lying there staring up at her, without saying a word. And this, late at night, in a city full of creeps.

"No," said Thren quickly, "no ambulance, please. I'll be fine."

"You don't look fine," said the girl, relaxing a little. "Are you sure you don't want a hand?" She offered her hand, more confidently this time. Thren took it, and let her help him to his feet. He was beginning to recover from the shock of the fall and realised that he hadn't done any lasting damage, but how did humans cope with such vulnerable bodies? He tried to take a step away from the girl, only to discover that his injured ankle couldn't take his weight yet. He really did need her help.

"You'd better lean on me, till you get where you're going," said the girl. "By the way, where are you going?" She glanced nervously at the wall about fifteen feet above their heads. There was no sign of Thren's impact on it, but they both had a pretty good idea about where he'd made contact.

"Nowhere special," said Thren, which was true enough really. He was just trying to get the hang of the place. It wasn't as if he *had* to go and check out that golden soul-light. Not right now. "Perhaps I'd better just head for home," he finished.

"Where is home?"

"The cathedral," he replied automatically, then his realised his mistake. "I mean, close by the cathedral." After all, nobody really lived in a place like that, except him.

"Then I'll walk you home," offered the girl. "I live near there too."

"That sure is kind of you," said Thren, genuinely grateful for the offer. As soon as he recognised the emotion he felt ashamed. Grateful to a *human* – what was wrong with him tonight?

"I can't quite place your accent. Are you American?" she asked, as she settled his arm more comfortably round her shoulders, and started to help him along the road.

Thren winced, and not just because of his ankle. The accent was a sore point. When he'd been told he was stuck with guardian duty, he'd done a bit of research about Earth. Not enough, as it turned out. Not if the incidents with soul-lights and brick walls were anything to go by, but some. The trouble was, on being told he'd need to learn to speak English, he'd done all his research on America. After all, the place was huge, they spoke English there, and it was bound to be where they'd send him, right? Wrong.

He was stuck in jolly old England, but all his speech patterns were American. He even thought in American and he couldn't change that now. It was just something else that made him stand out in the crowd. Of course, the wings did that too. She hadn't even mentioned those yet. Maybe she hadn't noticed.

"I've moved around the States a bit," said Thren, belatedly remembering to reply to her question. "I guess my accent is from all over." It was true. He'd done a whistle-stop tour as part of his research. Talk about a waste of time.

Thren tried not to lean on the girl too hard as he hobbled towards the cathedral. He wondered if fluttering his wings a little would help take the weight off his bad ankle, but didn't dare try it. The less attention he drew to his wings the better. He was sure the girl had seen them, but if she was too polite to mention the matter, who was he to raise the subject?

"What's your name?" asked the girl after another awkward pause. "I'm Becky, but most people call me Bex." To Thren, swapping names with one of these creatures seemed much too personal, but he couldn't get out of it now.

"Thren," he answered tersely.

"That's unusual," said Bex, then added cautiously, "but then you are a bit ... different, aren't you?"

Thren wasn't sure whether she was referring to the flying, the wings or the accent, so he ignored the remark altogether.

Bex looked embarrassed. "Sorry, I didn't mean to offend you."

"I'm not offended," lied Thren. "I just don't see what you're getting at. What way different?"

"Well," said Bex, pausing under a streetlight and glancing sideways at him, "wings are a bit unusual. I mean, I've seen people with fancy dress wings before, but yours are real, aren't they? They even work."

"Hey, it's just an illusion, like in the movies," said Thren quickly. "In fact, that's what it's all about. That's what I'm doing here in Chester. I'm an actor, making a movie, and as for the flying, it's all done with mirrors."

"Then where are the film crew, and the cameras? If you were making a film there'd have been loads of people there."

"Would there?" asked Thren. "I mean, there would – if we were filming, like *actually* filming, like we will be soon. I was just practising, you know, like actors do. Doing the actor thing."

"You mean rehearsing?" queried Bex.

"Is that what you call it over here?" asked Thren, trying to sound casual, and flicking his shoulder-length golden hair back the way he imagined a movie star would.

"That's what actors call it everywhere," replied Bex, unimpressed. "So, what are you? No, don't tell me. I don't think I want to know. Things are weird enough already."

They turned off the road and went under the arch that led to the cathedral close. The medieval building loomed above them in the darkness, while soft lights shone from the windows of the houses surrounding the green.

"This'll do fine," said Thren. "I can manage the last bit on my own, thanks."

"Well, if you're sure," said Bex. "Where exactly did you say you lived?"

"I didn't," said Thren, determined to finish the conversation as quickly as possible. This girl was far too smart to hang around with.

"Okay," said Bex, resignedly, "but if you did need to find me I live just over there." She pointed to a little house nestling beside the cathedral, much less impressive than the other buildings around the green. "My father's one of

6

the canons at the cathedral." She gave Thren a penetrating look. "I know he'd love to meet you."

"Mutual, I'm sure, but I'm going to be way too busy practising ... I mean, rehearsing – for the movie. I don't get much of a social life. Still, thanks for your help. It's been great to meet you. Have a nice day ... I mean ... night." Thren's list of excuses and farewells ground to a halt, and he turned and limped away, walking past the entrance of the cathedral and into the shadows beyond it. All in all he thought he'd done pretty well. Pretending to be an actor. Neat. He should have thought of that before. Actors could explain away anything, and be forgiven anything come to that. Earth was weird.

Bex watched him go. She was certain he wasn't any kind of actor. He couldn't even lie convincingly. But the only other thing he might be was ... well, too strange to even put into words. She thought about pinching herself to check she wasn't in the middle of some kind of dream, but she didn't need to. She could still feel the ache in her shoulder from supporting Thren's weight.

'Funny,' she thought to herself, 'I never thought of angels being heavy.' As soon as she allowed herself to even *think* the word 'angel' she began to feel nervous. If Thren really was an angel, what was he doing here? Why had he spoken to her? What was going on? The whole idea was so strange that she couldn't really take it in. It was exciting, but scary too, and she started to shiver, as much from shock as from the cold.

She turned and walked up the path to her house, and let herself in quietly. She dumped her bag and coat in the shabby hall and put her head round the door of the sitting-room. Her father was dozing in an armchair, in front of the embers of a dying fire. It was February, and the nights were still cold. The TV was flickering in the corner, with the sound turned down, droning away to itself like bees in a hive.

Bex went to the kitchen and returned with a tray, laden with two mugs of hot chocolate and a plate of digestive biscuits.

"Dad, are you awake?" Dudley Collins opened his eyes and smiled at his daughter. Immediately his tired old face lit up with pleasure. Dudley had a delightful smile. It was one of the things people always noticed about him. Years of prayer and contemplation, coupled with parish work, had never turned him in on himself. He was always alert to the needs of others, and enjoyed their company. Most of all he loved to sit and talk with his beautiful daughter. Well, to him she was beautiful.

Other more critical eyes might have noticed that her dark brown hair was always untidy, her chin was dimpled and her nose not quite straight, turning up slightly at the end. She looked pleasant, and sensible, and kind, certainly, but not beautiful.

Dudley, however, was a firm believer in beauty being in the eye of the beholder, and he never ceased to thank God for the presence of Bex in his life. He and his late wife, Sheila, had never been blessed with children, and had finally come to terms with a childless existence. Then a baby had been dumped in the porch of the cathedral one autumn night and Sheila had been the one to find her. Of course, the authorities were called, and attempts made to trace the parents, but to no avail. Sheila was convinced that this abandoned scrap of life was God's gift to them both, and Dudley, though less certain at first, had backed her efforts to claim the right to foster the child.

Against all the odds, for they were both in their mid-forties and childless, the authorities had given in, and placed the child in their care. That, more than anything, convinced Dudley that Someone's hand was at work. It was easier to move mountains than cut through red tape like that. And here was this mysterious child, grown into a young woman, sitting at his feet, sipping hot chocolate.

"Dad," said Bex, cautiously, "do you believe in angels?"

"Of course, my dear. They're mentioned in the Bible often enough."

"But what about here and now? Would you believe in an angel if you saw one in the street?"

"If I was wise enough to recognise the being for what it was, then I hope I'd have the faith to believe in it." Dudley glanced at his daughter to see if she was teasing him, but she looked serious enough. In fact, much more serious than usual. "Why do you ask?"

"Well," Bex paused. She wanted to talk to her dad about this. She could usually tell him about anything, but how could she explain what she thought she'd seen tonight?

"Go on," said Dudley. "You can't start a conversation like that and then leave me guessing. It's not fair."

So she told him, and he listened, nodding and smiling not at her but with her, and when she'd finished he said "I can't think of any other explanation."

"But he's hopeless," Bex pointed out. "I thought guardian angels were supposed to be –"

"Perfect?" finished Dudley.

"Exactly," said Bex. "And this one's incompetent. Letting me see him, crashing into the wall, hurting himself, and then making up stupid stories and thinking I'd believe him."

"Maybe he's new," said Dudley. "Everyone has to learn."

"Even angels?" asked Bex, incredulous.

"Why not?" replied Dudley. "Are there any more of those biscuits?"

***

High above the cathedral, wings fluttered, dark and heavy, and a satisfied sigh drifted through the night air. The rules had been broken – an angel had revealed himself unnecessarily to a mortal, so it was only fair that another 'invisible' would have the same chance. Mischief was about to begin.

Thren was back on the roof of the cathedral, and not by way of the stairs. He'd waited until Bex had entered the house and shut the door behind her, then he'd twitched his wings and flown up. It was a relief to take the weight off his injured ankle, so once on the roof he hovered a few inches above the slates and went back to surveying the city. None of the soul-lights he could see attracted him. He looked over at the house Bex had entered, but could only see one soul-light – a flicker of almost pure white, but slightly transparent which he seemed to remember was something to do with age. Her father's perhaps? So where was Bex's light, and what colour was it? He was alarmed to realise that she didn't seem to have one, but then everything about his first encounter with a human had unsettled him. Nothing had gone according to plan. Leaving aside his unpleasant experience with the wall, which could conceivably have been his own mistake, how did you explain the rest of it?

Should she have been able to see him? Should he have been able to read her mind for the first couple of minutes? What about the wings? If everyone noticed those, life was going to be tricky. And *she'd* helped *him*, which was not the way round it was supposed to be, for sure.

It made his skin creep to think that he owed anything to one of the sheep. Although, as humans went, the girl didn't seem that bad, he'd hated having to put his arm round her shoulders on the way back to the cathedral. He'd actually had to touch her. Ugh!

'I mean,' mused Thren, 'Angels are just not touchy-feely creatures, even amongst themselves, while humans always seem to be holding or hitting each other. All those mixed emotions churning around inside them, looking for ways to be expressed. So primitive.' He hoped all his contacts with humans weren't going to be so physical. Not for the first time he wished he'd paid more attention to his guardianship training while he'd had the chance. Now he was going to learn the hard way. He looked at Bex's house again. Still just the one soul-light. Maybe something was wrong. Not that it was his problem – with so many souls to look after, it wasn't as if you were actually expected to care about any one of them, right? You just did your best for the whole flock of them, in a general sort of way, and let them get on with it. That was going to be tough enough. If he were expected to be concerned about any of them individually that would be too much. Way too gross. 'So why doesn't Bex have a soul-light?' he muttered.

"She does," said a voice just above Thren's left shoulder. Thren spun round to see another angel hovering behind and above him. "It's just that you can't see it because it's none of your business." The angel fluttered her immaculate white wings and touched down. Having placed her delicate feet on the roof she was below Thren, but still managed to look down her nose at him. Quite a feat when he was a good four inches taller than she was, *and* floating just above the roof.

"What do you mean, none of my business?" said Thren, feeling strangely insulted. "I'm the guardian angel for this city – it's all my business."

"You really are ignorant, aren't you?" said the second angel. "Surely you had some training before you came down?"

"My Come Down was kinda sudden," said Thren, embarrassed. "I didn't have time for a whole lot of training."

"So it would seem."

The other angel settled into a sitting position on the parapet wall and smoothed her long golden hair with one hand. Thren didn't know why she bothered – she looked the kind of angel who never had a hair out of place, even in the middle of a whirlwind. She beckoned Thren to join her. The assumption that he would annoyed him. In fact everything about this trespassing angel annoyed him, from her cut-glass British accent to her graceful, confident movements, but most of all her smug air of superiority. That *really* wound him up.

"Who are you?" he demanded, determined not to take the seat she'd offered.

"I'm Mentor, but I'm usually addressed as Tor. I'm Bex's guardian angel."

"What do you mean? I'm the guardian here." Thren wondered why he was sounding so indignant about a job he didn't even want.

"Over the city, and most of its inhabitants, certainly, but not over every single individual. Those with their own personal angels don't come under your protection. And since you don't have to take any responsibility for them, you don't need to see their soul-lights."

"That's why I thought Bex didn't have one?"

"Exactly," said Tor. "Her soul-light will always be invisible to you, for as long as she's under my protection."

"How long will that last?"

"For life," said Tor, with the air of someone who has all the time in the world, which was, of course, the case. "Bex's life, that is."

"*Hold the phone*," said Thren startled. "You mean, I have to try and look after a whole city full of these disgusting creatures, and you get to baby-sit just one?"

Tor nodded. "That is *so* not fair," raged Thren. "I mean, talk about a cushy number. *One* human to look after for all those years. Piece of cake. How hard can she be to protect, right? I've got hundreds of thousands of the things crawling around down there. I'll never get a moment's peace and you'll just sit around all day doing nothing, that it?"

"That does rather sum up the situation, yes," said Tor contentedly.

"Wanna swap?" said Thren with his most charming smile.

Tor was understandably not charmed. Thren had never been any good at relationships with other angels. Not that they had relationships the way humans did. Girl angels and boy angels did not 'date' or anything close, but most angels were capable of forming strong bonds with others on an equal basis – the equivalent of human friendships, though these did tend to last longer, on account of angels being immortal. Thren, however, did not do friends, or charm, or consideration, and had consequently led a rather solitary existence up to now.

"I would never swap," said Tor. "I couldn't."

"Scared of breaking the rules, are you?"

"No," she replied. "I just couldn't bear to. I'm too fond of her."

"Run that by me again," said Thren. "Did you say *fond*? Of one of those creepy-crawly lesser being things?"

"That's right," said Tor. "And I certainly wouldn't put her in your hands with an attitude like that. In fact, I'm amazed you're on guardian duty at all. I wouldn't have selected you for it. For that matter, I'm surprised you chose to take up the post."

"I didn't," said Thren, defiantly. "I was sent down as a punishment."

"That explains everything," said Tor. "Except, of course, your total inability to do the job. Do you realise that I've protected that girl since she was a baby, and she's never even caught a glimpse of me? She has no idea that I'm with her, or even that I exist. Whereas you, within hours of your arrival, have revealed your presence to someone who wasn't even in your care."

"It's okay. I told her I'm a movie actor," said Thren, still proud of his inventiveness. "She doesn't suspect a thing."

"So why is she sitting talking to her father about guardian angels, even as we speak? My job will be much harder from now on."

"I'm sorry, but I still don't get it. If you've been doing

this guardian stuff for so long, how come you haven't moved up the ladder, been given more people to look after, got your own town, while me – Mr New Kid on the Block – I've got a whole city?"

"You really have no idea how this system works yet, have you?" said Tor calmly. "Oh well, you'll learn."

# Chapter 2

The next morning Thren looked down from the cathedral roof to see the city bustling about its business. Tor was gone, though she had given him a couple of useful tips, not so much to be helpful as to stop Thren from giving guardian angels a bad name.

For a start, he now knew what to do with the wings. Of course he'd always used his wings for flying, but nobody had told him before (or if they did he hadn't listened) that if he beat them at a certain frequency they set up such a disruption to the light pattern that he'd be almost invisible. Rather like the way you can't see the wings on a hummingbird when it's hovering in front of a flower. You just see a blur of movement. Well, with angel wings you didn't even get that. Just a very faint disturbance to the light, like a heat haze, around where the angel was standing. Most people wouldn't even notice it, and would look right through the angel, seeing whatever they expected to see. If an angel suddenly stopped beating their wings when they'd been using that frequency they'd still remain invisible for a few moments, until the light around them stopped vibrating, and the haze dispersed. However, if Thren did need to become visible he only needed to alter the frequency and the angle of the wing beats, allowing his body to be seen, while the wings remained a faint haze behind him. 'This is kinda cool,' he thought.

Armed with the confidence this knowledge gave him, Thren set out to get to grips with the city. He even walked down the stairs into the cathedral. (He'd found it difficult to fly and use the 'invisible' frequency at the same time.) He paused to absorb the glorious atmosphere in the building and felt a real tug of homesickness. Pushing the feeling aside he stepped out into the weak winter sunlight. Beating his wings suitably, he tried strutting up and down in front of the people hurrying around the green. It was working. None of them could see him. Terrific. He walked up to one elderly gentleman, who'd stopped to tie his shoelace, and pulled a face at him. A real Hall of Mirrors grimace. No reaction. This could be real fun.

Just then Bex came out of her house, walked down the path and waved at him, before heading for the archway. "Hi, Thren," she called out, before she disappeared from sight. Thren froze, horrified. She could see him, even with his wings beating. What was going on? He dodged the old gentleman, who'd been about to bump into him, and hurried after Bex.

"Hey, Bex, wait for me," he called. By the time he caught up she was walking along the road, heading away from the centre of the city. He strolled up beside her, trying to be casual, and making sure his wing beats were set to 'invisible' frequency. Bex stopped walking and looked at him.

"What are you doing?" she asked.

"Checking to see if you can still see me," said Thren, embarrassed. "You shouldn't be able to now I'm doing the wings right."

"Well, I can," said Bex firmly. "Though I wouldn't want to look at you for too long. All that flickering light is giving me a headache."

"Okay," said Thren, crossly. "Then don't look."

"Thanks, I won't," she replied, equally annoyed. "But it would be easier if you weren't here for me not to look at."

Bex knew she was being unreasonable, but she found

the whole situation so strange that she didn't know how to deal with it.

By the time Thren had worked his way through the tangled logic of that sentence, Bex was several paces ahead of him.

"Slow down," he called, running after her.

"Only if you tell me why you're following me around," she replied. "I mean, I think I know what you are, but I'm sure you're not meant to hang around me like this. It's embarrassing."

"I'm not meant to hang around *you* at all," snapped Thren, irritated. Well, nobody likes to be told they're an embarrassment, do they? "In fact, I'm supposed to hang around everyone but you. *You* do not rate my services; you are not on my list – you are off my radar – simple as that. Everyone else in the city, yes. You, no!"

Bex felt as if she'd been slapped in the face. One minute she thought she'd somehow earned herself her own personal guardian angel – embarrassing but quite flattering too, and the next she discovered that she hadn't. Worse – she was the only person in the city *not* to deserve the attentions of a guardian angel – if that's what Thren was. She wondered what she'd done wrong, but she didn't dare ask, it was too humiliating. She carried on walking.

Thren watched her go, wishing he knew a bit more about human body language. He thought it was supposed to tell you how they were feeling, but as with most of his training, he couldn't remember the details. However, he felt pretty sure that a bowed head, drooping shoulders and slightly dragging footsteps didn't suggest rapturous delight. He felt a twinge of something uncomfortable stir inside him as he watched Bex trudge along the road. Could it be guilt he was feeling? Whatever it was, it wasn't pleasant. And it wasn't fair. After all, being nice to humans wasn't part of the job. You didn't have to be sociable with them, just protect them from ... whatever. Thren was a bit vague about that part of the job too.

He looked around for someone to protect, but the sheep seemed to be going about their business much as usual. Even their soul-lights seemed to be the usual range of colours. He really must find out what the different shades meant. Since he couldn't see anyone requiring his immediate assistance he was left with three choices. He could explore the city, return to the cathedral or follow Bex. Of course, Tor would be really annoyed if he muscled in on her human, so what choice did he really have?

He followed Bex, keeping his distance this time. He was struggling with the idea of trying to understand and protect everyone in the city at once. Maybe if he could understand Bex a bit better, see her with some friends and get an angle on how humans behaved with each other, he'd feel easier about the job. After all, he needed to recognise the difference between teenagers just larking about and them getting into real trouble. He did remember being told teenagers were a major part of his responsibilities, and that even humans weren't very good at understanding them, so it sounded like dealing with them was going to be hard work.

Feeling smug at remembering at least some of his training, Thren followed Bex out of the city and on to a university campus. Bex greeted one or two people as she headed for class, but didn't turn round at any point, so was unaware of Thren's presence.

He followed her into a lecture hall and was relieved to see that no one else seemed to be aware of him either. Bex joined a boy sitting halfway back in the class, and got a file out of her bag. There followed a tedious hour where a middle-aged gentleman explained the principles of copper uptake in plant roots to a bunch of students who could think of nothing duller. The lecture over, the class splintered into small groups and made for other parts of the campus.

Still trying to avoid being seen by Bex, Thren walked behind her and the boy she'd sat with over to the canteen.

Three more students sitting at one of the wooden tables beckoned them over. Thren lurked behind a pillar, eavesdropping on their conversation.

"Hi, Bex, Tim."

"Hi, Nesta," Bex replied. "I thought you weren't in this morning."

"I mixed up the days. My new timetable's confusing."

Tim grinned. "Serves you right for changing courses mid-year."

"I had my reasons," said Nesta awkwardly. Thren noticed the girl had a bright yellow soul-light, but it dimmed for a moment.

"I thought you loved the Biology course," said Bex.

"Maybe at first," said Nesta, her soul-light getting even dimmer, "but it started to drive me crazy."

"Some lectures would drive anyone crazy," retorted Bex, still rattled after her encounter with Thren, "but we don't all chop and change like you. Not if we know what we want to do eventually."

"Get her," teased another girl. "Who's rattled your cage this morning, Bex?"

"Sorry," murmured Bex, with an apologetic look at Nesta. "I'm just in a funny mood today."

"That's all right," said Nesta, still subdued, but her soul-light brightened slightly.

"Well, I've got some news that will cheer everyone up," said the third girl. "Marty's having a party tonight. Just a small one. His parents are away so he thought he'd ask a few friends over. Do you want to come?"

Bex thought about the course work she'd planned to do that night and decided to ignore it. "Sure, Debbie, I'll come. Who else is going?"

"From our lot? You, me and Nesta. What about you, Tim?"

"Count me in," said Tim, "and you, Flint?"

Flint, a sullen young man, shrugged and said, "Why not,

got nothing better to do."

"Marty said anyone who wants to can stop over, so you won't have to worry about missing the last bus," said Nesta.

"T'rific" said Flint, without enthusiasm. "Is it bring a bottle?"

"And a couple of candles," said Debbie, grinning. "There's something Marty wants to try."

"Like burning the house down?" suggested Tim. "His parents will love that when they get back."

Thren gave up trying to follow their conversation, and observed their soul-lights instead. Debbie's was a soft pink, with flickers of orange in it. It seemed to grow and shrink with each turn in the conversation, depending on how interested she was. Tim's was a light green and fairly steady, Nesta's bright yellow and Flint's grey. Dark grey. "Something is *totally* not right with that boy," thought Thren. Even though he couldn't remember what the different colours meant he was pretty sure that dark grey couldn't be healthy. He wondered about warning Bex to give Flint a wide berth, then remembered that Bex wasn't his responsibility. Tor would not appreciate him butting in, that was for sure.

After a few more minutes the group broke up, heading off to their next set of lectures.

Thren, who'd been lectured out for one day, couldn't be bothered to follow any of them, but felt pretty satisfied with what he'd learned so far. He gathered they were all in their first year, enjoying the lack of restrictions which went with being free from school at last, but not really finding university quite as laid back as they'd hoped. Classes weren't so different from school really, except that they were expected to do their course work without being nagged. Nesta, Debbie and Tim were all living in the halls of residence, and that was where the difference really lay between school and university. They were experiencing life away from home for the first time, with the feeling of independence that can bring, but Thren sensed they weren't all finding it easy. Bex, though living at home with her father, was at least within walking distance of the campus, and included in everything.

It was Flint who seemed to be the odd one out. He was living at home with his parents, in a village some miles from the city, and didn't even have a car. Being tied to bus timetables didn't exactly fit in with a free and easy student life, making him a bit of an outsider.

Thren had studied their faces carefully, knowing he had to get over his 'all humans look the same' attitude. Maybe if he learned these five faces he'd start noticing the differences. Bex he could already recognise, and her friends didn't seem too difficult to tell apart. Tim had a cheerful, freckled face and curly brown hair. Nesta's hair was long and very dark, and she kept it plaited. She had slightly pointed, almost elf-like, ears and green eyes, and Thren thought that her smile was infectious. He found himself smiling when he looked at her. 'Cute chick,' he thought. Debbie, on the other hand, was more of a babe. As well as being well-built she had blonde hair and a slightly superior attitude. While the others all looked like they'd thrown on the first thing that came to hand that morning, Debbie was dressed to attract attention, and possibly pneumonia, given the time of year. Thren admired her style.

Which left Flint. Thren had to admit he would recognise him again. Easily. Flint had shoulder-length, wavy black hair, tied back in a pony-tail, and very dark brown eyes, but he rarely made eye contact with the others. His face was lean and fine-boned, and he could have been really handsome, if he didn't wear a permanent scowl. As it was he just looked like a sulky schoolboy. Not a happy bunny.

Thren noticed one other thing as the group left the canteen. Nesta took her chair with her, or to be more precise, Tim pushed it for her as she crossed the quad, the

21

wheels splashing through the puddles.

Thoughtfully, Thren left the university and made his way back towards the cathedral. As he reached town he noticed a very strange smell coming from one of the shops on the main street. The window was full of mottled yellow cheese, and although the aroma made Thren gag, he was determined to find out the attraction of the stuff, for the little store was packed with customers. There were tiny cubes of cheese to taste on top of the counter. Thren picked up a piece and put it in his mouth, realising too late that a piece of cheese apparently moving through the air of its own accord might attract considerable attention. Luckily in the crowded shop people were too busy to notice, so Thren was free to enjoy the flavour. That was some taste. Not that angels needed to eat, of course, but there was nothing in the rules to say that they couldn't. Not that Thren could remember anyway. After scooping up some more pieces of cheese when no one was looking, Thren left the cheese shop and walked further into the city thinking 'food-fest'. He checked out every food shop along the route, picking up little 'tasters' as he went along, deciding which foods he liked.

Pies and pasties were nice, and sandwiches and fizzy drinks, and cakes and ice cream, but the raw tripe he'd snatched from the butchers had been a bit disappointing. In fact, he was beginning to wonder if angels could chuck up. He was feeling very green.

Just then he saw two men fighting outside an old pub. Both their soul-lights were glowing redder and redder. One of them punched the other, sending him flying into the road, just as a car came speeding towards them. The soul-light of the one in the road turned icy-blue and flared up as the man realised the danger he was in. Thren leapt across the road into the path of the oncoming vehicle, putting out his hand to stop it.

The impact jarred Thren's arm and shoulder, but the car

stopped dead, a hand-shaped dent deforming its bonnet. The man in the road crawled to his feet and made it to the pavement, where the man who'd been thumping him a couple of minutes before supported him carefully into the pub. Their soul-lights had returned to normal.

'So red must mean anger,' thought Thren, nursing his injured arm, 'and ice-blue is fear. Well, that'll make it easier to know who needs my help in future, although at this rate I'm going to be in no fit state to help anybody. First the ankle, then the arm. This is *not* my idea of fun.'

Still feeling off-colour and aching all over, Thren headed back to the cathedral. After all, he reckoned he'd earned a rest. Thren walked under the archway and was about to cross the green when he noticed someone walking down the path from Bex's house. It was an elderly gentleman wearing black clothes and a clerical collar. Bex's father, Thren was sure of it, for there was the soft white soul-light that he'd seen the night before. Forgetting how vile he was feeling, Thren turned and followed the old man though the archway and into the city.

If Thren's first trip into town had been somewhat food-orientated, the second showed him a different side of the city. Bex's father was carrying a bag, but shopping was not on the agenda. Instead the old man was going up to various people who were sitting on the pavement. In each case he offered them some food from the bag, and made sure they knew the address of a local hostel where they could sleep that night. One or two of them turned nasty, shouting that they'd rather have the money, but most seemed grateful for the food, and the information. Bex's father obviously knew some of them quite well, for he sat on the pavement next to them and chatted for a while, like an old friend. When the bag was empty Thren followed the old man back to the cathedral precincts, where he disappeared into an office for what looked to be a very boring meeting. At that point Thren lost interest and climbed wearily up to the cathedral roof to lie down and rest.

Hidden by the parapet wall, Thren lay on the roof tiles and thought about what he'd seen. Bex's dad was obviously one of the good guys. 'Maybe that's what having a white soul-light means. All the impurities, like selfishness and greed, gradually melt away leaving the pure white light of goodness. Well, something like that anyway. This is kinda nice,' Thren thought, 'Lying here, soaking up the sunlight. I could even try the sleep thing. Humans do it all the time. And I do need to rest up. After all, I've got a party to go to tonight.'

Thren closed his eyes and slept, dreaming of Home. Memories drifted through his mind, the beauty of the place, the laughter, the sense of His presence, the joy of it all. His thoughts twisted in another direction, remembering larking about in guardianship classes, playing practical jokes on the angels who were teaching him, wondering why everyone else took it so seriously. Then the interview with Him, after Thren had made one too many jokes about humans, and His affection for them. If only he'd yelled at Thren, instead of looking so disappointed, it wouldn't have been quite so bad. Even in his sleep, Thren cringed, tossing and turning uncomfortably, muttering "No, don't send me there – I'm not ready – I don't know what to do." He woke with a start, glad the nightmare was over.

He didn't realise that the real nightmare was only just beginning. If he'd stayed awake that afternoon he might have seen trouble, in the form of a huge, dark-winged creature, invisible to human eyes, flying overhead in the direction of Marty's home. He might have been prepared for what was going to happen. He wasn't.

# Chapter 3

Bex was rooting through her rather limited wardrobe, trying to find something to wear for the party. Between her tiny clothing budget and the fact that her father was old-fashioned enough to prefer his daughter to be 'modestly dressed', which translated as being completely covered up, there wasn't much for Bex to choose from.

Usually she didn't mind. All through school she'd tried to resist the pressure from her friends to wear the 'right' clothes with the 'right' labels, especially since she knew her adopted parents couldn't afford that kind of stuff. Oh yes, she knew she was adopted, and where she'd been found. Both her parents were convinced it was better for her to know the truth as soon as she was old enough to understand it, so that she didn't have a horrible shock later, and feel that they'd deceived her over the years. Mostly she was fairly comfortable about her past, though she had spent a lot of time when she was younger wondering what her real parents were like. Now she was more mature she tried to dwell on it less. She knew she couldn't have had a warmer home to grow up in than the one Dudley and Sheila had made for her, or missed her 'real' mother more than she missed Sheila when cancer had carried her off so suddenly. Bex had chosen to study locally instead of going away to university, despite Dudley making it quite clear that he didn't expect her to stay at home just to keep him company.

All through her final years at school he'd emailed for prospectuses from universities across the country, and left them in her room as a way of indicating that she was free to make her own choice. Perversely she'd chosen to stay put. She couldn't bear to think of her dad living alone, without Sheila or herself to keep an eye on him. And she'd never regretted it until now. Even that slight feeling of being on the outside at university, because she was one of the few students living at home, hadn't bothered her. She really did enjoy her father's company, knew that staying at home saved money (always in short supply in her family) and could comfort herself with the knowledge that she was being a good daughter.

Well, enough was enough. She'd been a good girl, a good student, a good daughter for years and where did it get her? According to Thren she was the one person in the whole of Chester not to merit a guardian angel. Not that she actually wanted one, but, still, being told she didn't rate one was a bit of a downer. It appeared she'd slipped up somewhere in her life and didn't even know about it, which was really unfair. She felt as if all the things she'd believed in, and thought she'd understood, had suddenly been snatched away from her. As if the world had turned upside down, leaving her spinning like an astronaut in free fall.

Well, if she was so bad, perhaps she should dress bad. Bex discovered that if she approached even her unpromising wardrobe in this mood she could find something suitable to wear to Marty's party. Or rather, something her father would think was unsuitable, not that it was him she was rebelling against. It was everything, especially the fact that being good didn't seem to get you anywhere.

Of course, the scissors helped. Ignoring the fact that they would quickly fray and have to be thrown away, Bex cropped one of her tops and shortened a skirt in radical fashion. Finding she'd cut it at an angle by accident she went the whole hog and chopped off even more on the slant, leaving it just above the knee on one side and barely covering the hip on the other. She tried it on and looked in the mirror. It looked cool. Given it was February it looked freezing. Terrified that it made her look fat, and since she wasn't used to exposing her legs to the elements she hunted in her chest of drawers for a pair of leggings, which looked surprisingly okay with the rest of the outfit. Then she applied make-up, in quantities she hadn't used since her Goth phase, back-combed her hair and sprayed it with glitter left over from Christmas. She surveyed the result. She looked like a different person, which was just what she wanted to be.

After raiding the cupboard under the sink for candles, Bex set off for the party, not noticing that Thren was tailing her. At least he thought it was her, though her transformation had confused him momentarily. He wondered if everyone going to the party would be wearing fancy dress.

Apart from calling into an off-licence to buy a bottle of vodka (Bex usually played safe and stuck to wine but tonight was not a playing safe night), she went straight to Marty's house, which turned out to be close by the campus.

Bex was the first to arrive, and wished she'd timed it to get there a bit later. Worse still, when the others did turn up almost everyone else had decided to come casual, which made her feel ridiculous. She poured herself a vodka and orange and tried to get in the party mood.

It wasn't long before Tim and Nesta appeared, with Sarah and Cath, a couple of other students who lived on campus. Flint slouched in with them, the only one of the five to make an effort with his appearance. Since he hadn't had time to go home and change he'd raided the costume store at uni. He was studying Drama, so had access to the place. He'd chosen one of those big, white, period shirts with full sleeves, and a crimson waistcoat, and looked quite striking, but completely out of place. It made Bex feel better just to know she wasn't the only one who'd picked the wrong outfit.

Debbie was the last to arrive and she looked – just perfect, Bex thought. Glamorous but restrained, in a dress that must have cost more than the average student loan. Bex glanced down at her own hacked-up clothing and winced. Perhaps she could avoid being in the same room as Debbie all evening, so people didn't make comparisons. She could hide somewhere, under the stairs maybe. In the dark. That would do it.

Thren watched through the window as the party warmed up. Marty was a plain-looking young man, with a pleasant manner, and short blond hair. He was wearing a black t-shirt and chinos, and his soul-light was amber. The gathering was small. Just a dozen guests and Marty, who was busy for the first hour or so, making sure the others had enough to eat (well, there were crisps) and to drink (a wide selection). The students sat around chatting and arguing about the music they were listening to.

Listening to their conversation Thren gathered that the two girls who'd turned up with Nesta were both on the English course. Sarah was plump and lively, with frizzy fair hair and dimples. Her eyes were light brown and her soul-light was the palest pink Thren had ever come across. Cath, on the other hand, was tall and thin and very neat. Her clothes were smart, by student standards, without being showy like Debbie's. Her hair, her eyes and even her soul-light were brown. Thren didn't take to her – she reminded him of all the teachers he'd ever had, and he hadn't liked any of them. He hated being told what to do.

Sarah moved over to sit near the window, a glass of wine in her hand. Her earlier enthusiasm had evaporated and she seemed sad, but Thren had no idea why. This was supposed to be a party. Humans were supposed to enjoy parties. A boy moved nervously towards Sarah, and stood awkwardly looking down at her. His ran his hand nervously through his spiky hair, and cleared his throat, his yellow soul-light flickering.

"You've got a face like a wet weekend, Sarah," said the boy. "What's up?"

"Oh, hi, Graham. It's nothing really, I'm just being silly."

"Want to talk about it? It might help." Thren could sense that Graham really wanted an excuse to talk to her, but felt guilty about capitalising on her unhappiness.

'I'm getting real good at understanding these humans,' thought Thren smugly.

"Promise you won't laugh?" Sarah moved over so Graham could sit beside her.

"I promise," said Graham solemnly.

"Well you know we've been away from home for nearly six months now."

"Yes."

"And we're stuck in rooms on our own most of the time."

"Yes." Graham leaned forward hopefully, his heart beating a little faster, and his soul-light flickering wildly.

"I really miss my pet rabbit."

Graham laughed. Sarah glared at him and stood up.

"I'm sorry," Graham tried to apologise. "I didn't mean …" But it was too late, Sarah was already walking away.

'Okay, I take it back, I don't understand humans at all,' thought Thren, bewildered. 'And I'm not sure I want to.' He glanced round the room – everyone was talking, except Flint, who was staring at his mobile phone in horror. Thren guessed he'd just received a text message, but he wasn't near enough to read it.

"Shit!" Flint swore softly as he shoved the phone back in his pocket and glared at the others in turn. They didn't seem to notice. Flint went and poured himself another drink. A girl called Joanna moved over to talk to him, but

Flint didn't seem that interested. Thren couldn't think why not – the girl was beautiful, with her long blonde hair and gorgeous figure. Her blue soul-light brightened when Flint talked to her, and dimmed as he turned away.

"Hey, Flint, what's up?" said Joanna, "This is a party, we're supposed to be enjoying ourselves."

"Yeah, right, I'm having so much fun," he replied.

"Then why don't we jack this in and go into town?"

"I'm not in the mood, okay?" Joanna, offended, turned and headed for Graham, still sitting on his own where Sarah had left him.

***

'This is *not* a happening party.' Thren was bored, and decided he might as well move on. Just as he was leaving Marty called for silence.

"You may be wondering why I've invited you all here tonight," said Marty, in a spoof horror voice. "I called you here to explore the fundamental mysteries of the Universe".

"Oh, get on with it," said Tim. "Tell us what this is all about."

"All right," said Marty, grinning, and reverting to his normal voice. "There's something I saw in a horror film, and I want to give it a go. Did you all bring candles?"

Within minutes Marty had the group organised. The thirteen of them sat on the floor in a big circle. They had each brought two candles, which were placed in a second, smaller circle within the first. Marty stuck the letters of the alphabet, scrawled on Post-it notes, onto the candles, one on each, and then got out an empty bottle and placed it on its side on the floor in the middle of the circle. Most of the group groaned. It was just a Ouija board set up, on a larger scale. A glorified kids' game. They never worked anyway; someone always cheated and wrote something silly. Still, it was Marty's party, and no one could be bothered to argue.

And the circle of candles did look strangely impressive when they were lit. Everyone, except Debbie, had brought the normal white household sort but hers were from a fancy shop in town, multi-coloured and carved into ornate pillars. Marty stuck a note with 'Yes' written on it onto one and 'No' on to the other. As that left them two candles short they scrapped the letters Z and Q. Then Tim put the ceiling lights out.

They drew lots to decide who'd get to spin the bottle first and Debbie won. She asked the predictably boring question, "Is anybody there?" and spun the bottle. When it stopped spinning it was pointing to the letter D.

"You see," said Tim, "completely random."

A few more students had a go, and got similar random letters. Even writing them all down in order, as Nesta had volunteered to do, all you got was DTGASNIG.

Then it was Bex's turn. At first she thought about refusing. She knew it was exactly the kind of thing her father would hate her doing, even in fun. The other students were looking at her; half-expecting her to pass up her go. After all, she was the only so-called Christian among them, the only one who could be said to believe in all of this stuff. Because the down side of believing in good was having to believe that there must be evil too. Or at least something other – not human. But hey, she was already a lost cause, according to Thren, so what did it matter? Fortified by the unusual amount of vodka she'd been drinking, Bex reached out to spin the bottle.

Thren suddenly found he could read her mind again, briefly. He sensed the doubt that their encounter and his stupid comments had cast over her and the rebellion she was now expressing – that she was open to anything, and it was all his fault. He wanted to reach out and grab her arm, but he was on the outside and it was too late. He leapt to the front door, which was slightly ajar, and let himself in. Perhaps he could still do something to stop all this, or Tor could. Where was she anyway? Bex was supposed to be her responsibility.

The bottle was spinning.

Marty called out, "Go on, Bex, ask your question."

"Who's there?" asked Bex. The bottle stopped, pointing to the letter M then moved again, *without being touched*, to stop at the letter E.

"M-E – me," said Nesta, shaken. The whole room was silent. They had all seen the bottle move of its own accord. Suddenly it didn't feel like a game any more. The bottle began to spin again, slowly pointing to one letter after another. Everyone's soul-light flickered, turning ice blue.

"Write it down, Nesta," whispered Debbie, urgently, as everyone called out the letters that the bottle indicated.

"What do they spell?" asked Marty nervously.

Nesta made sense of the string of letters and read them out. "Don't you want to ask me anything? I've come all this way to see you."

Thren tried to use the power of his mind to stop the bottle moving, and failed. The force that was manipulating it was too strong. He'd have to fling himself across the bottle to stop it. He tried to move forward but there seemed to be an invisible force blocking his path.

Tim called out, "Who have you come to see?" desperately hoping it wasn't him.

Letter by letter the bottle replied: BEX, OF COURSE. I'M HER GUARDIAN ANGEL.

Bex stared at the moving bottle, horrified. "No," she screamed. "I don't want you. Go away."

The bottle kept moving, spelling out more words: THAT'S NOT VERY NICE, IS IT? WON'T SOMEBODY INVITE ME IN?

No one moved. They were all thinking, 'If this is a trick, it's a really clever one, and if it isn't, I want out.' Well, not quite all. Flint, who'd been silent throughout the proceedings, suddenly reached forward and turned the bottle, pointing it at the 'Yes' candle.

"Go on," said Flint. "Come in, I dare you."

Suddenly the bottle shattered under Flint's hand, cutting into his palm. A moment later the candles in the circle guttered, and dark, choking smoke began to spiral up from each of them, even though the flames returned to burning steadily. The black cloud swirled round the room, casting strange shadows, and making the students cough and splutter. The movement was eerie, as if the particles formed a living creature, with a mind of its own. The circling mist seemed to split into long tendrils, which trailed around and between the students' heads, spinning and twisting, some of the smoky tentacles snaking across the faces of Bex and Flint, in particular, before rising up to the ceiling, where it hovered, completely still.

"That's that, then," said Marty, faintly, in the silence that fell as the coughing subsided.

"It's gone, whatever it was," said Tim, trying to sound confident.

"No it hasn't", whispered Sarah nervously. "What about the stuff up there?"

"That's just a bit of candle smoke. It's not even moving any more." Graham tried to sound reassuring, but failed.

Flint, picking the bits of glass out of his hand, said, "I knew whatever it was wouldn't have the guts to show itself face to face," though he didn't sound completely convinced.

"You were wrong then," said a harsh, disembodied voice. Bex looked up into the fog above them. It appeared to be coalescing, forming a thickening oval around a more translucent centre, and the denser part of it was moving, in sync with the creature's words, like a mouth. How could a pall of smoke have a mouth?

"Don't bother to look for me," said the voice, "I'll find *you*, when I'm ready." The cloud became even denser, then there was a whooshing sound, and it shot out of the room, through the front door that Thren had left open, and away. There was silence in the room for a couple of minutes.

"Do you think it's really gone now?" asked Nesta.

"I hope so," replied Marty. "Better put the candles out."

They all leaned forward, eager to blow the tiny flames out and get back to normal. Pretend the evening never happened. But some of the candles wouldn't blow out. They seemed to re-light of their own accord whenever they were snuffed. They weren't even the fancy cake variety that was supposed to act like that. They were ordinary, common or garden, keep them for power cuts, domestic candles. And despite blowing on them, snuffing them and smothering them with wet tea towels the candles kept burning until they scorched the letters stuck on to them. *Then* the candles went out.

Nobody wanted to be the first to say it, but there was a pattern to the candles that kept burning. Or at least to the letters that were stuck to them. The charred letters – the only charred letters – were F, L, I, N, T, and B, E, X.

# Chapter 4

The party broke up rather fast after that. Nobody could think of anything much to say, especially to Bex and Flint. Unusually for a student party, everyone mucked in with the clearing up, as if eradicating all trace of the party would make the weirdness of the evening disappear. Not that there was any real chance of that.

Marty looked round awkwardly and asked, "Does anyone want to stay the night?" He wasn't really surprised when nobody did. Even those students who'd planned to stay over had rapidly changed their minds. Tim took pity on Marty. "I don't think you should stay here on your own tonight, either. Why not come back to the halls with us? Sleep in my room." Marty nodded gratefully and within minutes the house was locked up and the students were walking towards the campus. For some reason they preferred to stay in a tight bunch, instead of straggling along at different speeds as they usually did.

Nesta asked Bex if she wanted to stay in her room that night, but Bex, now the buzz from the alcohol was wearing off, was feeling ashamed and embarrassed. She wanted to get away and be by herself to think. She had a horrible feeling that the game had only stopped being a game the moment *she'd* joined in. That she was responsible somehow and if anything horrible happened it would be her fault. The fact that the letters of her name were burnt had completely freaked her out.

As they reached the campus Bex peeled off from the group and started to head for home.

"You shouldn't walk home alone," called Tim.

"Not tonight," added Marty.

Flint, who hadn't said a word since the candles were put out, not even to arrange a place to stay, suddenly announced, "I'll walk her home," and set off after Bex. The others were surprised. Flint wasn't usually that helpful. In fact, it was rare for him to put himself out for anyone, unless he wanted something from them. However, it was a relief when he was out of sight. His complete silence since the 'game' ended had been oppressive, and with Bex and Flint gone the rest of the group suddenly relaxed a little.

Thren was torn. Apart from Bex, everyone in the group was supposed to be his responsibility. All the students were shaken up. He could tell from the behaviour of their soul-lights, which had reverted back to their usual colours but were pale and shaky. But Flint was his responsibility too, and as for Bex, that moment when he'd read the anguish in her mind had made him realise just how much he was to blame for what had happened.

He followed Bex and caught up with her at the same time that Flint did. Which meant Thren couldn't try to talk to her. Not just yet, anyhow. He hung back so that Bex couldn't see him, and walked silently behind them until they reached the cathedral close.

"Are you all right?" asked Bex as they stood at the end of the path to her house.

"No," said Flint. "You?"

"Not really," said Bex. "You'd better come in."

Thren watched through the window as Bex made them both some coffee, and fetched a blanket and couple of pillows so Flint could sleep on the sofa. They didn't talk much, but each seemed to take comfort from being in the presence of someone who was as scared and confused as they were themselves. Flint's soul-light had turned to a darker shade of grey, but flickers of ice blue appeared in it every few seconds. He was still frightened. Thren was very much afraid the boy was right to be.

*** 

When Thren landed on the cathedral roof he found Tor waiting for him. He was surprised to find he felt angry with her for leaving Bex in the lurch like that.

"Terrific," snarled Thren the moment he touched down. "You've only got one lousy human to look after, and you can't even be there when she really needs you. Where were you tonight? Why didn't you stop her? Call yourself a guardian angel? Boy, are *you* in the wrong job."

Thren paused for breath, and only then did he notice that Tor looked blazingly angry. 'Way too angry,' he thought, '… almost … dangerous.'

"How dare you," said Tor, all the more unnerving for keeping her voice soft and even. Thren wished she'd shout and get it over with. "You're the one who broke the rules, who let a human see you, quite unnecessarily. Who *chatted* to her on the way to university this morning. Who let her think she was the only unprotected soul in the whole city. Don't you dare lecture me!'

"So I made a mistake," mumbled Thren. "I didn't realise she'd take what I said the wrong way. And I did not; repeat not *let* her see me this morning. She just sees me – full stop – end of story."

"Then keep out of her way," said Tor. "Do you have any idea of the damage you've done?"

"Are you kidding? I was there, which is more than you were. I saw the whole thing, and let me tell you, even I was freaked out."

"You're pathetic," snapped Tor. "Do you want to know why I wasn't there? Because I went Home, to get advice. It's perfectly obvious you're a liability. I was trying to persuade the High Council to suspend your punishment and send you Home – before you destroy everything I've done here. I knew it was a risk, leaving Bex unprotected, but I didn't think that even you could cause this much trouble in one day. Also, I was seeking permission to appear to Bex, and explain who I am. To correct the damage you inflicted earlier."

"Actually, I think she's kinda off guardian angels at the moment. *Big* no-go area. Steer clear."

"So you think I should just walk away and leave her in this mess, do you?" said Tor, with a threatening glint in her eye.

"Well, no. I didn't exactly mean that, it's just that with me saying that I wasn't … hers, that is … and the *thing* tonight saying it was … hers – she might not know what to make of you. Right now. Maybe." Thren gulped. "Actually, maybe it's time I took a turn over the city. Checked to see if anyone else needs a hand. Like, that's my job, right?"

"Wonderful," said Tor. "*Now* you remember you have a job. So why didn't you do it in the first place, instead of interfering with mine?"

Thren took a step towards the parapet wall, and twitched his wings. Maybe he'd come back later, when Tor had cooled down.

"You're not going anywhere," said Tor. "You're going to stay here till we've decided what to do for the best."

"I don't have to take orders from you, I'm in charge round here. This is my city," said Thren, challengingly.

"You really haven't grasped the rules, have you? It is your city, but I'm in charge – of you, at any rate. In human terms, I outrank you."

"Yeah, right lady – and you base this status on *what*? Having one itsy bitsy little soul to look after. I think not. No way. Nix."

Thren stepped off the wall, and flicked his wings. Nothing happened – with his wings, that is. They didn't move. His body on the other hand, that was moving – very, very fast. Downwards. Either that or the ground was moving upwards, and it didn't matter which way round you chose to look at it, the result was going to be the same. Messy.

'And to think that only yesterday I was wondering what this would feel like,' thought Thren, with a small part of his mind that was still thinking about things. The rest of his mind was busy screaming *Help!* very loudly.

Suddenly he stopped falling. He was suspended in mid-air. He didn't need to look to know that it was Tor who had caught him, and was now towing him back up to the cathedral roof. She went a few feet higher than she needed to, then released him so that he dropped on to the roof with a thump that knocked the wind out of him.

"That was something else I arranged with the High Council while I was Home. I have the authority to ground you."

"Literally?" panted Thren. "You might have warned me. That was a pretty close call, and getting intimate with paving stones was *so* not on my list of thrilling things to do in Chester."

"Will you shut up and listen?" shouted Tor, exasperated. "We are facing a major crisis here, in case you hadn't realised. Your total disregard for the rules has enabled one of the 'invisibles' to break through into the physical realm. You've jeopardised the soul of the human entrusted to my care, and at least one of those that you're supposed to be responsible for, and all you can do is make silly jokes."

"That's because I'm scared. I don't know what else to do so I try to lighten things up."

"Lighten things up? Things will not 'lighten up' of their own accord, Thren. We have to work together on this." Tor suddenly stopped sounding off and looked at Thren. "Did you say scared?"

"Yes," said Thren, softly. "I couldn't stop it happening, Tor. I tried, but once that thing broke through it was too strong for me. We're angels. We're supposed to be able to tackle anything, right? Well, I couldn't tackle that, and I'm scared."

"What are you scared of?"

"I don't know. Failing, I suppose. Not doing the job right. Being sent back in disgrace. Not that I want to be here, but still, nobody wants to be a loser, right?"

"And that's all?" asked Tor, sadly.

"I guess," said Thren. He felt he'd given the wrong answer. He could sense Tor's disappointment in him but he didn't know what she wanted him to say. If he'd have known, he'd have said it, whether he meant it or not, because right now felt like a really bad time to rock the boat.

"What's with the soul-lights?" asked Thren, trying to think of something positive to say, something to make him look like he was taking an interest in his 'duties'.

"I get that red is anger and blue is fear and stuff, but it's like a rainbow down there. How am I supposed to know what the all the different colours mean?"

Tor sighed. "You really didn't listen at all during training, did you? A human's soul-light expresses something of that person's personality, so *of course* they're all different. Very dark colours can suggest a person has something troubling them, and pale ones can be a positive sign but most people's soul-lights are in the middle of the colour range, though they can change over time."

Thren grinned. "So if I see someone with a sky-blue pink soul-light with orange polka dots, what do I make of that?"

"A joke, obviously," snapped Tor, glaring at him. "All you ever do is joke." She turned away from him and stared out over the city.

"Am I being sent Home?" he asked, after an awkward silence.

"No," said Tor. "The High Council refused my request. They said that He'd chosen to send you here personally, and they couldn't interfere."

"He must *really* be mad at me," said Thren in awe.

"Besides, it's too late to send you back now. You've done too much damage, and I'm going to need your help to sort it out."

"Just how are we going to sort it out?" asked Thren nervously.

"God knows," said Tor. "Unfortunately, He hasn't told me."

# Chapter 5

The cloud of dark particles that was Dross hovered above Chester looking for something. He'd had to put aside his demon body when he'd been invited through into the physical realm and he really needed somewhere to take up residence while he developed his plans. Shell-less, it was too easy for the spirit to be dispersed over a few hours, its essence being scattered to the winds. As it was, Dross was having to use most of his energy just to hold himself together.

He needed a body and he needed it dead. Human would be ideal, but anything would do to tide him over. He could always swap later, if something more suitable turned up. He checked the hospital, but there was nothing there for him. Funeral homes and graveyards were out. He didn't want to be trapped in a coffin and he didn't want to be rotten, not for what he had planned. He lingered over a boy sleeping in a shop doorway, trying to keep out the cold by wrapping himself in newspapers. He looked fairly healthy, so he couldn't have been on the streets long. The boy tossed and turned, muttering in his sleep. He was obviously having some kind of a nightmare. If Dross decided to take over his body, it would be a nightmare he would never wake up from.

Dross was tempted. It wouldn't be too hard to finish him off and use the body, but the boy was only about fourteen or fifteen, too young to mix with the set Dross was interested in. Still, he might come back and have some fun with him later.

He moved towards the ring road, planning to follow one of the major routes out of the city till he found some roadkill to occupy. Not that he wanted to be stuck in a squashed hedgehog or a flattened badger but it was nearly dawn and he needed a refuge. Finding the right body would have to wait till the next night.

He'd barely left the city when he had his lucky break. Or somebody else's unlucky break. Brake failure, in fact. A car was accelerating away from the city when a young man came running out of a side street and carried on straight across the road. The driver of the car slammed his foot on the brake, and nothing happened. The driver tried to swerve, and the young man, suddenly realising the danger he was in, attempted to dodge too.

Misjudging it, the runner bounced off the front of the car, and soared across to the central reservation. His body landed draped over the metal safety rails, lifeless. Dross saw a soul-light drifting over the body, but he couldn't move quickly enough to catch it. Pity, but there'd be others. For the moment he had what he needed. He paused, watching the soul-light circle the body until it got its bearings, then it shot up into the night sky and disappeared.

The car had crashed into a tree on the grass verge, and the driver scrambled out. The man ran across to the body to see if he could help, but it was obvious that the pedestrian was dead. Stunned, the driver walked back to his car, and got his mobile off the seat. He phoned the police, and asked for an ambulance, just in case, but he was sure the runner was dead. He turned back to the scene of the accident and froze. The body hanging on the railings was beginning to move. First the arms twitched, then the head turned, and the back straightened until the figure was standing up. It looked at the driver with blank eyes.

"What's happening? I thought I'd killed you."

The runner shook his head, carefully, trying to bring the world into focus. "Just winded, that's all." His lips seemed strangely out of sync with the words coming out of his mouth.

"I've called an ambulance," said the driver.

"I don't need one." The words were coming out more clearly now, the lips moving at almost the same time. "You have it. Now, if you'll excuse me, I've got to go." The runner turned and started to walk towards the city. His legs seemed a little unsteady, but he was whistling cheerfully.

"But the police are on their way. They'll want to talk to you,' called the driver, then sat down on the grass verge before his legs buckled under him. He looked at the front of his car. That was definitely blood smeared across the bonnet.

***

Dross was pleased with his find. Apart from a few minor cuts and bruises and one big gash across his chest, the body had a broken neck and a fractured leg. As long as the demon concentrated on holding those damaged bits in the correct positions he could get about all right. It wouldn't be too difficult to get the eye and mouth movements right, and in every other respect the corpse was perfect. Right age – early twenties, right looks – extremely handsome, and *fresh*. Couldn't be fresher. All he needed now was a name, and a bit of practice at animating the creature, and he was all set. Time to have some fun.

# Chapter 6

When Bex woke up the next morning, there was a hammering in her head. 'Must be the vodka,' she thought. Then she realised that the hammering was being underscored by a soft tapping sound.

"Come in," she called blearily. Her father walked into the room, carrying a mug of tea, and set it down gently on her bedside table.

"Sorry to wake you up, my dear, but it's nearly half past eight. I thought you might have overslept," said Dudley.

"I did," said Bex, reaching for the tea gratefully. "I had some horrible dreams last night. I suppose that's why I slept so badly – and when I did finally drift off, I was so tired I didn't hear the alarm." In her half-awake state, and with a pounding, alcohol-induced headache, Bex was easily able to convince herself that the supernatural events of the night before had just been an unusually vivid nightmare.

"I hope you don't mind my mentioning it, Becky," said Dudley, "but there appears to be a body on the sofa."

Bex sat bolt upright. "B ... body?" she stammered, realising with a sinking feeling that the horror of the previous night hadn't been a dream after all. "Do you mean ... dead?" she asked. After the strange occurrences of the last couple of days anything seemed possible. Perhaps whatever they had *disturbed* last night had come after Flint and killed him.

"To the world," said Dudley, smiling, "He's out cold. I

didn't have the heart to wake him. Now look, you've spilt
your tea all over the bedclothes. I'll go and get a cloth."

A few minutes later the spilt tea was mopped up, Bex
was dressed, and Dudley was in the kitchen poaching some
eggs. He was worried. Bex wasn't usually so nervous. He
could tell she had a hangover but that wasn't what concerned him at the moment; nor did he mind her bringing a
university friend back to stay – but why was she so frightened? He could hear her in the front room, talking to her
friend. He resisted the temptation to eavesdrop, but he did
wish Bex would talk to him about whatever was troubling
her.

Perched on the sitting-room window sill, Thren had no
such qualms about eavesdropping. In fact, as far as he was
concerned, it was essential. After all, he needed to know
what was going on. Next to him sat Tor. They weren't
exactly on good terms but they'd called an uneasy truce,
since it was clear that they were going to have to work
together to try and untangle the mess.

"Look, Bex," Flint was saying, "It's no big deal. We just
all got a bit worked up last night. It was ... collective hys-
teria, that's all".

"So, you're not frightened any more?" asked Bex, beginning to feel less nervous herself.

"Frightened of what?" said Flint, putting his shoes on.
"Nothing really happened."

"I suppose not," said Bex, willing to be convinced.
Inside, they were both still scared, but perhaps pretending
nothing much had happened was the best way to deal with
it after all.

Just then Dudley called them through to the kitchen to
have some breakfast. Neither Bex nor Flint was hungry,
but Dudley insisted they had something before they went
to university. He was concerned to see that they were both
still very pale, and Flint's hands were shaking as he but-
tered his toast, but if they didn't want to tell him what was

wrong, he couldn't make them.

When Bex and Flint set off the truce between Thren and Tor broke down.

"Look," said Thren, "I gotta go with them. Flint is my responsibility."

"So is just about everyone else in this city," said Tor. "Isn't it about time you took some notice of other people? I can keep an eye on Flint while I'm watching Bex."

"*I'm* going to follow Flint, so I'll watch Bex for *you*," said Thren.

"No," snapped Tor, "I don't want you anywhere near her. You've done enough damage."

"But I gotta check on the other students," protested Thren.

"Nonsense," said Tor, in her most nannyish voice. "I'm quite capable of keeping an eye on all of them – especially since they'll be together for most of the day. I suggest you go and do something useful in some other part of the city, and do try not to make any more mistakes."

Thren was left sitting on the window sill as Tor took off to follow Bex and Flint to the campus.

"Great," said Thren sarcastically. "Back to looking after a city I don't like, full of people I don't understand. How come Tor gets all the cushy jobs? Eternity is *totally* not fair!"

***

Tor caught up with Bex and Flint as they reached the campus, and observed them and their friends for the rest of the morning. All the students who'd been at the party were rather quiet and edgy, but none of them seemed keen to talk about the night before. As far as Tor could see, they were all taking the same approach as Flint, and pretending nothing had happened.

Debbie, in particular, had developed a new interest, and seemed to have forgotten all about the party. She had her eye on a newly enrolled student, David, who'd joined the English course that morning. He was tall and good-looking, and Debbie wasn't the only person who was attracted to him. Bex, too, seemed to be interested, which Tor was rather pleased about. She didn't want Bex to get too involved with Flint, and as far as she was concerned the two of them spent far too much time together. Tor had disliked the moody, secretive Flint from the moment that Bex had met him. David, on the other hand, seemed pleasant, open and intelligent – just what Bex needed.

Tor wished she could see David's soul-light, just to see if it confirmed the good impression that the young man had made on her. Of course, just as Thren couldn't see Bex's soul-light because she wasn't his concern, the only soul-light Tor could see was Bex's. However, Tor considered herself to be a good judge of character, and she was delighted to see that David appeared to be as taken with Bex as she was with him. Tor decided to give the relationship as much help as she could.

It was Graham who first referred to the party, approaching Sarah with a clumsily wrapped parcel when she walked into the canteen at lunchtime.

"Here," he said, awkwardly, handing it to her, "It's to make up for last night."

"Oh, yeah, and what did you to get up to last night?" sniggered Sam, Graham's friend, coming over to join them.

"Nothing," Graham was embarrassed. Seeing him squirm, Mark hurried over. Mark and Sam did pretty much everything together, especially winding up their friends.

"Did big, brave Graham comfort scared, little Sarah after the spooky party?"

"Oh, grow up, boys," said Sarah dismissively, as she opened the parcel, "It's not like you weren't scared too."

"That was just an act," bluffed Mark.

"Yeah," agreed Sam, "we were just trying to freak you

guys out even more. It wasn't like there was really any-thing to be frightened of."

"It was just some stupid trick Marty set up," added Mark. "We knew it all along." "Though the smoke effects were pretty clever," Sam chipped in.

"Why a photo frame?" Sarah asked Graham, as she turned the gift round in her hands, looking at it with surprise.

"I thought you could put a photo of your ra–." Seeing that Mark and Sam were still standing there, Graham stopped mid-sentence. If they knew Sarah was homesick for a *rabbit* she'd never hear the end of it. "… of your family, or anything else you were missing … in it."

"Hoping she'll use it for a photo of you?" goaded Mark.

"Piss off," said Graham, knowing he'd never get any-where with Sarah while the Terrible Twins were hanging around.

Sam and Mark were both on the Biology course and had teamed up together within the first week of the September term. Although they didn't look alike, Sam being short with close-cropped ginger hair while Mark was tall and elegant, they been given the nickname within a few days and it had stuck. Getting bored with teasing Graham and Sarah, they wandered off to get some lunch, leaving the other two in peace.

"Thanks for the frame," Sarah smiled. "It's a nice thought."

Graham wandered if this was a good time to try asking her out, or if that would be a bit unsubtle. He realised that Sarah was looking at him curiously.

"How did you find time to go and buy this? We've had lectures all morning."

Graham panicked, and stupidly blurted out the truth. "I didn't buy it … I already had it … my mum gave it to me … it had a picture of her in it …"

Sarah looked disgusted. "You mean you threw out a picture of your own mother, just to try and impress me?"

"I didn't throw it out," he protested, "I pinned it to my notice board. I just thought you'd like the frame." Seeing the look Sarah was giving him he decided now was definitely not the time to ask for a date. "Oh, I give up," he finished, and walked away.

Sarah grinned as she watched Graham walking towards the food counter. If she wanted to go out with him it looked like she was going to have to do the asking. She tucked the frame carefully into her bag, and went to get some lunch. Tor sighed, and decided to leave them to it, thankful they weren't all her responsibility.

*** 

Thren, meanwhile, was taking a turn over the city. For the first time he flew high above it, looking down, taking in its ancient sites and modern buildings. The city had long since spread outside its old stone walls and Thren's responsibilities included the surrounding suburbs, the industrial estates to the south, and even the zoo to the north.

Since he couldn't see any call for his services in the city below him, and Tor had forbidden him to go to the campus, Thren decided to explore the zoo.

'After all,' he thought to himself, 'I deserve a bit of a break. I mean, it's not like I asked to come down to do this job, and even He took a holiday one time. Besides, it's just the kinda thing that'd really wind Tor up. She'd reckon it was irresponsible. Works for me!'

Thren flew over the zoo, feeling like a kid in a candy shop. He couldn't decide what to look at first. He swooped under the waterfall arch in the elephant enclosure, sending spray flying in all directions, and splashing not only the elephants but also their keeper. The man took off his cap, scratched his balding head and looked around, trying to work out which of his beloved animals was responsible for showering him. One of the younger elephants, Uphali, was swinging his trunk with pleasure. "Bloody teenager," muttered the keeper, as he returned to his work.

Thren criss-crossed the zoo, trying to dry out, and adjusting his wing beats to see which speed was the best for drying feathers. He discovered he could fly at a speed where his shadow was visible, even though he wasn't. He thought everyone would be much too busy to notice, but one of the keepers, a keen birdwatcher, spotted the shadow as it slid across the guanaco paddock. The young man looked up, eager to see what kind of bird was creating such a shadow, but there was nothing there. He rubbed his eyes and looked again.

He could definitely see a large, winged shadow moving back and forth across the paddock, but not the bird that was making it. He was about to radio through to the Bird Section, to ask if any of the condors could have escaped, but then thought better of it. Reporting an escaped bird was one thing, but radioing through about an escaped shadow was something else. The kind of something else that earned a lot of comments about how much alcohol you'd had the night before.

The guanaco paddock was next to a huge building labelled 'Twilight Zone'. Thren was intrigued, so he landed on the path and walked into the building. It was large, lined with rockwork up to the roof, and filled with jungle plants set around a pond. It took a few moments for Thren's eyes to adjust to the darkness, then he realised that the building was full of bats, fluttering and feeding on the fruit that had been put out for them on the trees. There were agile little bats fascinated by everything around them, and large impressive bats, that flew about high above people's heads with slow, steady wing beats.

Thren was delighted, and promptly decided to join them. He shot up to the top of the rockwork and soared through the air beside a very confused fruit bat. "Nice day, how ya doing?" said Thren to the bat. The bat, understandably, didn't reply. It came to rest next to a piece of watermelon, and made chattering noises to tell Thren to get lost.

Thren banked and swooped, taking one final turn about the building. He opened his wings to full stretch – and knocked someone off the top of the rockwork. It was another keeper, who'd been climbing up the rocks to put out more fruit for the bats. The man lost his footing and started to fall towards the stone pathway below. Two women in zoo uniform looked up from the path and froze.

Thren saw their soul-lights flicker with fear as their friend lost his balance and heard the smaller, dark-haired woman cry, "Oh no, I knew he'd fall one day."

The angel dived under the plummeting man, and flicked his wings upward, propelling the man back up into a safe position on the rocks. "You oughta be more careful," said a voice in the keeper's ear. "You really gotta get some safely equipment round here. I do not have time to hang around the place playing catch with you."

The keeper nervously ran his hand over his bearded chin, trying to make sense of what had just happened. "I'm going mad," he muttered to himself, "mad as a snake. How am I supposed to explain this to anyone?"

Thren was feeling so smug about having accomplished another successful rescue (even if it was him who'd caused the accident in the first place) that he didn't look where he was going. He flew lower than he meant to and crashed into a branch in the semi-darkness. The impact knocked him out of the air and he landed in the pond with an enormous splash.

The two women came running, but there was no sign of whatever had crashed into the pond. One of the women checked on some rather startled catfish, who usually led a very quiet existence, un-enlivened by falling angels. She had long, blonde hair, and Thren couldn't resist giving it a tug as she leaned over the water, so that she nearly over-balanced and fell in herself. The other woman searched round the pond to see what could have caused the splash, but all she could find were some damp footprints leading away from the pond and out of the building.

Thren, wet and bruised, decided to go home. He caused a localised shower as he flapped across the zoo, dripping on a presenter trying to give a talk about sea lions to the assembled visitors. Stoically, the woman kept talking in her soft, Scottish accent, hardly pausing in her speech as she enthused about Nemo, the male seal lion.

The angel swooped down to look over the shoulder of an artist who was sketching some wallabies. The woman flicked her long, dark hair out of her eyes and studied the animals closely. 'Kinda like me studying humans,' thought Thren, pleased with the idea. Her drawings captured the creatures perfectly, but as he leaned forward for a closer look, his wet feathers dripped onto the paper, ruining her work. She looked round, puzzled. It didn't seem to be raining on anyone else.

Just as Thren was about to leave the zoo he noticed a man dragging a little girl by the arm. The man's soul-light was a simmering red, while the girl's was green, flecked with gold, which turned to blue whenever the man shouted at her – which was often. Thren landed and squelched along behind them as they marched towards the giraffe enclosure.

The man was hauling the girl along as he told her off. "Now look, Amy," said the man, "I brought you here to cheer you up, and stop you whining, so just shut up and enjoy the animals."

"But I don't want to," protested the girl, who looked about nine years old. "Not today. I want to find Luke."

"Luke's gone," said the man, sharply, "and we're here. You've been pestering me to bring you to the zoo for weeks, and now I have, so will you stop moaning?"

"But I wanted you to bring Luke, too," said the child, starting to cry. "It's no fun without him."

The man raised his arm and cuffed the girl hard across the ear. She squealed with pain and tried to pull away from the man, but he was still holding on to her. He twisted her round until she was facing the giraffes, and whispered fiercely "Don't say another word, Amy, just look at the animals like a good girl, otherwise Daddy will take you straight home."

"You're not my daddy," shouted the girl, "you're just Harry!"

"Well, I'm all the daddy you've got, so you'd better start doing what I tell you to, or else," threatened the man.

Thren stood there helpless. He wanted to help, but couldn't think of anything he could do. 'This just ain't right,' he thought. 'The guy's a monster, treating a little kid like that. I really do not understand humans. If this is meant to be some kinda treat for the kid he's going about it all wrong. And I can't even step in and help. I mean, I could rescue the girl from a speeding car, or something, but not from her own father – or whatever he is. What the heck am I meant to do in a situation like this?'

Since Thren couldn't come up with an answer to his own question, he left the pair of them and flew back to the cathedral. He was surprised to find Tor waiting for him.

"Where have you been?" asked Tor, before he'd even landed, "And what on earth have you been doing? You look as if you've been swimming."

"Something like that," said Thren, trying to sound casual, "I've been saving someone's life. How about you? Shouldn't you be with Bex and the others?"

"No need, there's nothing to worry about, at the moment," said Tor, complacently. "It's just a normal day. They're hardly talking about last night at all. The boys don't want to admit they were frightened, and the girls are busy flirting with a new student."

"Maybe I'll just drop by the campus and see for myself," said Thren.

"Don't interfere," said Tor. "I've already told you, everything's fine."

Which just goes to show how wrong even an angel can be – because if Thren *had* gone to check out the campus, he might have noticed something odd about the new student who was getting on so well with Bex and her friends. Like the fact that the guy didn't have a soul-light.

# Chapter 7

Bex and David were sitting drinking coffee in the canteen in the middle of the afternoon. Not that they were alone; pretty much everyone who'd been at the party was with them, but somehow David made Bex feel like she was the only one there. She didn't realise he was also having this effect on all the other girls at the same time, and even the boys were really impressed with him, though they tried not to show it, as they talked interminably about cars.

"I hope McLaren gets its act together before the season starts," Tim was arguing, "otherwise it will be just like last year, with Red Bull winning every race."

Marty couldn't let that pass, "Why shouldn't they win if they've got the best cars? That's what Formula One is all about."

"Maybe," replied Tim, "but it gets boring. What's the point of watching the race if you always know who's going to win? Not that some of us will be able to watch the races live any more, not without shelling out for the Sports channel, and I can't afford it. I'll just have to settle for the highlights."

"You can always come round to my place to watch the races live," Marty offered.

"Your parents would love that – especially at six o'clock on a Sunday morning."

"Can't you talk about anything but cars?" interrupted Debbie, who was getting fed up.

"We're not talking about *cars*, we're talking about Grand Prix racing," protested Marty.

"Which is a completely different thing," added Tim. "The new season is about to begin and ..."

"So you keep telling us," interrupted Debbie, sarcastically, "and we're all very pleased for you. Now cut it out, you're boring David."

"Don't mind me," David replied, "I have rather a ... personal interest in cars myself."

David stood up to fetch himself another coffee. He asked who else wanted one, but only Marty said "Yes."

While David was queuing Debbie said to Bex, "Well, what do you think?"

"He's really nice," said Bex, struggling to take her eyes off him.

"Nice!" said Debbie. "He's a hunk, and he's mine, so stop making eyes at him."

"I wasn't," said Bex, indignantly, "but I'm not sure it's you he's interested in."

"Of course it's not," said Nesta, much to everyone's surprise. "It's me he's asked out this evening." Everyone turned to stare at her. "Not that I'm going to say yes," Nesta looked briefly at Tim, then looked away again. Everyone knew that Nesta had fallen for Tim almost as soon as they'd met. Everyone except Tim that is, who was trying to keep a long-distance relationship going with someone he'd been at school with. As far as Tim was concerned, Nesta was his best friend, nothing more, and Nesta didn't expect he'd ever feel anything else for her. Still, she couldn't help how she felt about him. Which meant she wasn't ready to go out with David, even if everyone else was drooling over him.

"I expect he only asked me to be kind, anyway," said Nesta, nervously. She felt uncomfortable with everyone staring at her like that.

"You said no?" Debbie was stunned.

"Not yet, but I will, once I get a minute on my own with him."

"I think you *should* go out with him," said Tim. "You ought to get out more, Nesta, and David seems like a really decent bloke."

The rest of the group glared at Tim as Nesta muttered some excuse about going to the library and wheeled herself away.

"What have I done?" asked Tim, puzzled.

Sarah looked up from her magazine. "If you don't know there's no point in us telling you." She turned to Joanna, "Listen to this – the weekend will see the start of a great romance, be sure to let your crush know how you are feeling!"

"*Your crush*? What rubbish are you reading?" Joanna grabbed the magazine, looked at the title and flung it on the table in disgust. "You're not still reading *that* are you? I gave up those things when I was fourteen."

"Besides," added Debbie, "everybody knows horoscopes are rubbish. You can't base your life on what they say is going to happen."

"You can if you *make* it happen," said Sarah, grinning.

"You're not going to ask David out, are you?" asked Joanna, concerned. At this rate she'd never get a look in.

"What makes you think it's David I fancy?" said Sarah, enjoying the speculation she was causing.

The mobile in Flint's pocket beeped, and he got it out to read a text message. He went pale, and looked round the other members of the group, suspiciously. "OK, who's doing this?" The others looked at him blankly.

"Who's doing what?" asked Bex, confused.

"Who's the tosser who's sending me these sodding texts?" No one answered.

Flint stormed out, and the others stared at each other in surprise. There was an embarrassed silence as David came back with the coffees. He carried them a little awkwardly, but no one noticed. As he sat down Marty said "Which uni have you transferred from, David? You never said."

David looked at him for a moment, then turned to include everybody. "Oh, I don't believe in looking back-wards, ever. I've come here 'cos I liked the look of the course, and I wanted to make a new start, so why talk about the past? Ugh, this coffee's bitter, it must have been stewing for hours. Sorry about that, Marty."

Marty tasted his coffee and pulled a face, but said politely, "That's all right David, it's not your fault." He carried on drinking it, so that David wouldn't think he was being too picky. Pulling a packet of cigarettes out of his pocket, Marty wished he could light one and take a long drag on it, to mask the taste of the coffee, but he couldn't smoke indoors, and didn't want to leave the group to go outside. Seeing the pack in his hand, Debbie glared at him – she hated him smoking.

Joanna nursed an almost cold cup of coffee in one hand, while with the other she absent-mindedly picked at the tender scabs where her latest piercing was just begin-ning to heal over. She caught David looking at her and blushed. She'd hoped he'd been interested in her and now she'd blown it. She tried fidgeting with her hair instead, but that wasn't any better. David turned away, and smiled at Sarah.

"Nesta said to tell you she's busy tonight," said Debbie, when she managed to catch David's eye, "But I'm free, if you're still looking for a date."

Marty choked on his coffee. He and Debbie had a kind of on/off relationship going. At the moment it was off, admittedly, but it was still a bit much to be expected to sit and watch her chatting up David.

Marty stood up to go, and David called after him. "Hey, Marty, you haven't finished your coffee. It wasn't that bad, surely?"

Politely, Marty turned, downed the rest of his coffee,

then left. Debbie carried on chatting to David as if nothing had happened, and after a couple of minutes David said to her, "Look, I didn't mean you to think of it as a date. I just asked Nesta if she fancied coming to the cinema with me. I hate watching films on my own, but if you're free, and you'd like to join me, then why not?"

Debbie smiled, satisfied, and Bex felt crushed. She'd been sure David was going to ask *her*. Bex was surprised at just how disappointed she felt. It wasn't like her to fall for someone the moment she met them. But then, she hadn't been behaving like herself for the last couple of days.

Debbie and David finished making their arrangements to meet that evening, and David stood up to go. He reached out to pick up his bag and accidentally knocked it to the floor. He cursed and was about to reach down for it when Tim dived under the table to collect the bag and the pieces of paper that had fallen out of it. One of them was a student enrolment form – for a Mr David Ross.

# Chapter 8

Blissfully unaware of what was happening at the university, Thren spent the afternoon with Dudley. The angel followed the old man out into the city, and watched him distributing more food to the homeless for an hour or so. After seeing how the man at the zoo had treated the little girl that morning, Thren found Dudley's generosity strangely reassuring.

Not that Thren expected much of these creatures but still, he reckoned taking your frustrations out on kids was pretty taboo in any culture. To see that some humans did have better qualities made him feel his job wasn't quite so pointless. After all, what's the point in trying to help beings that don't deserve it? But if there was some good in some of them ... maybe that's why He was so interested in these things. Well, not so much interested as obsessed.

Thren could sort of understand getting fond of one or two of the nicer ones, now he'd seen a few of them close up to compare them. It would be a bit like having a pet. But to worry about *all* of them? That was taking it too far. But the word at Home was that that's what He did. Thren gave up trying to understand it. All he knew was that he wouldn't do it that way.

If he had to make a choice in a crisis, he'd save someone decent, and let the rest suffer. Take that man at the zoo, the one with the kid. Thren certainly wouldn't mind if *he* suffered ... he wondered if there was anything in guardian angel duties that included punishing the little squirts if they got out of line. Maybe he could ask Tor.

Dudley's bag was almost empty when he found the boy in the doorway, the one that the demon had been interested in the night before. The boy was only fourteen, and obviously frightened. He must have run away from home pretty recently, but when Dudley suggested contacting his parents the boy panicked, and said he didn't have any. The old man gave the boy the last of the food he had with him, and talked to him reassuringly while he ate.

Then he offered to take the boy to the hostel for the homeless, so that at least he'd have a bed for the night. The boy was pathetically grateful, and it wasn't long before the two of them were walking along the road side by side with Thren following a little way behind them.

The hostel was in a rundown part of the city, but the people who ran it obviously made an effort to keep the building neat and cheerful. Dudley introduced the boy to one of the members of staff, who took him away to find a bed and settle him in. Then Dudley went into the office to say hello to the woman who ran the project. Though she was usually delighted to see him, today she didn't even smile when Dudley entered the office.

"Janet, what's the matter?" he asked, seeing how serious she was looking. She held out a letter for Dudley to read, and he scanned it quickly. "Notice to quit?" he said, looking up from the page.

"Yes," said Janet, "it arrived this morning. The landlord wants us out by the end of the month, so he can sell the block to a developer."

"But the hostel?" said Dudley. "Has he offered you anywhere else?"

"No, he hasn't," said Janet, leaning back in her chair. "Why should he? He never wanted it in the first place. He said it 'lowered the tone of the area,' but since nobody else would pay him rent for this dump of a building, he was prepared to take our money – while it suited him."

"Perhaps we can do something," said Dudley, trying to encourage her. "Perhaps we could go and speak to the council and get them to help."

"Perhaps," said Janet, but she obviously didn't feel very hopeful.

Thren left Dudley with Janet and returned to the cathedral. As far as he could see, people led very complicated lives. The old clergyman and the woman who ran the shelter didn't *need* to get so stressed about things. After all, it wasn't as if the place gave either of them a roof over their heads. And yet it was the very fact that they were concerned for others that made them people he was interested in – in a detached sort of way. Thren thought about what Tor had said; that she was fond of Bex. Thren couldn't imagine that at all. Taking a mild interest was one thing, but caring … oh no, that was *not* going to happen … not to him. He wasn't too bothered about his fellow angels and what happened to *them*, so getting attached to a human being was out of the question.

***

Looking down over the edge of the cathedral roof he saw Bex trudging up the path to her house. She looked tired, which was hardly surprising given how little sleep she'd had. She also looked fed up. As she settled down to type up some lecture notes, she couldn't help thinking about Debbie, and how she'd thrown herself at David, and right in front of Marty too. It wasn't fair. Bex didn't have a boyfriend, and she was sure David was interested in her, and then Debbie stepped in and hijacked him. Okay, they were only going to the cinema, but Bex liked movies too. Besides, once Debbie got her hooks into David, none of the rest of them would have a chance. Bex knew it was stupid to feel jealous, especially about someone she'd only just met, but she couldn't help it.

Thren hovered outside her bedroom window. Again he found he knew what she was thinking, but he didn't think it was the time to show himself. Tor would strangle him if he let Bex spot him again.

Bex stood up and walked over to the window to close the curtains against the winter darkness. Thren kicked his heels and soared up to the roof to stop her seeing him. He drifted down again a few minutes later. Good, there was still a thin gap he could look through. He opened his mind and tuned into her thoughts again. They were very jumbled. Her brain was like a butterfly, flitting from one idea to another. She kept coming back to David though, whoever he was. Thren decided he must be the new student Tor had mentioned. Then he noticed she was thinking about Flint too, and about a text message that had stressed him out in the canteen. Thren remembered the text that had troubled Flint at the party, and wandered what was going on. Not that it was any of his business.

Bex was still worrying about Flint. She didn't know what to make of him. 'Well, that makes two of us,' thought Thren. In Bex's mind, Flint was rather intriguing. He could be really friendly sometimes, but he had such a chip on his shoulder. There were moments when Bex just wanted to tell him to grow up. Not that she ever said it, but she wanted to. Thren decided she was on the right track. Of all the students, Flint was the one Thren had the most trouble understanding. He just couldn't figure him out, no way. Not that he'd tried that hard yet; there was nothing about Flint that made Thren want to make the effort.

Just then Tor appeared at Thren's shoulder, and started giving him an earful about muscling in on her human again.

"Okay, okay, I'm just going," said Thren. "Keep your wings on! I just want to know how she is."

"*She* is none of your business," snapped Tor, "whereas the other students, and the rest of the population of the city, are, so go and spy on them."

"Hey," said Thren, "I wasn't spying. You make me sound like some two-bit peeping Tom. I'm just taking an interest, is all."

"Well, take an interest in someone else," said Tor, raising her voice, "or I'll ground you again."

"Ground yourself," Thren shouted back.

The angels were so busy arguing that they didn't notice Bex pulling back the curtains and opening the window.

"Stop it, will you!' cried Bex, looking Thren directly in the eye. "You've made it clear you don't think I deserve your attention, so just go away and leave me alone. Stop hanging around outside my window shouting at me!"

"I wasn't shouting at you," said Thren. "I was shouting at her."

"Who?" asked Bex. "I can't see anyone except you."

"You may not be able to see her but believe me she's there."

"Who?" asked Bex, again.

"Your guardian ang–" Thren didn't finish the sentence. In fact, his face took on a rather squashed appearance as Tor clapped her hand firmly over his mouth.

Bex watched, as Thren appeared to shoot backwards, his arms and legs thrashing helplessly in the air. What she couldn't see was Tor, dragging him by the wings in an effort to get him away from Bex before he caused any more chaos.

Bex leaned her elbows on the window sill and sank her head in her hands. She couldn't work out what was going on. She was sure Thren had started to say the words "guardian angel" – a phrase that left her cold at the moment. Just hearing it made her think of the party, and the chilling voice that had seemed to come from the smoke that had hovered above them at the end of it. That had claimed to be her guardian angel too – and Bex was certain that she didn't want anything to do with the owner of that voice. But Thren had been talking about a female, Bex was sure of that, and the voice at the party had been male – hadn't it?

Suddenly Bex had an overwhelming urge to go and speak to her father about what had been going on. She knew he'd disapprove of what had happened at the party – worse, he'd be disappointed with her for joining in, but at least he might be able to help her make sense of things. She had a niggling doubt at the back of her mind that perhaps she was going out of it – her mind, that is. Perhaps she was going mad. That would explain everything, almost.

Just then she heard the phone ringing, and after a few moments Dudley hurried up the stairs and stuck his head round the door.

"I'm sorry, my dear, but that was Tim on the phone. Your friend Marty's been taken ill. He's just been rushed to hospital. Tim thought you'd want to know."

"Of course. Where's Tim now?"

"On his way to the hospital, he thought Marty might want someone there. I gather the boy's parents are away."

"Right, I'll go down there and join him," said Bex, grabbing a jumper off the back of her chair. "Has he phoned Debbie?"

"He didn't say," said Dudley, but Bex was already out of the room and halfway down the stairs.

# Chapter 9

Debbie was at the cinema with David, watching a horror film. It wasn't really her thing – especially after what had happened the night before – in fact, she'd be happy never to have anything to do with anything like that again. She wasn't sure horror was David's thing either. He certainly didn't seem that interested in the film. Debbie wondered if he'd only chosen it in the hope that she'd cling to him during the scary bits – which she was more than happy to do.

She held his hand, which felt surprisingly cold, and leaned against his shoulder. He was wearing an expensive aftershave, which Debbie rather liked, but underneath it was a smell she couldn't quite place, and definitely *didn't* like. For a moment, she wished it was Marty sitting next to her, then brushed the thought aside. She was sitting next to the best looking boy on her course – the one all the other girls fancied. Who in their right mind would want to swap him for boring old Marty?

She felt David's arm round her shoulders, and then his face against hers. He was trying to kiss her, but for some reason Debbie didn't feel like being kissed just then. Not in public, anyway. She turned her face away and pretended to be engrossed in the film. David sat back in his seat and waited. He could afford to wait, at least until they left the cinema. She was bound to kiss him sooner or later, and one long kiss was all he needed. Eventually the credits began to roll, and the audience started to shuffle out of the cinema.

Somehow Debbie and David found themselves at the back of the crowd of cinema-goers. The auditorium was still dimly lit and as they reached the doorway David suddenly swung Debbie towards him, wrapped his arms around her and leaned down to kiss her lips. He braced himself to concentrate all his energy on her. It was a long time since he'd tried this method of collecting soul-lights, but he was sure he still had the knack, and it attracted much less attention than murdering someone in public.

Just as his lips touched Debbie's, her mobile phone began to ring. It had been out of range in the centre of the building, but now they'd moved nearer the exit, it could just pick up a signal.

David cursed and released her, pretending not to notice how relieved she looked as she fumbled in her bag for the phone. She suddenly realised that she didn't want to kiss David after all. In fact, she didn't even want to walk home with him. For some reason she couldn't explain, he frightened her. She just wished Marty was there. She held the phone to her ear and heard Bex say "Debbie, can you get down to the hospital as soon as possible? Marty's here, he's asking for you. He's really ill, Debbie."

Debbie said she was on her way, then turned to David to explain what had happened. To her surprise he offered to go to the hospital with her, so the two of them set off to find a taxi.

Though he seemed calm enough on the outside, inside David was seething. If the phone had rung just thirty seconds later, he'd have completed the kiss and collected Debbie's soul. And what made it worse was that it was his own fault. He'd been in too much of a hurry to deal with two of them at once. But then he hadn't expected Marty to get sick so quickly. Usually the poison took longer to work. David hadn't expected Marty's soul to be ready for harvest for at least another four hours. Now one plan had counteracted the other. He almost shoved Debbie into the cab when they found one, but she was too shaken to notice. They were both desperate to get to the hospital quickly, but for very different reasons.

# Chapter 10

Up on the cathedral roof, where Tor had dragged him, Thren was still arguing with her.

"I wasn't making things worse, I was putting them right, *right*," he was protesting. "I mean, the whole problem started 'cos she thought she didn't have a guardian angel, and everyone else did."

"No, Thren, the whole problem started when you decided to have a little chat with a human. She's not supposed to be able to see you. She's not supposed to be able to see any of us."

"So? Is it my fault that she breaks all the rules?"

"She doesn't break them, Thren, she doesn't even know they exist. You, on the other hand, *do*, which means *you're* the one who's supposed to obey them. That's why He made them. If we angels deliberately, willingly, break the rules, then we upset the balance that He's trying to hold the world in. It gives the other side a chance to break through. For every rule we break, the demons can break one too. For every random, unnecessary contact we have with a human, they're allowed access too. That's how it works."

"But that thing last night, it made contact with a lot more than one person. That's not fair, right?"

"That's because demons cheat. They're bad, remember? Besides, the students invited it in."

"Can't we cheat too?", pleaded Thren. "It would make life way easier."

"No. We're supposed to be good. You do remember that, don't you? And angels don't cheat!" Tor paused, looking at him despairingly. "I can't believe we're even having this conversation. This is all so basic, even a cherub would know it."

"I guess I'm a bit rusty about what guardian angels can and can't do," said Thren, offended. "I mean, I am absolutely thrilled to have been given this job – *not*! In fact, I'm not going to do it any more. I didn't ask to come here, and I sure as heck didn't ask to have you breathing down my neck all the time, and pushing me about. You towed me along by my wings ... my *wings*, damn it. Look at my feathers! They may never be the same again ... and *that* when I was trying to help! Well, I'm not going to help any more. Not you, not them. Stupid sheep! Well, I'm no shepherd. I am *not* my brother's keeper. I don't even have a brother, and I'm not about to put myself out for a bunch of dumb *humans*!" Thren spat out the last word as if it was a swear word, which, in his terms, it was just then. He flew off the roof and fluttered around the green, finally coming to land on the window sill of one of the more imposing houses facing the cathedral.

The room was lit, and half a dozen men in clerical dress were sitting around a table talking. Thren would have moved again just to get away from human voices, but he couldn't think of anywhere else to go, so he just tuned them out.

He'd been sitting on the window sill for some time sulking, and thinking about how unfair life, or in his case immortality, was when he began to catch the odd sentence drifting out from the meeting behind him.

"Need a younger man," said a tall, thin member of the clergy, who the others addressed as Pearson.

"Too stuck in his ways," said another, backing him up.

"Surely not, Poole," said a gentle, middle-aged vicar.

"He doesn't know when to take a softly, softly approach,"

said Poole, a short, plump, smug sort of man. "Of course, he's a good man …"

"Of course," agreed Pearson, "but too outspoken … in the wrong sort of way. We need someone younger, trendier, more in keeping with the times."

"Absolutely," nodded Poole. "After all, he has earned his retirement."

Poole and Pearson seemed to be doing an effective job in steering the other four men around to their way of thinking. Thren, sitting on the window sill, began to feel sorry for whoever they were talking about. Not that he had much sympathy to spare. He was saving most of it for himself. Still, the clerical Mafia in there certainly had the knives out, and was getting ready to stick them into somebody. Not that it was his problem. He was out of it. Lying low. On strike. He'd washed his hands of the whole business.

Just then he felt a prickle up his spine as he caught the name of the man they were discussing. Some canon or other? Dudley Collins. Dudley? Bex's father!

Thren felt a wave of indignation washing over him. These callous cathedral crows were trying to get rid of that generous-spirited old man. Why, he was worth ten of any of them. Thren had a good mind to go in there and tell them so. Reveal himself in all his robed and feathered glory. That would make them rethink their ideas on the relevance of an old-fashioned approach. You can't get much more old-fashioned than an angel, guardian or otherwise.

He stopped himself just in time. Considering the trouble a little conversation with Bex had caused, he didn't dare guess what a confrontation with half a dozen clergymen might lead to, and didn't feel that now was the time to find out. He felt completely out of his depth, just as he had that morning when he'd seen the little girl at the zoo.

If he was meant to be able to help in complicated situations like these, he had no idea how. Of course, Tor could probably tell him, but that would mean asking for her help.

Boy, did that idea stick in Thren's throat. 'I mean, feeling sorry for one of the little sheep is one thing,' he thought, 'but doing something about it – especially when it means having to crawl to another angel – is not in my game plan. The old guy will just have to sort it out for himself.'

Thren sat on the window sill for another five minutes, then reluctantly he took off and headed back up to the cathedral roof, rehearsing various approaches in his head. He finally decided to go for a grovelling apology and a restrained request for help, but he didn't get the chance to say more than, "Look, Tor, there's something I gotta say ..."

It was at that point that Thren glanced over Tor's shoulder at the city, and realised that all hell had broken loose, from a soul-light point of view – and most of the soul-lights that were flickering dangerously looked familiar.

Thren took off, heading for the hospital. Tor turned to see what had sent Thren off in such a hurry, and saw Bex's soul-light, touched with streaks of icy blue. Tor, too, headed for the hospital.

# Chapter 11

They were gathered in the corridor outside the intensive care unit. Tim was holding Nesta's hand, as much for his own comfort as for hers. Bex had her arms round Debbie's shoulders, while Flint stood a few feet away, staring out of a window. David leaned against the wall, and looked at them all.

Here they were in one place – five of his potential 'targets' – and he couldn't do anything about it. Not just yet, anyway. Of course there were others. There had been thirteen people at the party, and he had worked out how to get to all of them, one by one.

The trouble was if you rushed things, like he had that night, they tended to go wrong. That was how he'd lost his chance with Debbie. But if you didn't rush them, well, it wasn't as if he had that long – a few days at the most. Then people would begin to smell a rat, or rather a corpse.

The door to the intensive care unit opened and a solemn-faced doctor came out. He looked round at Marty's friends.

"I'm afraid we're losing him. We've tried everything we can think of, but without knowing the cause of the illness, it's hard to apply the right treatment. He's regained consciousness but he's very weak."

"Can we see him?" asked Debbie, anxiously.

"He's asking for you," nodded the doctor, "but don't all go in together. You'll tire him, and I want him to save his strength. We'll give you a few minutes alone with him, but we won't be far away." The doctor pointed to the nearby nurses' station.

Tim glanced at Debbie. She was still trying to grasp the seriousness of the situation, so he stood up and moved towards the door. Inside the unit he found Marty lying on a bed with drips going into him, and leads linking him to the surrounding equipment.

"Looks like they're monitoring you more closely than Jenson Button's car."

"Great," said Marty weakly. "Fix some Pirelli tyres to the corners of this bed and I'll be off," but they both knew Marty wasn't going anywhere.

Tim tried to think of another Formula One joke, but his mind went blank, so he just listened to the messages the boy wanted passed on to his family, held Marty's hand and told him how much his friends wanted him to get better. When Marty had said his goodbyes to Tim, he asked if Debbie was there.

"Of course she is," said Tim. "She came as soon as she heard. I'll send her in." Tim stepped out into the corridor and beckoned Debbie towards him. Debbie nervously walked towards the door, Bex at her elbow to support her. Then David stepped forward, put his arm around Debbie's shoulders and led her into the room.

Bex stopped, surprised. David hardly knew Marty, it didn't seem right for him to be present at a time like this. Still, as Debbie's date for the evening, perhaps he did have the right to be there for her, regardless of how little he knew them all.

Debbie started to sob again when she saw Marty lying there. He opened his arms weakly, and she moved forward and gently laid her head on his shoulder. David stood back discreetly as Marty and Debbie talked softly.

"I'm sorry, Marty," wept Debbie, "really sorry. About David, I mean. I didn't mean to upset you, going out with him."

"You're a free agent," murmured Marty, smiling. "No strings, that's what we agreed."

"But there *are* strings," protested Debbie. "We both know that. You *do* know how much I care about you, don't you, Marty? That's why you've got to get better. So we can get back together. Here's me, just realising what you mean to me, and you go and–" she stopped, unable to complete the sentence.

"Die on you?" said Marty. "Sorry, Debbie, can't help it. Guess it's going to be a bit of a one-sided relationship from now on. I'd stick around if I could. You know that, don't you?"

Debbie could only nod, weakly. She couldn't bear to see him looking so frail. He'd always been so fit, so full of energy.

Suddenly, Marty's breathing started to fail, his eyes closed and the equipment around him started to beep and flutter. Debbie turned and ran out of the room to call for a doctor, a nurse, anyone, but there was no need. Two of the nurses were already hurrying towards the intensive care unit.

What nobody noticed was that when Debbie left the room, David remained. He knew he'd only have a moment before the place was full of medical staff, but that should be long enough. He watched the dying boy intently. There was a moment after Marty had stopped breathing and before the nurses arrived when something left his body and hung briefly in the air above it. It was Marty's soul-light, still amber, but now touched with glints of gold. David leapt forward and caught it in his hand, just before it shot upwards and out of his grasp forever. He shoved the soul-light into his mouth and swallowed. He felt the energy he'd captured surge through him, strengthening him as it did so.

The demon licked his lips, savouring the (literally)

sweet taste of success. He could almost feel the surprise of Marty's spirit as he hijacked it, preventing it from reaching its planned destination, and that added to his pleasure. This was what he had come for – souls. To be a soul-catcher was one of the highest ambitions of a demon, and he was one of the best. He put on a sorrowful expression as the medical team reached the room and attempted to revive Marty. They were unsuccessful, of course. After all, there was nothing to revive.

David slid out of the room, unnoticed by Marty's friends, who were too wrapped up in their grief to be aware of his departure. As he walked away down the corridor, whistling softly to himself, he glanced back over his shoulder at the remaining students, thinking, "One down, twelve to go."

# Chapter 12

Thren and Tor reached the hospital too late to help Marty. They stood in the intensive care unit looking down at his lifeless body, as the medical staff left the room.

"He was your responsibility," said Tor. "Perhaps if you'd done your job properly, instead of interfering in mine, he'd still be alive."

"Thanks," said Thren. "That's just what I need to hear. I *really* appreciate your support – like I'm not feeling bad enough right now."

Thren was horrified to realise that he was genuinely upset about Marty's death.

'I mean, what's *that* all about?' he thought to himself. 'Like, I hardly knew the guy, and anyway, he's a human. There are millions of the things crawling around down here. What's one more or less?'

But Thren wasn't fooling anyone, not even himself. He felt guilty. He hated to admit it, but Tor was right. Marty had been his responsibility, and Thren hadn't been there when the boy needed him.

"Still, you can't blame me for him getting sick, right?" said Thren, trying to make excuses for himself. "I mean, getting ill, it's natural; we're not meant to get involved in that kinda thing, right?"

Tor turned to him. He could tell from the look she gave him how much she despised him, and he stepped back a little in surprise.

"Don't you know anything?" she snapped. "There *are* times when we can interfere in an illness, but that's not the point. Marty wasn't ill, he was poisoned!"

Thren looked at her in amazement. "Just how can you tell that? You some kinda quack?" He grinned at Tor. "And I thought those wings meant you were an angel, not a duck." He knew the joke was lame, but he was trying to use it to push away the truth of what was happening – to stop himself feeling so bad.

Tor just glared at him, and then she turned and pointed at the body saying, "Shut up and look at him."

Thren did look, and noticed something strange, almost like a little grey cloud hovering just above the boy's stomach. Even as they watched it started to disperse.

"And that tells you he was poisoned?" asked Thren. "How do you know he didn't just eat something that made him sick to his stomach?"

"Then the cloud would be blue," said Tor, simply. "Those clouds are supposed to help us diagnose what's wrong so that we can help."

Thren sighed. "I sure wish these humans came with colour charts – this is all way too complicated for me. I've barely gotten the hang of soul-lights yet. Hey, hold on a minute … what happened to Marty's soul-light? I didn't see it go anywhere, and I was looking directly at the hospital all the way here."

"It should have ascended the moment that he died," said Tor, puzzled.

"Well, it didn't," said Thren. "I'd have seen it. It just … disappeared."

"It's been snatched," said Tor decisively. "A soul-catcher must have taken it … in which case …"

Suddenly Tor reached over and pressed the red emergency call button, then she leaned over Marty and kissed him full on the lips, breathing life back into him as she did so. After a moment a nurse walked in, looking rather confused. After all, the patient had been certified dead almost five minutes before. How could he possibly be pushing the call button? The nurse looked at the body, and saw Marty's chest rise and fall as Tor alternately breathed into his lungs and pressed the air back out by pushing down on his chest with her hands.

Thren was completely bewildered. "Tor, what are you doing? The boy's dead, his soul's gone. What's the point in reviving him? Do you want to turn him into some kinda zombie?"

"Can't talk now," gasped Tor, between breaths. "Take over here, I've got something else to do."

"You mean *kiss* the guy? On the lips?" said Thren, revolted.

"He's your responsibility. Take over!" ordered Tor, and Thren did. He continued to help Marty to breath while the nurse ran out of the room and came back with the full medical team. They couldn't understand what was happening or how, but their patient appeared to be breathing, and they were determined to keep it that way. A few seconds later Marty was wired up to the machines again. Thren stepped back, and when the doctors saw Marty stop breathing they rapidly put him on to a life support machine.

"Now will you tell me what you're doing?" demanded Thren, scrubbing his lips with the sleeve of his robe.

"Giving him a chance," said Tor. "Now shut up, I'm busy."

She went over to one of the doctors and appeared to whisper in his ear, then she moved to the next and did the same thing. Tor kept going until she had tried to communicate with each of the medical staff in turn.

"What's the point in that?" said Thren, when she'd finished. "None of them can hear you."

"Humans don't only hear with their ears. Sometimes you can speak to their minds or their hearts. Of course, they'll never realise where the idea you've given them came from, and they can choose to ignore it, but it's worth a try," said Tor, rather tiredly.

Suddenly one of the doctors picked up on the idea Tor had whispered to him. Another rushed to fetch a stomach pump while a third took another blood sample and went to phone the lab to have it analysed at once.

"What did you say to them?" asked Thren.

"Quite a lot, but it looks like all they picked up on was the word 'poison'. Still, that's enough. Come on, we've got work to do."

"But what about Marty? I can't leave him," protested Thren, as Tor took his arm and tried to lead him from the room.

"You can't help him by staying here, Thren. All we've done is buy him some time. The doctors can identify the poison and deal with it, now they know that's what caused the problem, but that won't do him any good unless we can get his soul back. He'll just stay in a coma indefinitely."

"Is that what happens when a soul is taken? The person goes into a coma?"

"It depends how it's taken," Tor explained patiently. "Marty was poisoned, and his soul taken after death. If he wasn't hooked up to all that equipment he wouldn't stand a chance. As it is, the doctors might be able to treat him for poisoning, and get his body functioning again …"

"But if we can't get his soul back?"

"He'll never revive."

They stepped out into the corridor, but the students were gone. They must have left when the doctors told them Marty was dead, so they didn't know their friend still had a fighting chance.

# Chapter 13

They were in Nesta's room in the halls of residence. Debbie was lying on Nesta's bed sobbing, and none of the others could think of anything to say that would console her.

Tim had his arm round Nesta and they were both trying not to cry, while Bex was attempting to make a pot of tea, but her eyes were blurred with tears. Flint was the only one who appeared to be unmoved, but he sat on the bed and held Debbie's hand, and tried not to flinch when she gripped his hand so hard that it hurt. She was so distressed she wasn't even aware she was causing him pain.

The tea made, they sat in silence drinking it. None of them knew what to say, but they still appreciated each other's presence. Just being together was a comfort.

There was a tap on the door, and they all looked at each other in surprise. It was two o'clock in the morning. Who'd call round at that time? Tim stood up and went to open the door. David was standing there, looking very composed, a slight smile on his lips.

"It's been quite a night, hasn't it?" said David. "May I join you? I thought Debbie might want cheering up."

Bex and Nesta looked at David, stunned. How could he be so tactless? What Debbie needed just then was Marty; 'cheering up' wasn't on the agenda, the situation was far too serious for that.

Flint spoke, for the first time in ages. "Well, Debbie, how do you feel? Do you want David to stay?"

Debbie shook her head, and moved slightly so that she was behind Flint. The uncomfortable feeling she'd started to have about David at the cinema was back with a vengeance. She didn't want him anywhere near her, especially just then.

David saw the repulsion in Debbie's eyes and cursed silently. If only he'd managed to kiss her earlier. Now he'd lost his chance. He noticed the whole group seemed to draw together, shutting him out. Flint stepped forward and spoke politely but firmly.

"I'm sorry, David, but Debbie's very tired and she'd like you to leave now."

David glared at Flint, but turned and walked away. He couldn't tackle them all at once, and he realised picking them off one by one would be more difficult from now on. He'd forgotten how seriously humans took life and death, and how much they needed each other's company to deal with grief. It would be hard to prise that little group apart for a few days. Still, they weren't the only names on his list. There had been other students at Marty's party. Students who didn't even know yet that their friend was dead. Perhaps it was time to tackle some of those, before they found out and it became harder to get them on their own.

They lived in the halls of residence too, so David checked each of their rooms in turn. He could tell by their soul-lights that most of them were asleep, but one of the girls, Joanna, was out, and Graham was still up, supposedly working.

David decided it was too late at night to wake the sleepers without making them suspicious, so he'd start with Graham. He savoured his plan to eliminate the other students and then go back and deal with Flint and Bex. It appealed to his sense of the dramatic to leave those two till last. They owed him that delicious pleasure, and once they realised what was going on they would feel more and more guilty, as one friend after another died at his hands. He liked the taste of guilt, it lingered in people's soul-light giving them a distinctive flavour. He was particularly looking forward to catching Flint's little grey soul-light. That was *full* of guilt, he could tell from the colour. David thought he and Flint would have a lot in common. After all, Flint was the one who'd invited him into the physical world in the first place. Flint liked living dangerously and danger was certainly what he was in, although living wasn't something he'd be doing much of in future. Not once David had finished with him. And as for Bex, she was the one who'd started the whole thing off. The one who could see angels. Strange, that.

David frowned – the others would have to wait, it was time to deal with Graham. David fetched a bottle of Southern Comfort from his room and knocked on Graham's door.

The young man opened it, and stared at David, trying to place him.

"Hi," said David. "I'm David ... David Ross. I saw you in class today. I've just started here, on the English course. My room's just down the corridor, and I saw your light was on, so I thought I'd drop by."

Before Graham could think of anything to say David had strolled into the room and sat down on the only chair.

Graham found himself sitting on the edge of the bed, looking at this almost total stranger with surprise.

"Actually," said Graham, "I can't talk right now. I'm supposed to be finishing this essay. It's due in tomorrow."

David glanced at the papers spread out on the table, dismissed them with a snort of laughter, and turned back to Graham.

"Running a bit late, aren't you?"

"Yes, well, I've got a bit behind on my work this term, but I've decided it's time I caught up," said Graham, not wanting to add that this was a new resolution, made after the shock of what had happened at Marty's party the previous night.

David smiled knowingly. "Too many parties and pub crawls, eh?"

"Something like that," said Graham. "Anyway, I want to get back on top of my course work, not waste any more time."

"Couldn't agree more," said David. "You can waste so much time going out boozing. Much better to buy a bottle and drink in your room." And he got out the bottle of Southern Comfort and placed it on the table. "Want some?"

"Thanks, but the essay ..." said Graham, looking longingly at the bottle.

"Can wait," said David firmly. "Why, the assignment's not even late yet, and how much more useful work are you going to get done at this time in the morning?"

Graham let himself be convinced fairly easily after that, and why not? He was an easy target. He'd slept very little after the party, spent the whole day trying to pretend he wasn't bothered about what had happened, messed up yet another chance to get together with Sarah, and approached his neglected course work at full pelt, trying to live up to his new resolution. He'd even skipped going to get some food that evening, so he could spend more time on his essay. He deserved a drink. At least that's what David kept telling him. In fact, David seemed to think he deserved several, which is why he kept topping his glass up.

Graham had always thought he had a pretty good head for alcohol, but tonight its effects on an empty stomach and tired brain were almost immediate. He could hear his speech starting to slur and feel his lips going numb.

"Sorry, David, I'm feeling a bit rough, let's just call it a night, okay?"

"Nonsense," said David. "All you need is a bit of fresh air. Let's go for a walk."

"But it's half past four in the morning," said Graham, with some difficulty, after glancing blearily at his watch. "We can't go for a walk now."

"Why not?" said David cheerily. "It's the best time of the day. Nice and peaceful, no traffic, lots of stars to look at." He put his arm round Graham's shoulders and half led, half dragged him out into the corridor.

David's broken body didn't find it easy, but, strengthened by Marty's soul-light, he managed to tow Graham out of the halls of residence and towards the city.

"Come along, Graham, time for a nice moonlit walk on the walls."

They passed under the massive arch of the Northgate, and turned to walk up the steps to the city walls.

"Put some effort into it, Graham, we're supposed to be going on a walk, not a crawl."

Graham, trying to cooperate, managed to climb the stone steps up onto the city walls.

"This way," said David, steering him along the walkway to the right.

Graham tried to stroll along beside his new friend, but his feet were determined to be disobedient, meandering off in all directions, so he had to let David guide him. There were a few shops opening onto the walls just there, but they were closed and locked at that time in the morning.

"Music shop," said Graham, eagerly, as they passed. "Second-hand books. Great place, you'll like it."

"I'm sure I will," said David, patiently, "but not at the moment, it's shut."

"Oh yes, of course," said Graham. "Silly of me," and they staggered on until they reached a corner. The walls and walkway carried on to their right, but ahead of them, built into and above the walls, was an old stone tower, with steps leading up to its doorway.

"See that tower," slurred Graham, "It's the King's … no … Charles's Tower. No. That can't be right … Prince

Charles ... not the king yet ... how can it be King Charles's anything? It's a tower anyway."

"So I see. Look, Graham," said David, pointing to the steps. "The view will be even better from up there." Graham nodded and started to stumble up the steps, with David trailing behind him.

The boy stood, leaning against the sloping stone wall which ran up beside the steps to the locked door of the tower. David looked at him, or rather through him. He could see the boy and the flickering yellow soul-light within him, and, as if the boy were transparent, he could see the stars beyond.

"Beautiful," said Graham, leaning further over the wall to point to the stars. "Really beautiful ... maybe I should have studied astrol – astrom – astronomy instead." He turned and grinned at David. "I'm going to bring Sarah up here show her the stars – she'll appreciate that. Better than a rabbit ... or a photo frame. If my mum knew I gave it away, she'd kill me."

"Don't worry," said David, "She won't have the chance," and shoved him over the wall.

David waited for the thud, as Graham's body hit the ground, but it didn't come. He leaned over the wall to see what had happened. Graham had managed to get a grip on the rough sandstone blocks that made up the wall. He was hanging there, just out of reach, his fingers grappling to maintain his hold on the stone slabs.

"All right," said David, "we'll do it the hard way." Carefully he heaved his broken body over the wall and began to climb down to where Graham clinging. The young man was desperately trying to find a foothold, before his fingers slipped out of their crevices, but his shoes had smooth soles and he couldn't get a grip. He could see David moving towards him, but he didn't dare move in case he slipped.

"Why are you doing this?" he gasped, but David didn't

bother to answer. He quietly edged closer and closer, until he was just above Graham. Then he reached out his foot and began to kick Graham's fingers, where they were wedged into the rockwork. David cursed silently, as he used his fractured leg to kick Graham loose, annoyed at the effort he was having to spend on what should have been an easy kill. He needed his good leg to support himself on the rockwork, or he'd slip too, and his body would get even more damaged if it fell to the ground below.

He glanced down. He could see Graham's fingers. The knuckles were beginning to bleed where his kicks were landing, one more good kick should do it. Graham let go with one hand and made a grab for David's leg, but he missed, and the swinging foot caught him full in the face as David, too, lost his balance.

Graham's other hand lost its' grip, and he started to fall, still trying to grab hold of his attacker. David flattened himself against the wall and managed to cling on. He heard Graham's scream then silence. He looked down to see the broken body lying on the ground below the tower, stretched out on the grassy area between the city walls and the canal. David waited impatiently, hoping to grab the little yellow soul-light before it shot up into the sky, but the soul-light, though weak and flickering, remained inside Graham's body. The boy was badly injured, but he was still holding on to life.

David was about to climb down to finish him off when he heard a shout. A cyclist was pedalling up the towpath towards where Graham was lying. Reluctantly, David decided he'd have to leave before accomplishing his task. If the cyclist got a good look at him, he might be able to give the police enough information to identify him. That would blow his cover, and mean he'd have to find a new body, in order to get close to the other students. As the cyclist crouched over Graham's bleeding body, David began his uncomfortable climb back up the wall. He cursed the rules that meant he couldn't just attack the cyclist and finish him off as well, but he knew that if he attempted to take a life he had no right to, he'd find himself back in the invisible realm, having forfeited his chance to go after the other students.

The cyclist glanced up in time to see someone pulling himself over the top of the wall and disappearing from view, but didn't catch a glimpse of the man's face. Once back on the city walls, David took a moment to straighten himself up. His broken neck was getting harder to control, but then he hadn't expected the evening's activities to be quite so physical. He made his way back to the halls of residence, and let himself into Graham's room. He wiped the almost empty bottle and the mug he'd used to remove any fingerprints, then left the bottle and Graham's dirty mug on the table. After all, it was only fair to leave some clues to help the police piece together what had happened – hopefully they'd just assume that the boy had had too much to drink, gone for a walk on the walls and had a nasty accident. David was pretty sure Graham would be in no fit state to tell them anything. The boy had looked barely alive after his fall. David smiled. That little yellow soul-light might be coming his way yet.

# Chapter 14

For the second night in a row Flint walked Bex home. She was tempted to stay in the halls with the others, but she didn't want to have her father worrying about her.

At first they walked in silence as they left the campus and headed for the cathedral. Then Flint started talking. Having said hardly anything for twenty-four hours, suddenly he couldn't seem to stop.

"It's my fault, you know that, don't you? It's all my fault."

"How can it be your fault Marty – got sick?" said Bex, trying to calm him down.

"I don't know, but it is. It's as if, since the party, everything's turned nasty – and it's all my fault. I was the one who invited – whatever it was – in. Told it to appear."

"But it didn't appear, did it? None of us saw anything, except for that horrible smoke."

"No, but all of us heard it. That *thing* is out there somewhere, and that's what killed Marty. I'm sure of it."

"Do you really think so?" asked Bex, nervously. Marty's death had put the incident at the party right out of her head for the last few hours, but suddenly the fear came flooding back. "'Cos if you're right," she said guiltily, "it's my fault too. It was just a silly game till I joined in. That's when something started to talk to us. I shouldn't have got involved. I should have known better."

"Why, because you're a Christian?" sneered Flint.

"Sort of, I suppose. 'Cos I believed there could be something real there, and played the game anyway."

"Well, don't think you've got a monopoly in believing things. I believe in stuff too. I believed that thing was real when I asked it in."

"Good real, or bad real?" asked Bex, softly.

"Bad real, of course, and I still invited it in."

"Why?" asked Bex, bewildered. "What made you do it?"

"I don't know, I just thought it would be interesting."

"Isn't there an old Chinese curse about that?" asked Bex, trying to lighten the conversation. "Something like 'may you live in interesting times'?"

"A curse is what this feels like," said Flint morosely. "But I'm the one who deserves it, and Marty's the one who's dead."

"Stop it, Flint, don't talk like that."

"Why not? It's true. Maybe that's why the letters of my name were burnt on the candles – 'cos it's all my fault. Maybe the thing will come after me next."

"My name was burnt too," said Bex so softly Flint could hardly hear her.

Flint shut up, but he took her hand comfortingly as they carried on walking.

There was silence for a few minutes until they were nearly at the cathedral. A cold wind was starting to blow, making the night seem even more sinister.

"It said it was my guardian angel," said Bex, suddenly.

"It was lying," Flint tried to reassure her. "A guardian angel would be something good. This wasn't. Anyway, there's no such thing."

"Yes, there is!" said Bex resolutely.

"Oh, yes, and I suppose you've seen one?" teased Flint.

"As a matter of fact," Bex stopped abruptly. She couldn't tell Flint about Thren. He'd think she was mad.

"What?" asked Flint.

"Nothing, come on, we're almost there."

They approached the arch that led to the abbey green. The shadows beneath it seemed very dark. Bex squeezed Flint's hand more tightly and he swore under his breath.

"What's wrong?" asked Bex, and held his hand, palm upwards so she could see it by the light of the street lamps. The palm was cut and sliced in several places, and fresh blood was smeared across it.

"It was the bottle, last night," explained Flint. "I didn't get round to doing anything about it, and then tonight, when Debbie was squeezing my hand, it started bleeding again."

"Why didn't you say something?"

"What, complain about my poor little cut hand when Marty's lying there dead?"

"Well, let's get inside, and I'll get some antiseptic for you."

They took a deep breath and stepped into the darkness underneath the archway, only breathing out when they were safely the other side of it. They walked up the path to the house, and Bex got out her key, but the door opened before she could use it. Dudley had waited up for her, and within a few minutes he had them both sitting in front of the fire in the study telling him what had happened at the hospital, while Bex cleaned up the cuts on Flint's hand.

Inside the cathedral Thren and Tor were talking too, taking shelter from the rising wind.

"I just don't get it," said Thren. "How are we gonna get Marty's soul back when we don't even know who stole it?"

"We do know who stole it," said Tor patiently. "The demon who came through to the physical world at the party last night. We just don't know what form he's taken."

"Well, how are we gonna find out?" persisted Thren.

"It should be perfectly straightforward now we know what he's trying to do," said Tor, in her explaining-things-to-an-idiot voice. "He's going to try and eliminate each of the students who were at the party, and collect their soul-lights."

"But that doesn't make any sense," said Thren. "I mean, those guys are the ones who invited him over. You'd think he'd be grateful, right?"

"No," said Tor, firmly. "As far as he's concerned they took a step towards darkness by playing that game, and asking him in. That gives him rights over them."

"That's not *fair*!" protested Thren. "They didn't know what they were doing. It was just a silly kids' game."

"And silly kids can get hurt," snapped Tor. "However, now we know what he's planning we should be able to protect them. We must be extra vigilant at the moment. He could attack any one of them at any time."

"Terrific, so I've got twelve potential victims to look after plus a whole city full of other sheep to protect."

"Eleven," said Tor, primly. "I'll take care of Bex."

"Gee, that's swell, I'm *so* grateful. One less to worry about, now there's a weight off my mind, *not*."

"Speaking of grateful, you haven't thanked me yet."

"What for?"

"Saving Marty's life," said Tor smugly. "Well, buying him some time while we try to get his soul back."

Thren squirmed uncomfortably. Trouble was, he realised he actually was grateful to Tor for saving the boy. Which was weird, because what's one human more or less, right? Even weirder, his relief wasn't just about her getting him, Thren, out of trouble. It was for the boy's own sake, for *his* chance to carry on with his life. Still, the words stuck in his throat when he came to say them. Having to be civil to Tor was bad enough, but grateful, ugh!

"Thanks," said Thren, abruptly. It was the best he could do.

Tor smiled. Not the broad, open smile of a friend, but a small, purse-lipped, satisfied smile. The smile of an angel who had got her own way.

"By the way, Thren," she said. "What was it you were about to ask me, before we dashed off to the hospital?"

Thren suddenly remembered his other problems. The things he didn't know how to deal with. Non-physical stuff like Pearson and Poole trying to get rid of Dudley, and the homeless shelter that was about to close, and the little kid at the zoo. He found himself pouring it all out to Tor, including his frustration at not knowing how to help.

"I mean, it's *so* not right, all this stuff, and I don't know how to stop it. There's gotta be a way, there's just gotta, so how come I just stood there like a dummy not knowing what to do?"

Tor stared at him amazed. He was actually bothered. He was starting to care about what was happening in people's lives, or at least some of them. He didn't seem to realise the significance of what he was saying, and she knew better than to point it out to him. He'd only deny it, and start to back off from his involvement. So she shrugged, and tried to make her answers sound casual, but for the first time she started to see that he might have some potential after all.

"You saw what I did at the hospital," she said. "Just try that. It's called influencing. Keep whispering in the ears of the people you're trying to change. Some of them will tune you out, but some will pick up on the idea with their mind, or the feeling with their heart, and start to act on it."

"Seems kinda hit and miss. Can't we just appear to them, tell them what to do?"

"No," said Tor. "Though there are times when I wish we could. If we worked that way, people would obey us out of fear. By influencing them, they still have a choice. We remind them of what's right, but it's their decision about whether to behave that way. All we can do is prod their conscience a little."

"But don't they realise it's us doing it? If an idea just pops up out of nowhere you'd think they'd start to figure it out. Just how dumb are they?"

# Chapter 15

"We're not dumb at all," said Bex, stepping out of the shadows.

"What the heck are you doing here?" said Thren, startled.

"I came to see you. You said you live here," said Bex firmly, "so I borrowed my father's keys to the cathedral and here I am."

Out of the corner of his eye Thren could see Tor frozen with horror. This was not supposed to happen. Humans weren't supposed to come looking for angels. They weren't supposed to be able to see them.

"Make yourself invisible," ordered Tor.

"I can't," shrugged Thren, "the kid can always see me, whatever I do."

"I'm not a kid," said Bex, crossly. "And who are you talking to?"

Thren looked at Tor who shook her head. Personally, Thren thought that Bex needed to know the truth, but it wasn't his decision.

"No one," he lied, turning back to Bex. He could sense her mind again, and knew she knew he was lying. He blushed.

"Sorry," he corrected. "Fact is, I'm not supposed to tell you. I'm not supposed to talk to you at all, but to be fair, you're not supposed to be able to see me."

"I could hardly miss you," said Bex. "You're so – obvious."

Thren didn't know how to take that remark, so he decided to change the subject. "Why did you want to see me? Tonight, I mean."

"I have to know what I did wrong," said Bex. "Why I'm the only person in Chester who doesn't – why you're not my guardian angel. I have to understand what's happening."

Thren turned to Tor. "Did you get clearance when you went to the High Council?" Tor nodded.

"Then you answer her, because I am *not* equipped to deal with this."

Suddenly, Bex saw another angel materialise next to Thren. The being smiled at Bex and said, "You don't need him to be your guardian angel, my dear. You've got me."

"Who are you?" asked Bex, suddenly nervous in a way she wasn't with Thren. "What's your name?"

"We're not supposed to get on to first name terms," said Tor, formally.

"Oh, for pity's sake," said Thren, annoyed. "We're way past all that. Bex, this is Tor, short for Mentor. She's your personal guardian angel. She's looked after you all your life. In other words, she gets the cushy job of protecting little old you, while I have to try and look after everyone else in the city, all by myself."

"But, why?" puzzled Bex. "I didn't think I was so bad that I didn't deserve your help, but I'm not so good I'm special either."

"Don't ask me," said Thren sulkily. "Nobody tells me nothing round here. Zilch! Big fat zero!"

"You don't need to know, Becky, my dear," said Tor. She really did sound like a nanny sometimes. Bex could understand why Thren pulled a face.

"Why can't I see you, but I can see Thren?" Bex asked.

"We don't know. You're not meant to be able to see any of us, ever, unless we choose to let you. The only reason I'm allowed to show myself to you now is because I got special permission from the High Council, so I could correct *his* mistakes."

"What mistakes?" asked Bex curiously.

"Where do I start? He let you see him, he chatted to you, he teased you about not being your guardian angel. In other words, he's responsible for everything."

"What do you mean, responsible?" asked Bex, confused.

"Well, he broke the rules by letting you see him, by making contact, so now the other side has the right to make contact too."

"You mean, the thing at the party?"

"Exactly," said Tor.

"It said it was my guardian angel."

"It lied, big time," said Thren. "Just keep away from it."

"I would if I knew where it was," said Bex.

"We mean it, Bex, the creature's dangerous," said Tor, urgently. "If you have any idea of where it might be, what form it's taken, we need to know, as soon as possible. We have to stop it before it does anything else."

"What do you mean, anything else?" Bex paused, horrified. "You mean Marty, don't you? Flint was right ... Marty didn't just get sick, did he? That *thing* got him somehow, and Flint and I are to blame." Suddenly Bex turned and looked Thren full in the eye. "Were you Marty's guardian angel?"

"Yes," said Thren guiltily. He could feel himself blushing again.

"You didn't do a very good job, did you? Why couldn't you save him? If you were meant to be protecting him, why is he dead?"

"He isn't," said Tor coolly. "Not any more, we revived him, or at least his body."

"He's alive?" said Bex, wonderingly.

"In a manner of speaking," said Tor. "Though if we can't find the creature that's stolen his soul-light, and return it to him, he'll never actually recover."

"Soul-light?" questioned Bex, looking from one angel to another.

Thren turned to Tor, looking thoroughly smug. "You said the s-word, lady, not me. It never crossed my lips."

"Shut up, Thren," said Tor, embarrassed.

"Why should I? You're Miss Perfect, never-make-a-mistake, 'Wonderwings' and you just said the s-word. You just broke the rules."

"Oh, well, what does it matter?" said Tor crossly. "Things can't get any worse."

Wrong.

# Chapter 16

Thren walked Bex back to her front door. It was almost five in the morning, and still pitch dark.

"Look, Bex," he said awkwardly as they walked up the path. "I am sorry about Marty, I really am. I didn't see this coming. To tell you the truth, I'm kinda new to all this."

"That's what Dad thought," said Bex. "When I told him how hopeless you were he said you must be learning the ropes."

"Not fast enough, I'm afraid. I've gotten so much to do, I just can't keep on top of it all. It's scary."

"*You're* scared?" asked Bex.

"Sure, I'm starting to be. I mean, I'm supposed to be responsible for all these sheep – I mean, people – and I don't know what I'm doing. Like the thing with Marty. I wasn't expecting that."

"But you did save him, didn't you?"

"Kinda. Tor did it really, but all we've done is bought him a bit more time, while we deal with whatever did that to him. And it could go after anyone of you, any time. I can't be everywhere at once, Bex, so you better be careful, okay? You and all the others. And I got other things to deal with too, like this little kid, and your dad, and the ..."

"My dad?" interrupted Bex. "What about him?"

"Me and my big mouth again," said Thren. "Look, it's nothing, right, just a little situation I'm trying to deal with for him. Pretend like I never said it, right?"

"All right."

"And I'm sorry I upset you, the other day," added Thren. "It was mean of me. I'm just so hopeless at this stuff. Talking to humans – ugh! This is *not* my thing."

"But you're talking to me now," Bex pointed out. "And you helped Marty."

"Yeah and I had to kiss him on the mouth to do it. Gross! What is it with the kissing thing anyway? You humans do it all the time. It makes my skin crawl."

"Does it?" said Bex smiling. She reached up and kissed him on the cheek. "Thanks for doing it, anyway."

"Hey, stop that," said Thren, pulling a face. "And get inside, it's freezing out here. I don't want you catching your death."

"I'm not your problem, remember?" said Bex, teasing him.

"Maybe not, but if anything happens to you, you can just bet Tor will hold me responsible for it."

"Night, Thren, and thanks," said Bex, and she entered the house and closed the door behind her. Her head was spinning as she climbed the stairs, kicked off her shoes and crawled into bed. There were such things as guardian angels, and she had one. In fact, it felt more like she had two really. Oddly enough, she felt more comfortable with Thren than she did with Tor. She was sorry she'd had a go at him earlier. She suspected he was feeling as guilty as she was about what happened at the party, and what that thing had done to Marty. Best of all, Marty was still alive, sort of, which at least meant there was hope. Bex closed her eyes and began to drift off to sleep, as the wind rattled the windowpane and the rain began to fall.

When Thren got back to the cathedral Tor was pacing up and down miserably. "Hey, what's up?" he asked her. "Apart from all the ways I've goofed up already."

"She doesn't like me," said Tor, miserably. "I've watched

over her all her life and now she's finally met me she doesn't even like me."

"Of course she does," said Thren, trying to be reassuring. "She's a nice kid, you're a … nice angel, she's bound to like you, just give her time."

"She prefers you."

Thren looked at Tor in amazement. She was sulking, no doubt about it. Come to that, she was jealous of him. Of how comfortable Bex seemed to be with him. Which was really weird. She was supposed to be the sensible, sorted one, while he floundered around unable to cope. And here she was getting all upset because Bex preferred him. He'd have found it funny if Tor hadn't been quite so upset.

"You don't know what it's like," said Tor, turning on him. "You haven't been doing the job long enough. For that matter, you don't want to be doing the job at all. Otherwise you'd realise, when you look after one person all their life, really care about them, you imagine what it would be like if they knew you existed. How many little incidents in the past would suddenly fall into place once they knew about you, that sort of thing. How close you'd be to them – and we're not. She doesn't want to get to know me at all."

"She will," said Thren, putting his arm round Tor's shoulder. "She's just got a lot going on right now, that's all. She probably feels like she's got information overload, can't take it all in at once. She'll be fine with you, you'll see."

"But that was my one chance," said Tor, rather weepily. "I got permission to show myself to her *once* to correct your mistakes. I'm not meant to hang around so that she can get to know me better. So if she doesn't like me now she never will."

"Did the High Council *say* you could only appear once."

"No, but those are the usual rules," sniffed Tor.

"Scrap the 'usual rules'. If they didn't actually say once, I reckon you should stick around. Give her a chance to get to know you. After all, what harm can it do? She knows you exist now, so why should it matter if she sees you once or a hundred times?"

"Do you really think so?" said Tor, looking a little more hopeful. "After all, even if I do keep appearing she may never actually like me. She didn't seem to take to me tonight. What did I do wrong, Thren?"

"Well, you were a little stiff, you know. Kinda formal and 'nanny knows best'. I guess she just wasn't ready for that tonight," said Thren, sympathetically.

"I was nervous," said Tor, defensively. "Besides, I don't know any other way to be. And get your arm off my shoulder!"

Thren withdrew his arm hastily. What had got into him? There was way too much contact going on. Getting mouth to mouth with Marty, being kissed by Bex, putting his arm round Tor. Maybe he was sickening for something ... like Home. He sure did miss the place. Earth was so – so physical, so demanding. He was starting to feel the pressure. There was so much to do, and he couldn't be everywhere at once. Which reminded him that it was time he got back to work. He hadn't checked out the city for hours. Anything could be happening, and when he got up to the cathedral roof, he saw that it was.

# Chapter 17

Given it was so early in the morning, and most people were still asleep, there seemed to be an awful lot of active soul-lights.

'Must have been some party!' thought Thren, as a group of hazy soul-lights staggered out of the city centre and headed for the halls of residence.

Then there was routine activity – people on early shifts starting to stir and head for work. Some other soul-lights were shaking or flickering, as if their owners were unhappy, or ill, and a group at the edge of the city walls was blazing like fury. Thren didn't know where to start. 'Like, how is one little old angel to deal with all this?', he thought.

Then he spotted the little gold light. It was the same one he'd noticed a couple of nights before. The one he was heading for when he'd crashed into the wall and met Bex. On that occasion it had been flickering erratically – now it was so faint it was barely there at all.

Thren decided to check it out and flew towards the light, but this time he didn't try to fly through the wall. Oh no, he'd learned his lesson – once was enough! He landed beside the building, a corner shop with a flat above it, and gently pushed the side door. He heard the lock click and the door seemed to swing open of its own accord.

'Cool,' thought Thren. 'I guess there are some advantages to being an angel.' He climbed the stairs. The flat was small and shabby, and all the doors were ajar. In one room a young couple slept deeply, while in the next a baby was asleep in its cot.

'So that's who the little light belongs to,' thought Thren. He looked round. There were medicines on the chest of drawers, just over the counter stuff, but it sure didn't seem like they'd done the kid much good. Her breathing was laboured, and her flickering soul-light was now so faint he could barely see it.

Suddenly the child gasped one final, rasping breath, and fell silent. Thren watched in sorrow as the remnants of the little soul-light began to float free of the body.

"Oh no, you don't," said Thren and, acting on instinct, he leapt up to the ceiling and spread his wings wide. The tiny light bumped against his outstretched wings, trying to escape upwards, but it couldn't pass through him.

"Gotcha," whispered Thren, then wondered what to do next. He tried to push the soul-light back down towards the child's body but it wouldn't budge. Stalemate.

Then he had an idea. He took a deep breath and blew hard, slamming the bedroom door shut with a loud bang. He heard the couple in the next room start to stir, but they still didn't come to see what was going on.

Thren took another breath and blew the medicines off the chest of drawers. "Oops," he murmured, as the sticky pink medicine started to seep into the carpet, but at least the noise of the bottles crashing into each other brought the parents stumbling into the room.

They went straight to the body of their child, then the woman starting screaming, while the man, after a few moments' shocked hesitation, ran to the phone and called for an ambulance.

The soul-light was still bobbing insistently against Thren's wings, but he found he could stop it escaping by furling his wings slightly, so that it was trapped in his feathers. It felt strange, sort of warm and tingly, and Thren squirmed with the sensation. "Hey, stop that, it tickles." He held on to the light while the parents waited in stunned silence for the ambulance, which arrived within a few minutes.

"Stand clear," said the ambulance woman as they shocked the baby, trying to start its heart beating again. After three goes the baby's body responded, and Thren could feel the soul-light struggling amongst his feathers. He unfurled his wings and it shot back down and into the child.

Thren was thrilled. He'd never done that before – saved a child's life. He heard the ambulance team questioning the parents. How long had the baby been ill? Why hadn't they taken it to the doctors? It turned out the child had been sick for a few days, but both parents had to work to bring in enough to survive on. By the time they collected the child from the childminder each night, the doctor's surgery was shut, so they just bought medicines at the chemist. She was their first child, and they just weren't experienced enough to know she was really ill.

The ambulance team reckoned the kid had a bad chest infection, so they put her on oxygen and took her to the hospital, the parents thanking them all the way. Of course, they couldn't thank Thren, as they didn't know he was there, or the part he'd played. If he hadn't hung on to that soul-light, it would have been gone before the ambulance team arrived, and the baby couldn't have been revived, however hard they tried.

Of course, from Thren's point of view, death wasn't really such a disaster for the person concerned, it was just the next step of a most amazing journey. But a death that came too early, or for the wrong reasons, that was one of the things Thren was there to prevent, and he'd done it.

The child still had a whole lifetime of exciting possibilities ahead of her, and the potential to do or be anything she set her heart on.

'Hey,' thought Thren, as he headed back to the cathedral, 'maybe this ain't such a bad job after all.'

# Chapter 18

Thren found Tor waiting for him on the cathedral roof. "You'll never guess what I've just done," he began, excitedly.

"Your job?" asked Tor disdainfully. "Surely you don't expect congratulations for that?"

"But there was this little kid, just a baby, and it stopped breathing, and I ..."

Tor interrupted rudely. "You left the students unattended. Was that wise, with a demon on the loose?"

"Like, what was I supposed to do, huh? Let the baby die?"

"Well, it's your decision, of course," said Tor, primly, "but you do have a particular responsibility to the students, since it's your fault the situation arose in the first place."

"No wonder Bex didn't take to you," sniped Thren, angrily. Tor shut up, and Thren felt guilty when he saw the hurt in her eyes, but he wasn't going to say sorry. No way. He changed the subject. "How are they? The students?"

"Bex and Flint are still asleep in the house. I have no idea about the others."

"You might have kept an eye on them for me."

"How can I? Unless they're up and moving around, I can't find them. I can't see their soul-lights, remember, only Bex's."

"You mean, they could be in trouble, and you wouldn't even know it."

"Exactly," said Tor, crossly.

Thren stood up and looked out over the city. No sign of trouble on the campus, that he could see. None of the students were up yet. It was only six o'clock and not even light yet. Then he saw the soul-lights blazing at one corner of the city walls. They'd been there earlier, but he'd decided to ignore them while he went to check out the dying baby. Now he thought he'd better investigate.

"Come on," he said to Tor. "Time to go."

"But I should stay here, in case Bex needs me."

"She won't be up for a while, she didn't get to bed till five," said Thren. "Besides, I may need your help. I can't work out what's wrong with those soul-lights, the ones by the wall. They're not blue or red or anything – just burning very intensely."

"Strange," said Tor. "That's usually what happens when someone's had a shock." The two angels looked at each other, then dived off the roof and headed for the city walls.

Within a few seconds they were standing on the steps of King Charles's Tower, looking down on the ground below. Between the outer wall of the city and the smooth curve of the canal was a grassy area, where a team of ambulance staff were carefully lifting Graham onto a stretcher.

"One of yours?" asked Tor in a whisper, not that the police and associated professionals milling around below could hear them. Thren nodded in reply.

"At least he's still alive," she continued, "it could have been worse."

"Not much," muttered Thren, "look at him, he's been smashed to pieces. He's barely breathing."

"But he does still have his soul-light?" Tor questioned.

"Yes," Thren replied, "so it can't have had anything to do with what happened the other night. Graham must just have had some kind of an accident."

"Of course," said Tor, sarcastically. "A demon soul-catcher is stalking a group of students, one of them suffers an unexpected and grisly mishap and you think that there's no connection? Come on."

The two angels fluttered down to the ground to pick up what information they could.

"And what time was this?" asked a policeman, who was taking notes in his little black book. He was speaking to a young man wearing a cycle helmet and fluorescent jacket. The man's bike was on its side on the towpath, a few feet from where Graham had landed.

"I told you, same as I told the last two coppers who asked me," said the cyclist. "It was about quarter past five. I was just taking a short cut, along the towpath, when I saw him fall, from up there. There was another bloke hanging on the wall too, but he climbed up and out of sight before I could get a good look at him. I used my mobile to phone the police and an ambulance and that's all I know. Now can I please go? I'm late for work."

"In a moment," said the policeman, "as soon as we have your details." A few minutes later the cyclist was allowed to leave, and the police began searching the area to see if there was any evidence of Graham's fall being anything other than an accident. Thren and Tor left them to it, choosing to follow the ambulance to the hospital.

Graham was given immediate treatment, but the doctors didn't look too hopeful. The boy had two broken legs, a dislocated elbow and a punctured lung, but his most serious injury was a severe skull fracture. The hospital sent for his family, uncertain if they would be able to keep Graham alive until his parents arrived from Rotherham.

The angels stood by the bedside of the unconscious boy, Thren staring at the weakening soul-light as if mesmerised. "Can't you fix this one, Tor?" he asked.

"I'm afraid not, Thren," said Tor, speaking more gently than usual. "This one is down to the doctors, there's nothing we can do."

# Chapter 19

Dross had already chosen his next target. Although the soul-light he'd consumed had given him strength, and reduced his rate of decay a little, he still had no time to lose. He had the right to try and take the soul-lights of all thirteen students before he returned to his own realm. If he succeeded then the power he would take back with him would raise his status considerably, and enable him to take control of his own section. Then he could do to some of his so called superiors what they had been doing to him for as long as he could remember – make every moment of existence miserable.

Of course, he could return with just some of the soul-lights, but he knew his fellow demons would count that as a failure. He was determined to get them all. After all, he'd waited long enough for his opportunity. The rules didn't get broken very often, and when they did there were hoards of demons waiting for the chance to come through into the physical realm. They all wanted their opportunity to collect human soul-lights and increase their own power. Dross himself had only had one other chance, and that had been centuries ago, in human terms; an eternity to him.

He'd had to argue long and hard to be given this opportunity, and had only been chosen because of his past relationship with Thren. Not that the angel knew who he was dealing with, not yet.

Dross had to act quickly, but he couldn't afford to attract

too much attention. That's why he would have preferred to kiss the soul out of Debbie. It was so much less obvious. By the time anyone realised what was wrong with her, Dross would have been back where he belonged. He'd missed his chance, and it wouldn't be so easy to get another one with her, but he'd find a different way to collect her soul later. He decided to forget about Debbie for now, and tackle his next victim before she joined her fellow students and discovered what was going on.

He waited until he saw Joanna's soul-light start to stir. Then he gave her a few minutes to get up and dressed. He checked his watch. It was ten o'clock and most of the other students had headed for their lectures, but Joanna had been out clubbing the night before. She'd returned late, overslept and woken up with a terrible hangover. David knew she hadn't seen any of the other students who'd been at the party since yesterday, which gave him an advantage. As she hadn't been told about Marty yet, she wouldn't be on her guard, or upset and in need of her friends' support. Just as well for him that she wasn't as close to Marty and Debbie as some of the others were. The girl had no reason to be suspicious of him at all.

Joanna groaned when she heard someone knocking on her door. She thought it would be Cath, telling her she was late for a lecture, but when she opened the door, there was David, the new student. The extremely handsome new student, and he was offering her a bunch of flowers.

"Are these for me?" asked Joanne, flattered.

"Well, I'm not carrying them round just for the sake of it," said David with a charming smile. He stepped into her room. "Shall I put the kettle on, make us a coffee?" he offered. "You look like you could use one."

Joanna stared at him, perplexed. She wasn't so keen on someone barging into her room uninvited, and making free with her kettle. On the other hand, the flowers were beautiful, and so was he, and it was morning. Dangerous creeps only come out at night, or at least that was her theory.

"Okay, if you like," she said, a little nervously. "If you'll excuse me, I need to get ready. I've missed my first lecture, but I should still make the next one."

She took a brush and started to untangle her hair. It smelt of stale cigarette smoke but she could hardly wash it with him standing there. Upending yourself over a sink is not the way to make a good first impression, so she settled for brushing her long blonde hair into reasonable shape then scooped it up into a loose ponytail and tied it with a wispy scarf.

David made two mugs of coffee, and handed one of them to her. She took it and had a sip. Bliss. The joys of caffeine. Her head was still throbbing from the hangover, but at least, as the caffeine started to take effect, she thought there was a chance she might survive after all. She looked at David over the rim of her mug.

"Shouldn't you be in class?" she asked. "I know I overslept, but what's your excuse?

"I just thought I'd take the chance to get acquainted," said David, at his most charming. "I noticed you yesterday but didn't have the opportunity to speak to you alone. That Debbie girl pounced on me. Even got me to take her to the cinema last night. I could hardly get out of it, not without being rude, but the person I really wanted to spend the evening with was you."

He smiled romantically into her eyes, taking a step towards her as he did so. She smiled timidly back. Joanna was not naturally a shy girl. In fact she'd had a string of boyfriends in the six months or so she'd been at university, but she did find it a bit strange to have a total stranger closing in on her at that time in the morning.

David thought she'd be a walkover. One quick kiss was all he needed, and she was an easy target. He'd noticed her the day before, and her pathetic attempts to attract his attention revolted him. He'd known at once that she wasn't the self-confident woman she pretended to be. She was little more than a schoolgirl pretending to be a grown-up, but he could also tell that she was used to having men running after her. She was obviously a pushover. He took another step towards her, so close that it would be easy to put his arms round her and close in for the kill – sorry, kiss.

For a moment Joanna stared into his eyes, almost hypno-tised, as he drew nearer and nearer. Then her brain kicked in. How dare he treat her like this, as if he knew she'd just fall into his arms? He might be extremely good-looking, a factor always high on Joanna's list of priorities, but that was no excuse. He barely knew her – and what was that peculiar, rancid smell?

Revolted, she stepped sideways; just as David attempted to wrap his arms round her and kiss her. His lips missed hers, and he was furious.

"I think I'd like you to leave now," said Joanna, strug-gling to pull away from him. His fingers caught in her hair and snagged on her scarf, and he tugged it loose, twisting it in his fingers. David was angry. He'd lost his chance with her, just as he had with Debbie, and he wasn't going to be cheated twice. It was obvious that she wasn't going to let him kiss her, not now, and from the revulsion on her face, not ever. Well, there was more than one way to get what he was after. The thin scarf would do to strangle her with, then he could swallow her soul-light. "Have it your own way" he whispered, "but you'll regret it." He stretched the scarf out between his hands, and dived forward, about to loop it round her throat.

Joanna wrenched herself away from him, flinging herself towards the door. She could hear footsteps in the corridor. Someone was walking towards her room.

"Joanna, are you up?" called a voice from the corri-dor. It was Cath. Joanna could have wept with relief at the sound of her friend's voice. "I overslept, I thought you might have done too. Are you coming? Our next lecture starts in ten minutes."

Joanna reached the door handle before David could stop her, and jerked the door open, practically flinging herself on top of Cath in her relief at getting away from him. The door banged shut behind her, hiding David from Cath's sight, and Joanna began to tow her friend swiftly along the corridor.

She knew it was foolish to leave him in her room, but she wasn't sure what else to do. With a bit of luck he'd get bored of waiting for her and go away. Then she could go back and pack.

***

Joanna had just decided that university life wasn't for her. She wanted her mum, even though she knew she'd be in trouble for quitting her course, and her dad would flip when he saw how many piercings she'd acquired since he'd last seen her. It would be worth it just to feel safe. She wondered what she'd done to attract a creep like David, if she was giving out some kind of a signal without even realising it. Why did he think she'd be such an easy target, either to kiss or – whatever? Well, she wasn't going to stick around and ask questions, or wait for him to try again. Joanna wanted to tell Cath what had just happened, but all she could have said was that David had tried to kiss her, which was hardly a crime. She didn't know how to explain just how menacing he'd seemed, how convinced she'd been that he was about to hurt her. It would all sound so stupid, as if she was a scared kid, so she let Cath ramble on about course work and essays as they headed towards what Joanna had already decided would be her last English lecture.

Back in her room David was furious. He couldn't believe that Joanna had got away from him. Well there'd be no more mistakes, no more missed opportunities. He'd make sure of that. He straightened his broken neck, which had twisted out of position when Joanna had pulled away from him, and smoothed back his ruffled hair. He checked his appearance in the mirror over the sink. Very smart, and no visible signs of decay yet. If only he could get rid of that smell. He thought it must be his internal organs starting to rot, not that it mattered to him physically, but it seemed to be putting the girls off.

He dropped the twisted scarf on the floor, cursing yet another wasted opportunity, and stepped out into the corridor. He checked his watch. Only ten thirty. He just had time to buy some mints to freshen his breath, before going to his next lecture, and choosing another victim. This time there would be no escape, no second chances. Time was running out.

# Chapter 20

By twelve o'clock that morning most of the students were in the canteen drinking coffee. The ones who had been at the hospital with Marty were gathered together, talking animatedly.

"Are you sure he's still alive, Bex?" asked Tim.

"Yes, but if you don't believe me phone the hospital."

"If this is some kind of horrid joke ..." said Debbie tearfully.

"I wouldn't do that to you ... to anyone," said Bex, taking Debbie's hand comfortingly. "But I honestly know he's alive."

"They should have phoned us," said Tim. "They took all our details last night."

"Has your phone been on?" queried Bex.

There was the usual automatic hunting in bags and pockets for mobiles.

"You're right," said Tim. "I switched it off at the hospital, and forgot to turn it back on."

"Mine too," sniffed Debbie. "There didn't seem much point."

Tim checked his voicemail and grinned at the others.

"You were right, Bex," said Tim, delightedly. "There's a message from the hospital. Something must have happened after we left last night. Marty is in a coma, but at least he's alive."

While the other students grinned and slapped each other

on the back in delight, Flint looked at Bex and asked, "How did you know?"

"Just a hunch, that's all," said Bex evasively.

"You knew as soon as you woke up this morning, didn't you? I thought you seemed surprisingly cheerful, after all that's happened."

"I – I dreamed it," said Bex, who wasn't about to tell Flint, of all people, that she'd got her information from a couple of angels. Flint teased her enough about her faith as it was.

"Anyway, at least now we can both stop feeling guilty," said Flint quietly. "Everything's back to normal."

"I don't know about that," said Bex. "Marty's still in a coma."

"Compared to being dead I'd say it was a significant improvement," replied Flint, grinning at her.

Just then Miss Caldwell, one of the student counsellors, walked in, looking pale and serious. She called for silence, but nobody heard her over the general noise of the place, so she picked up a food tray and banged it down on the nearest table. Everyone shut up abruptly and turned to look in her direction.

"I'm afraid I have some bad news for you. I believe some of you know Marty Watkins was admitted to hospital last night. He is currently in a coma, and the doctors suspect some form of poisoning. Apparently, the last thing he swallowed was some coffee, probably yesterday afternoon. Does anybody know where he drank it?"

"Here," said Debbie, very quietly.

"I was afraid of that," said Miss Caldwell. "I think it would be best if we closed the canteen down, while we investigate the cause of the problem."

Students all around the canteen stared nervously into their coffee mugs, then put them down on tables and window sills, handling them carefully, as if they feared the contents might explode if shaken.

A few of the students stood up to leave, but Miss Caldwell gestured for them to stay put.

"I'm afraid I have some more bad news," she said solemnly. "Graham Conley was found badly injured this morning, and is in a critical condition. It seems he fell off the city walls last night. It also appears he'd been drinking heavily. If any of you knows anything about what happened please report it to the police. They will be coming round later to ask questions, and I'd appreciate it if you all gave them your fullest cooperation." She paused then added, less formally, "I'm sorry to be the bearer of such bad tidings, but I thought it was better to tell you officially than have all kinds of rumours going round. If anybody needs to talk about what's happened, I'll be available all day."

There was silence after she left the room. Nobody knew quite what to say. The students who'd been at the party were the most stunned, since they were friends with both Graham and Marty.

"I can't handle this," said Tim. "We spent all night grieving for Marty, who turns out to be alive and then just as there seems to be some hope we discover that Graham might die too."

"What do you mean?" wailed Sarah, "She didn't say Graham was going to die".

"She said he was critical," answered Tim, gently, "that means they don't know if he's going to make it."

"I can't take it in," said Sam, "I mean, what was he doing out on the walls last night anyway? He said he was staying in to work on an essay."

"And he wouldn't have been drinking on his own," said Mark. "It's not like him."

Thren watched the students through the window. Luckily, Bex had her back to him, but he could see the faces of the others.

"Humans are weird," he thought to himself. "They're

all reacting in different ways. So unpredictable."

He decided it was time he got up to speed on the rest of the students who'd been at the party. He'd been so busy concentrating on Bex and her closest friends that he hadn't taken the time to get to know the others. Which was how Graham had got hurt without him even noticing. He didn't want that happening again, so he set himself to studying the others. 'Thrillsville,' he thought to himself.

Even in the short time that Thren had been observing the students he'd realised that Sam and Mark were a couple of jokers, but they weren't joking now. Sam's copper-coloured soul-light had dimmed and was grey-edged since he heard the news. His green eyes were misty with tears, which he was blinking back, hoping no one would notice. Mark looked less concerned, but his soul-light, already a very dark green, was turning almost black round the edges.

Most of the others were fussing round Sarah, who was weeping uncontrollably, her pink soul-light paler and fuzzier than ever. She kept repeating "Graham can't die … he can't. I was going to ask him out …"

Which left one student sitting alone at the edge of the group. Thren gathered that his name was Paul, and judging by the textbooks sticking out of his bag, he was studying Art History. The angel wondered why Paul was hanging out with this group of students. Apart from Flint they were all studying either Biology or English.

'Art History,' thought Thren. 'What kind of subject is that?'

Paul had large blue eyes, half-hidden behind thick glasses. His hair was mousy-coloured and he was really tall and thin. He reminded Thren of a stick insect. His soul-light, however, was a beautiful mixture of sky blue and lemon yellow, blending to green sometimes. Thren had no idea what that meant, but it made Paul more interesting. "Maybe there's more to him than meets the eye."

'That's all of them,' thought Thren, glancing round the

group and failing to notice that Joanna wasn't with them.

Debbie decided to skip her lectures for the rest of the day, and go and sit with Marty at the hospital in case he woke up. Thren would have liked to tell her not to bother. The only way Marty was going to recover was if he and Tor could figure out how to get the boy's soul back and they weren't even close yet. Still, the kid thought she was helping, and he wouldn't have wanted to take that away from her anyhow.

Tim and Nesta, also cutting classes, offered to go with her, and the three of them set off. Then Cath stood up, announced she was going to her next lecture, and tried to persuade Sarah to go with her.

'Definitely teacher material,' thought Thren.

"I can't just go to a lecture as if nothing's happened," sobbed Sarah. "Please, don't make me."

"I'm not trying to *make* you," said Cath, defensively, "I just thought it might help, take your mind off things."

"Well, it won't. I – I need to go to my room, be on my own for a bit." Sarah stood up to leave.

"I'll walk you over," said Sam, suddenly. He picked up Sarah's bag for her, and they walked slowly out of the canteen, leaving Cath staring after them.

Mark leapt out of his chair abruptly, knocking it over in the process, "I need a sodding drink," he announced, "Anyone coming?" and he hurried out of the room.

Paul also left, muttering something about classes, but Thren noticed that when he got outside the canteen his shoulders were shaking, and he had to wipe the tears from the inside of his glasses so he would see where he was going. Thren felt terrible. This whole mess was his fault and look at all the pain it was causing. Suddenly he understood Cath's reaction; the fact that she'd decided to go to her lecture anyway. She wanted to keep busy.

Thren felt the same. He didn't reckon there was anything he could do for the students just then, and at least now he'd learnt the colours of all their soul-lights, he could keep an eye on them from a distance. Besides, if he stuck around, Bex was bound to catch sight of him, and she was sure to blame him for what had happened to Graham. Thren couldn't handle that yet – way too much guilt flying around already, he thought. He decided to go somewhere else, where he could be of some use. He turned his back on the remaining students and headed for the cathedral.

Bex and Flint hadn't moved or spoken since Miss Caldwell's announcement.

"Is this your idea of 'back to normal'?" asked Bex.

# Chapter 21

Thren decided to follow Dudley again. Something about the old man always made Thren feel better, and he could do with cheering up right then. Not that the canon looked very cheerful himself, as he set off towards the council offices.

Thren glanced back to see Tor hovering over the campus. He figured the students would be safe enough in her care for a while, and he could do with a break, so he decided to put them out of his mind and concentrate on helping Dudley.

At the council offices Janet, the woman who ran the hostel, was waiting for the old clergyman. From their brief conversation Thren gathered that they were going to try and persuade the council to find some alternative premises for the hostel. Thren reckoned that was where he came in; time to try some of that influencing Tor had talked about.

At two o'clock Dudley and Janet were shown into an office which belonged to a Mr Simpson, and they set about trying to persuade him of the importance of the hostel.

Mr Simpson was lean and angular. His desk was covered in columns of figures; his grey eyes flashed like the display on a calculator. His soul-light was pale orange and he kept looking at his watch as Janet and Dudley tried to put their case.

Janet spoke passionately about what the hostel was doing for people, and Thren thought she was terrific. He hadn't taken much notice of her the first time he saw her, but now he was impressed. She was in her mid-forties and sensibly dressed – designer clothes obviously just weren't a priority compared to the issues she dealt with every day. Her light brown hair was just starting to turn silver-grey, but she had so much energy, so much commitment to the work she did, and the people involved in it, that she seemed younger. Her soul-light was silver, a pretty good colour, Thren guessed, but however eloquently she spoke, and however persuasively Dudley supported her arguments, Mr Simpson didn't want to know.

Phrases like "planning pressures", "zoning" and "not really a council responsibility" rolled off his lips like olive oil, as he showed them to the door.

'Right,' thought Thren, once he was alone in the room with Mr Simpson. 'Time to try that influencing thing.' Thren sidled up to Mr Simpson's right ear.

"Why don't you give it a go?" whispered Thren. "After all, what harm could it do?"

Mr Simpson didn't seem to be responding at all, so Thren tried again.

"Just think how you could boast about it, Simpson, if you were the one to stand up and offer them somewhere for the hostel. Everyone would reckon you were a real decent guy."

Still no response. Thren was getting bored. He wanted a reaction. He stood in front of Mr Simpson and yelled, "*Give them a building, scumbag!*."

Mr Simpson reached down and opened his desk drawer, drew out a personal stereo, and put the headphones over his ears.

Thren groaned and walked out.

"So much for influencing."

# Chapter 22

Thren was stamping about in the cathedral. To say he was annoyed was putting it mildly. He hadn't managed to help Dudley save the hostel, he hadn't had a chance to find that kid from the zoo, Graham was on the critical list, Marty was in a coma, and he had no idea how to deal with whatever was attacking the students. On top of which, he was being bossed around by Wonderwings, who was sure to make all kinds of cutting remarks when she found out he'd failed *again*. Like she was so perfect ...

He heard voices coming from the Chapter House. Voices he recognised, so he strolled in to check it out. He found Pearson and Poole huddled over some papers. In their clerical robes they really did look like crows, and Thren noticed they both had matching purple soul-lights. Unusual.

"It really is time we made a move," said Pearson, the tall, thin one. Beside him Poole nodded and smiled before asking "But how?"

"We need to discredit him, show him up for the blind old fool that he is. Then the others will see that it's time he retired."

"But how?" repeated Poole insistently.

"I don't know, but he's got to go. He spends too much time out in the city doing ..." Pearson paused.

"Good works?" filled in Poole, helpfully.

"Don't call it that," snapped Pearson, "That's half the trouble; everyone admiring him, expecting us to follow his example. He should spend more time here in the cathedral where he belongs – not waste his time with the down and outs."

"But aren't we supposed to …"

"Shut up, Poole, I'm thinking. The television company won't keep their offer open for long, you know. If I don't get the papers signed soon, they'll go and use some other cathedral."

"Would that really be so bad?" asked Poole innocently.

"Of course it would be bad. They want me to front the programme – the whole series. I'll never get another opportunity like this. Quite apart from earning a substantial fee for the job, it's my chance to get noticed, to show that I'm bishop material. At the very least it's my chance to become a 'media vicar', the kind they roll out for current affairs programmes. It'll do my profile the world of good."

Poole surveyed Pearson's profile. He couldn't see that it needed any improvement and said so.

"No, you idiot, my media profile. It's the only way to get on these days; establish a strong media personality, get yourself noticed," said Pearson, smoothing back his raven hair, which was so dark Thren was convinced he dyed it.

"But the programme is about the life of the cathedral," said Poole. "Its history, how it functions, who works here. So why don't you just do the programme and leave Collins out of it? As you say, he's hardly here. The film crew might not even realise he exists."

"They want to interview everyone, in depth," growled Pearson. "They want to find out what makes them tick, what they think about the issues of the day, that sort of thing. Of course, they won't use all the footage. They'll edit it down later, but if they interview him about his ridiculous charity work, it'll show the rest of us up. That won't do my image much good. Besides, he's so – biblical. He's bound to say something controversial, and that won't help my career."

"Why not?" asked Poole. "Don't the telly people want controversy?"

"Of course they do, they love it, but I'm the one who'd have to respond to whatever he said," explained Pearson. "If I disagree with him, I might come over as too liberal. If I agree I'll sound old-fashioned. Better not to express an opinion at all."

"But what's the point of being on telly if you've got nothing to say?" puzzled Poole.

"The idea is to appear to have good, sound opinions, without ever making it quite clear where you stand," said Pearson slowly, as if he was explaining it to a child. "That way you don't offend anybody, everybody thinks that you believe in the same things they do, and they all like and respect you. That's the way to get on in this business."

Poole was about to ask, "Is this meant to be a business?" but seeing how annoyed Pearson was looking, he thought better of it. Instead he asked nervously, "Why don't you just sign the papers for the TV programme and worry about the rest of it later? They're not going to film for a few months yet. You never know, Collins might go away on holiday or something while the film crew are here."

"The bishop said I had to get everyone's agreement before I could finalise the deal and Collins would never agree to it."

"How do you know? You haven't asked him yet."

"I know his sort. He's an old stick-in-the-mud. He'll think television is a bad influence," said Pearson. "And once he says no, the other waverers will change their minds and vote against it too. Then I'll have no chance. No, better to get him out of the picture before he has any say in the matter."

"Which comes back to my first question," said Poole. "How?"

# Chapter 23

Bex was at an anatomy lecture. It was the last place she wanted to be just then, but she thought that at least if she went along and took notes it would help Tim and the others catch up later. It felt slightly surreal, sitting there copying diagrams from the digital whiteboard as if everything was normal, when it was perfectly obviously that everything wasn't.

Behind her sat Tor, although Bex didn't know it. While Tor had decided she might go along with Thren's suggestion of appearing to Bex more than once, now didn't seem to be the time. So Tor just sat there, happy in the knowledge that she was doing her job, protecting Bex from danger, though she would have been happier if she'd had some idea what form the danger might take.

Unfortunately, this meant that Tor wasn't keeping an eye on the other students; the ones in the English class, for instance. She had meant to flit about the campus a little, and check on them all, but the lecturer had moved on to wing structure, and she just couldn't tear herself away.

Which was a shame, because it left David plenty of opportunity to approach Cath at the end of class, and invite her for a coffee.

"I hope you don't mind," he said smoothly. "I know what a bad day this is for everyone, but I gather you've got a full set of notes on the Brontë lectures. With changing courses mid-year, I've got to make up as much time as

I can."

"Of course you have," said Cath sympathetically. "It must be difficult for you, working out which elements we've covered already, and where the gaps are."

Since the canteen was still closed, David suggested they walk into town to find a coffee shop. Cath agreed, since she was planning to go into town that afternoon anyway. She needed some more folders and pens, and besides, she was keen to delay going back to the halls of residence. She knew all the other students would be speculating about what had happened to Graham and she didn't want to get caught up in it.

She didn't like talking about things that distressed her; she preferred to keep busy and pretend everything was all right, and although she hadn't shown it earlier, Graham's accident had distressed her – a lot. She was fond of him – well, more than fond really, and she knew Graham liked her. He'd asked her out in the autumn term, but she'd refused to go out with him. She said it was because she had a lot of course work on that week, which was true, but Graham had taken it as a personal rejection, and hadn't asked her again. She'd worried about him skipping lectures and getting behind with his work, but when she'd approached him about it, and offered to help him catch up, he'd just grinned, and told her to lighten up.

That was the main reason she'd gone to the party at Marty's house. It was Graham who'd casually invited her and Sarah, and Cath wanted to show him she could let her hair down sometimes. But the party had been a complete disaster, not her kind of thing at all. Graham had obviously decided he liked Sarah better than her, and now he was lying in hospital critically ill. She hadn't let herself cry in the canteen, she didn't feel she could, especially with Sarah weeping and wailing like that, but she'd wanted to. She'd been brought up to control her feelings, taught that emotional displays were a sign of weakness, but today she'd really envied Sarah her ability to express her misery. Cath wished she could have done the same, and had everyone being supportive and concerned for *her*, but she just couldn't bring herself to talk about how she felt.

She and David hardly spoke as they walked into the city. He steered her into a side street, and picked a coffee shop, a dimly lit one. It was half past four and almost dark outside. Inside the café there was barely enough light to read the menu, or see each other's faces. David chose a table with a padded bench seat so that they could sit side by side. Cath hardly noticed.

The strain of pretending that everything was all right was beginning to get to her. Now that she was away from the other students, sitting in the semi-darkness, her self-control began to slip. David could sense it, and since that was exactly what he wanted he began to talk to her about Graham.

"Of course, I haven't had a chance to get to know him," said David, "but he seems a pretty decent bloke. I ran into him in the corridor – my room's only a few doors down from his."

"He is," said Cath, trying to blink back the tears.

"Hard worker too, I gather."

"Whatever gave you that impression?" said Cath, surprised. "He was getting really behind with his work."

"Strange. When I saw him last night he said he was staying in," said David. "There was an essay he wanted to finish."

"What a waste," said Cath, unable to hold back the tears.

"What, finishing an essay?"

"No, the rest of it. Everything he's left unfinished … his whole life, if he dies…" and that was as far as she got, before she found herself in tears.

"It's all right," said David, putting a comforting arm round her shoulders. "It's all right. You just let it all out."

Cath continued sobbing and choking; she couldn't seem to stop. She was vaguely aware of David's arm supporting her, making her feel safe. She felt him plant a light kiss on her forehead, and looked up at him in surprise.

He looked lovingly down into her tear-filled eyes, leaned down and kissed her on the mouth. She jerked back in surprise, but it was too late. His lips were firmly connected to hers, and he concentrated all his energy on drawing her soul-light directly out of her, up through her mouth and into his. He swallowed, savouring the taste, then released her.

'Two,' he thought to himself.

Cath felt strange, rather hazy and disorientated. She stared at David, puzzled. "What were you doing?" she asked.

"Making you feel better," said David. "You don't feel sad any more, do you?"

Cath thought for a moment. Her body felt exhausted from crying, but she didn't seem to feel sad now. She didn't seem to feel anything at all.

"What were we just talking about?" she asked.

"Your friend, Graham. You remember, the one who's in hospital."

"Oh, him," said Cath, feeling nothing. "Is it time to go home now?"

"I think so," said David. "I'll just pay for the coffee, then I'll walk you back to the campus."

Cath stared down at her empty coffee mug. She couldn't remember drinking it. She couldn't even taste the coffee in her mouth. All she could taste was the sharp sting of mints and something else, something horrible, behind it. Something that reminded her of rancid meat.

Suddenly Cath made a dive for the ladies' toilets and was violently sick. She splashed some water on her face and made her way out of the coffee shop. David was waiting for her in the alley. He offered her a mint to suck.

"Here, it'll take away the taste," he said casually.

She accepted the sweet, and David led her back towards the campus, and left her outside her room in the halls of residence. They didn't talk on the way there – there was nothing to say.

# Chapter 24

When Thren left the Chapter House he was seething. Pearson, and his selfish plan to get rid of Dudley, made him really angry – and Poole was not much better. He'd raised the odd objection but then allowed himself to be led along anyway.

"How could they?" raged Thren out loud. "They call themselves Christians. They dare to refer to themselves by His name, and then act like *that*. Well, I know what I'd like to do to them, and it sure don't involve making that scumbag Pearson rich and famous. There's just gotta be a way to stop them, if only I could figure it out."

Thren was too angry then to figure out anything much, so he took himself off and flew over the city. It was just getting dark as he did a quick circuit over the campus, to check on the students' soul-lights.

They all looked safe enough to him, none of them flickering blue with fear or anything, so he reckoned they were fine.

He did spot Cath's soul-light, walking into town about then, but she was under the overhanging rows of shops, so he couldn't see her physically. Since there were no other soul-lights keeping hers company, he figured she was on her own.

"Typical teacher material," he muttered. "Everyone else is in a state of shock and she's going shopping."

If David's body hadn't been hidden by the overhanging

rows, Thren would have known something was up. Even though David had swallowed Marty's soul-light, it didn't show, and a body without a soul-light would certainly have attracted Thren's attention right then. But Thren couldn't see him at all, and Cath's soul-light looked as brown and steady as it had that morning, so Thren flew off to make himself useful. Of course, he'd have done things differently if he'd known what was about to happen to Cath, but that's easy to say afterwards. Dealing with the guilt is harder.

Thren zigzagged across the sky above the city. He was looking for a soul-light. A little green soul-light flecked with gold, and eventually he found it. The simmering red light was there too, as Thren flew down to check out the cramped terraced house in a run-down area near the racecourse.

Thren peered in through the kitchen window. Gee, the place was a dump. The sink was full of dirty dishes, there was stale food on the table, and it smelt like nobody had put the garbage out for a week, he thought. It didn't look like anybody'd done the laundry either. Amy's school uniform was looking kinda grubby, and Harry's shirt was gross. Spilt food all down it. They were in the middle of another argument.

"But I have to have it," protested Amy. "It's for school."

"Tough," said Harry. "I'm not forking out good money for a new blazer."

"But I can't wear it like this," said Amy, holding up something that was supposedly a school blazer, but looked rather more like a dust rag. "I'll get into trouble." One sleeve was ripped off, and the rest of it was torn and covered with mud.

"Then you should have looked after it better."

"But it wasn't my fault," said Amy, nearly in tears. "It was the big girls. They stopped me on the way home."

"Then learn to stick up for yourself," said Harry, unsympathetically. "There's no point in me buying you another blazer until you do – it'll only get wrecked the next time they gang up on you."

"But I don't want there to be a next time," said Amy. "Can't you stop them?"

"Not my problem," said Harry. "It's a tough world, Amy, you have to learn to deal with it. Fight back."

"But I'm only nine, and they're bigger than me," she wailed. "Anyway, I'm not supposed to fight."

"Then let them bully you, it's not my problem."

Amy stood there, frustrated, her eyes brimming with tears.

'How can a child argue with a grown-up, when they're the ones who make the rules?' thought Thren.

"If Luke was here, he'd have helped me," she whispered.

"Shut up about Luke."

"But we ought to look for him."

"Why? He's a big boy. He's made his own decision."

"He left 'cos you hit him. If we found him and you said sorry, he'd come back," pleaded Amy.

"We don't want him back, he's just another mouth to feed."

"He doesn't eat very much," said Amy. "I could share my dinner with him."

"Shut up. It's not about how much either of you eat," shouted Harry, impatiently. "It's the fact you're here at all. Why should I be stuck with looking after you? You're not mine, either of you. Just because your mother moved in with me, and dragged you along too. It's not my fault she died."

"Yes, it is!" shouted Amy. "You hit her and she went to hospital and never came back."

"Get out," screamed Harry. "Get out before I hit *you*!"

Amy grabbed her schoolbag and shot out of the room.

Thren heard her scramble up the stairs, and then a door banged shut. He flew up and looked in through the child's window. Her room was a little tidier than the kitchen, and someone had painted a rather clumsy mural on one wall. It was of a jungle, with the heads of various animals with cartoon smiley faces peering out from between the palm fronds. The colours were beginning to fade.

Amy was sitting on the bed trying not to cry. She missed her brother, she missed her mother, she even missed Harry, in a way. The person downstairs was nothing like the friendly, laughing man they'd moved in with. To Amy it seemed like even the real Harry had gone away, and left her with a terrifying stranger.

"It must be my fault," she whispered into the ear of a battered toy elephant, "I must be doing something wrong. That's why they've all left. If Luke was still here, he'd be able to tell me what it is, then I could make it better … but Luke's gone too." Flinging herself full-length on the bed, Amy burst into floods of tears.

Thren turned in mid-air. He didn't know how to help her, and he couldn't bear to watch her cry. He fluttered down to peer through the kitchen window again. How could Harry just sit there when a little girl was sobbing her heart out upstairs?

Harry wasn't just sitting there. He was slumped forwards in his chair, with his head in his hands, and he was weeping. The man was angry and frustrated and bitterly miserable, and Thren couldn't think of anything that he could do to help.

# Chapter 25

Thren flew back to the cathedral feeling totally confused. He couldn't stand Harry, and the way he bullied the kid, but now he'd seen the guy in tears, Thren wanted to help him.

"What is happening to me?" worried Thren. "Maybe I'm sick or something. The guy's a thug – probably a murderer. Not the kind of person I'm supposed to help – no way. At least, not that I recall."

Actually, Thren couldn't remember enough of his training to be sure if he was supposed to be selective or not, and stressing about it was making him feel uncomfortable, so he decided to forget the whole thing.

There was no sign of Tor at the cathedral, so Thren headed down to the campus to look for her, and find out what had happened that day.

She was in the library, watching Bex and Flint who were attempting to study. Well, Bex was, Flint just sat on a chair, with his feet on a table, staring at the ceiling, as he fidgeted with his mobile phone.

"Can't you put that thing down for a moment?" teased Bex, "Anyone would think you're welded to it."

"Well, I'm not. In fact I can't stand the thing.' Flint slung the mobile roughly down on the table and it slid to the far end on the smooth surface. He flung his chair back and wandered over to the nearest bookshelf. "Who reads this stuff anyway?" he muttered as he glanced at the titles in the psychology section. "It's all psycho-babble anyway."

Thren reached out from behind the shelves where he and Tor were hiding and picked up the mobile. He punched a few buttons and finally got into the text messages. He scrolled through them quickly, hoping that Flint wouldn't turn round and notice his phone was missing. The most recent one read "Well? Decided yet?" The one before said "What's it worth?" and the earliest one, dated the night of the party, read "WE KNOW YOUR SECRET." They were all sent from the same number.

Thren slid the phone back onto the table just as Flint returned to his chair and reached forward to pick up the mobile.

"Bex!" Flint's voice was tight with anger, "What do you think you're playing at?"

He waved the phone, still displaying the last message Thren had looked at, under her nose. Thren had forgotten to come out of the inbox before returning the phone.

Bex, who hadn't noticed the angels in the library, or seen Thren pick up the mobile, didn't know what Flint meant. "What are you on about? I haven't touched your phone."

"I thought I could trust you. I should have known better. You don't go reading someone's private messages, right!"

"I didn't," she protested. "Maybe you knocked a button or something when you threw the phone down – I don't know, but if you keep holding it in front of my face like that I can't help but read it." Flint snatched the phone away and shoved it in his pocket, but it was too late.

"What does it mean?" asked Bex. "WE KNOW YOUR SECRET. What secret?"

Flint sunk back into his chair and refused to answer.

"Be like that then," said Bex, annoyed that he wouldn't trust her, "but if you're being blackmailed you ought to get some help."

"Who says I'm being blackmailed?"

"It's just that kind of message, isn't it? WE KNOW

YOUR SECRET ... WE KNOW WHERE THE BODY'S BURIED ... that kind of thing." Bex paused, "You don't think it's got anything to do with ... everything else that's happened, do you?"

Flint looked at her, tempted to leave her with that idea, and get himself off the hook. It would be so easy, but then she'd be worrying about that too. Better to come clean, a least a little.

"No, it's not. The first text came *before* we played that stupid game at the party."

"First text? You mean there've been others?" Flint handed her the phone and she scrolled through the messages.

"They're all from the same number," said Bex, looking up at him, "Do you know who they're from?"

Flint shook his head.

"Have you tried phoning the number?"

"Of course, but all I get is the phone cutting off. They must recognise my number as soon as I dial."

Flint gave her a wry grin, "I did try phoning from a call box but they hung up as soon as they heard my voice ... It's driving me crazy!"

Bex looked at him nervously. She knew he'd hate her for it but she had to ask.

"What is your secret, Flint?"

She expected him to lose his temper, but he just shook his head and said "You really think I'm going to tell you?"

Seeing how worried she was looking he added, "I don't want you to know – I don't want anyone to know, that's *why* it's a secret, but trust me, it's got nothing to do with what's going on at the moment."

"Okay," said Bex , deciding that it wasn't fair push him to tell her more than that if he didn't want to. She tried to turn her attention back to her work, although she found it hard to concentrate with so many other things on her mind. What was Flint's secret? Behind the bookshelves Thren and Tor exchanged glances. They wanted to know too.

"I knew he wasn't good enough for her," whispered Tor.

"How can you say that?" Thren found himself arguing. "You don't even know what his secret is."

Bex leaned back in her chair. "It's no good. I can't concentrate. There must be something we can do before this … thing gets anybody else."

Flint looked up. "We ought to make a list."

"What?"

"A list of everyone who was at the party," he explained. "Then we can go and check if they're still all right – warn them to be careful."

"They'll think we're mad!" she protested.

"So, which would you prefer? Dead friends, or ones who doubt your sanity?" Flint looked at her solemnly. "There's got to be a connection between the thing at the party, and what happened to Graham and Marty. You know there has – and it could be after any of us. It's only fair to warn them."

"All right," said Bex, knowing he was right. Her conversation with the angels had told her as much. She just didn't want to admit it yet. It was all too strange to take in. She picked up a notebook. "All right, we'll make a list."

Just then Debbie walked in, followed by Nesta and Tim.

"We thought we'd find you here," said Debbie. "With the canteen closed it's the only place to get together."

"What makes you think I wouldn't be here usually?" asked Flint.

"The fact that none of us ever sees you in here," said Tim.

"How's Marty?" asked Bex.

"Still unconscious," replied Nesta. "We sat with him all afternoon, kept talking to him, but it didn't seem to make any difference."

"His parents are there now," said Debbie. "The hospital

got hold of them and they came back from holiday early. We thought we'd better leave them alone with him."

"We asked about Graham, too, while we were there," added Nesta. "They wouldn't let us see him. The only people the police are allowing in are his parents."

"The police?" Bex looked puzzled, "What have they got to do with it?"

"They don't think what happened to Graham was an accident," Tim explained. "They suspect someone was trying to kill him, so until they work out what's been going on, they're keeping him under police protection." Tim glanced at Flint and Bex. "So what are you two doing?" asked Tim. "You don't usually study together. In fact, Flint doesn't usually study at all."

"I'll ignore that," said Flint. "We're making a list of everyone who was at the party. We think …" he paused nervously, "we think there may be a connection between that, and what's happening to people."

He waited for the others to laugh at him, but they didn't.

"That makes sense," said Tim. "I know we've all tried to pretend it didn't happen, but it did … And if whatever spoke to us at the party is here …"

"It is," said Bex firmly. "I'm sure of it."

"What can we do?" asked Nesta.

"Work out who else was at the party, and warn them," said Flint.

"They won't believe it," said Debbie. "I'm not sure *I* believe it."

She looked at the others. They all looked so serious. They were sure they were on to something, and deep down she knew they were right. "Oh all right, we'll do it."

Thren and Tor watched from behind the bookcases as the students started writing their list.

"At least they're starting to take it seriously," whispered Tor to Thren. "The more alert they are the less chance that the demon will be able to get to them."

"I guess so," replied Thren. "But how can they fight one of the invisibles? Even we don't know quite what we're up against, so what can *they* do?"

"Stick together for a start," said Tor. "That should make them a little less vulnerable." She was afraid 'sticking together' would mean Bex and Flint spending even more time together, but it couldn't be helped.

"And the best way that we can help them is to try and find out more about whatever it is we're dealing with. Come along."

Tor dragged Thren out of the library and the pair of them started scanning the city for any sign of the demon.

Meanwhile, Flint was glaring at the list. "We missed some," he muttered. "There were thirteen people at the party. There must have been, 'cos we had twenty-six candles."

"How many names have we got?" asked Tim.

"Eleven," said Flint, reading them out. "Me, Marty, Debbie, Nesta, Bex, Tim, Graham, Sam, Mark, Cath and Sarah."

"What about Paul?" suggested Nesta.

Flint nodded. "I'd forgotten he was with us. He's always so quiet." He added Paul's name to the list.

"Joanna," said Debbie suddenly. "She was there. Has anyone seen her today?"

Nobody could remember seeing her.

"Let's go and check her room," said Flint, standing up abruptly.

"I'll stay here," said Nesta.

The others remembered that Joanna's room was on the second floor in one of the older buildings. Nesta's wheelchair couldn't get onto that level.

"I'll stay with you," said Tim, adding to the others, "It's better not to go round on our own – just make sure you come and tell us when you've found her."

In the halls of residence, Debbie, Flint and Bex were knocking on Joanna's door, but getting no reply. They were just turning away when David appeared from further along the corridor.

"Looking for Joanna?" he asked casually. "I ran into her earlier. She asked me to give you a message. She said she's decided to go home for a few days. She seemed a bit upset. I expect it was the news about her friends."

Not that David realised how close to the truth he was in saying that Joanna had gone away. If he'd known, he'd have been furious that she'd escaped from him so completely. He still had plans to catch up with her later, and savour that tasty blue soul-light. He was just making up a story to keep the others from talking to her, in case she said anything about his visit to her room that morning. "See you around," said David, walking on.

"Doesn't it strike you as odd?" asked Flint. "This guy appears from nowhere the day after the party, and starts chumming up with all of us."

"You think he tried to kill Marty?" asked Debbie.

"I don't know. I just think we should be very careful around him."

"Suits me," said Debbie. "He's a creep. Wait a minute … do you think he might try again … with Marty, I mean?"

"Who knows?" said Flint.

"Right," said Debbie, "I'm going back to the hospital. I'm going to stay with Marty and make sure nothing else happens to him."

Debbie hurried off down the corridor, leaving Bex and Flint alone.

"What are we going to do?" asked Bex.

"Follow David."

*** 

After the others had gone Nesta and Tim waited in the library beside Bex's abandoned books. Tim noticed Nesta scanning the open files on the table.

"Why are you reading that? You've changed courses, remember?"

"I hadn't forgotten," replied Nesta defensively. "I'm just interested, that's all."

"So how's the English course going?"

"Fine," she replied, but Tim wasn't convinced.

"Look, Nesta," he said, hesitantly, "I thought we were friends."

"We are!" said Nesta, wishing that wasn't all they were.

"Then why won't you tell me what's going on? You gave up Applied Biology, which you loved, and transferred to English, which doesn't seem to interest you at all. There must be a reason."

"Of course," she said, "I just decided …" Her voice petered out. She hated lying, especially to Tim.

"The truth, Nesta. I can tell when you're bluffing."

She hesitated briefly, then admitted, "I was getting a lot of flak from some of the other students on the course. They kept saying I wouldn't be able to keep up, pull my weight, once we started doing fieldwork. They didn't see the point in me studying something when I wasn't going to get the chance to put it into practice later. That I might as well change to some other subject. Something where the chair wouldn't get in the way."

"You should have told me. I'd have known how to deal with them."

"It's not your problem, Tim."

"Yes it is. You're my friend, my best friend, and I'm not going to let them treat you like that."

"But …"

"No buts," said Tim decisively. "What about all that stuff we talked about last term. Who our heroes were? Yours were all explorers and naturalists, remember? You wanted to be like … like …"

"David Attenborough and Gerald Durrell ..."

"Michael Palin and Steve Irwin ..."

"Except I'm not that keen on wrestling crocodiles," said Nesta, grinning. "Maybe I'd rather be Diane Fosse – gorillas are much more interesting. Have you read her book?"

"That's more like it," Tim grinned back at her. "How can you follow in their footsteps if you don't even finish the course?"

"But none of them were in a wheelchair!"

"Do you think it would have stopped them if they were?"

Nesta thought about it. She couldn't imagine any one of the people she admired *not* working in the field they loved. Maybe they wouldn't have had the *same* career, but they'd have found *some* way of working with the creatures they considered so fascinating.

"You're right, I suppose," she admitted, "perhaps I should have stuck with the course and seen where it took me."

"Of course you should! I just can't understand how you let yourself be talked into leaving it in the first place."

Nesta hesitated. She wanted to explain to him how she felt sometimes, but she was afraid he might think less of her for it – but if she couldn't talk to Tim, who could she talk to?

"You don't understand, Tim. You're always so confident, you probably don't know how it feels to get depressed, what it does to you."

"Depressed?" He looked at her in surprise. Nesta never struck him as being depressed, she always seemed so cheerful.

"I can't help it. I try not to do the 'why me' thing, not to wonder what life would be like if I wasn't in this chair, but I just can't help it sometimes. That's when I get depressed. I don't have much confidence, not really. I was really scared about coming here, living independently, but I was just about coping with it. When the others started knocking me, telling me I didn't have a chance, I just wasn't tough enough to ignore them."

Tim felt guilty. "I never noticed. Whenever I see you, you always seem so on top of things."

"It's when you don't see me that I'm in trouble. When I'm really down I just hide in my room. I can't cope with coming out and talking to people. I just want to crawl under a rock and stay there."

"Next time I'll come looking for you."

"Will you?"

"I promise … Now what are you going to do about this course? It's not too late to change back, you know. You've only missed a few weeks."

"But what will I do about the fieldwork?"

"We'll find a way to manage."

"But it's not your problem."

"It's not a problem at all," said Tim. "You just have to see your course tutors. See if you can change back to Biology. If you explain what was going on, I'm sure they'll understand."

"But what about the other students?"

"Just ignore them. I'll back you up. Who was it, anyway?"

"The boys mostly: Sam, Mark, Peter and Fliss."

"Sam and Mark are supposed to be your friends."

"They probably thought they *were* being …"

"They ought to know better. Honestly, I could kill them for this."

Nesta looked at Tim, "Not funny."

Tim looked away embarrassed, "No, it wasn't. Sorry."

# Chapter 26

David was looking for Sarah. He'd decided that she'd be the easiest one to pick off next, with her friend Cath out of the way. He checked her room, but the girl wasn't there so he started to search the rest of the campus, casting about for Sarah's fuzzy pink soul-light.

Behind him Bex and Flint were trying to keep track of David without being seen.

"He's bound to notice us soon," whispered Bex.

"Not if we're careful," replied Flint, dragging her back round a corner as David glanced behind him. "Besides, we're students here too. We've got as much right to be anywhere on campus as he has."

"But if he is what you think he is?" said Bex quietly. "Won't he realise what we're doing and come after us next?"

"He's going to come after us anyway," said Flint.

"Oh," said Bex, softly. She knew Flint was right, but she really didn't want to hear it put into words. "Maybe we're wrong," she said, hopefully. "Maybe he's just another student."

Flint glanced at Bex and shook his head. He was certain that David was the 'thing' from the party. Certain that 'it' was going to try and destroy everyone who'd been there that night, including himself and Bex. Especially himself and Bex. He was almost certain that 'it' would succeed, too. So far life hadn't given Flint much cause to be optimistic.

They followed David as he turned and started to stride quickly towards the chapel. He hesitated outside the door for a moment, then reached out, turned the handle, and stepped inside.

Sarah was sitting there, hunched up on a pew, sobbing. She couldn't understand what was going on, any of it. She'd never had to deal with anything like it before. She'd reached the age of nineteen without ever having come face to face with grief, or loss or fear. All her troubles had been little ones, and they hadn't equipped her to deal with the situation she was in now.

Graham, who she'd just started to fall for, was critically ill, Marty was in a coma and now Cath was being funny with her. After sitting alone in her room for a while, trying to calm down, Sarah had decided that she didn't want to be on her own after all. She had gone to Cath's room a few minutes before, knocked on the door and called her name, but Cath hadn't answered. Sarah knew she was in, because she could hear her moving about, so why was Cath refusing to come to the door? It was all too much, so Sarah had wandered off, feeling miserable, and found herself in the chapel, without even knowing why.

She wasn't religious, though her parents were, and had only stuck her nose into the chapel once since she'd started at university, but suddenly it was where she wanted to be.

It was quiet and peaceful in there, and she didn't feel she had to hide her feelings. She could let the tears out with no one to criticise, or try to cheer her up before she was ready. Somehow the place itself seemed comforting, calming her down even as she cried.

She reached into her bag and pulled out the magazine she'd been reading the day before. She opened it at the horoscope page and read the prediction for her star sign again: 'The weekend will see the start of a great romance.' But Graham had been injured before the weekend even started. '… be sure to let your crush know how you feel'. She hadn't let him know, had she? She'd chickened out every time. It wasn't that she didn't care about him. She did, she really did, and she wanted to go out with him, but she'd been frightened of what he might want from the relationship. She knew a lot of the girls in her hall were sleeping with their boyfriends, everyone seemed to expect it. Bex was probably an exception, because she was a Christian, but Sarah didn't share those beliefs.

It was just that she didn't feel ready for that yet, but she was ashamed to admit it. She'd wanted to ask some of the other girls for advice, but she was too embarrassed – they all seemed so much more experienced, she thought they'd laugh at her. She was afraid that if she told Graham, he'd lose interest in her, decide she wasn't worth bothering with. So she'd kept avoiding the issue when she thought Graham was about to ask her out, and now it was too late. Just when she'd decided that *she* was going to ask *him* out, that she could trust him not to rush things, he was in hospital. The doctors weren't even sure he'd live. She tore the horoscope page out of the magazine and started to shred it into little pieces.

She heard the door creak open and turned to see David standing there. Her heart sank. She didn't want company just then, and she certainly didn't want a stranger around.

"Can I help?" asked David, turning on the charm. He could see her fuzzy pink soul-light flickering with emotion, and suddenly felt very hungry. He forced himself to be patient. It wouldn't take long. The soul-light would be his in a few minutes. All he had to do was either kiss her or kill her. Easy. And she was hardly the strongest of the group, emotionally or physically. Getting hold of her soul-light would be like taking candy off a baby. David moved forward and sat down on the pew beside Sarah.

"It's good to have company at a time like this, isn't it?" said David. He smiled at her.

"Actually," said Sarah, nervously, "if you don't mind,

I'd rather be alone." She felt embarrassed. It seemed rude, rejecting his company like that, but she really didn't want him there. Somehow, he'd ruined the peaceful atmosphere of the chapel. In that setting David seemed to jar on her nerves, as if something wasn't quite right about him. He was out of place there, in a way that she wasn't, strangely enough, even though she hadn't spent time there before.

"Everyone needs a shoulder to cry on sometimes," said David, eager to kiss her and get it over with. Then he could get out of there. Being in the chapel made him physically uncomfortable, and somehow weaker. The less time he spent in there the better, but he didn't want to just kill her, not if he could help it. Too many suspicious deaths or accidents at once and people might start to work out who was behind them. Of course, if the police arrested him he could just ditch this body and get another, but the one he had was useful, and gave him easy access to the students. He slid his arm gently round Sarah's shoulders.

A shudder ran through her at his touch. She felt as if something horrible was wrapping its tentacles round her, and she pulled away from him. She couldn't understand it. He looked perfectly normal, but when he'd touched her Sarah had felt a real sense of … evil.

"Keep away from me!" she snapped, then shut up, shocked at her own reaction. A voice at the back of her mind was saying, 'Are you mad? What do you mean by evil anyway? You don't use that word. You're going to be *so* embarrassed about this tomorrow. What must he think of you?' Sarah pushed the thoughts away. She stood up and edged out of the pew. She felt safer with a bit of distance between herself and David. "I'm sorry," she said, "I didn't mean to be rude, but …"

David stood up and started to move towards her. Sarah felt paralysed, like a rabbit watching a stoat. She wanted to run away but her legs wouldn't move. Her mind was still telling her not to be silly, that he wasn't going to hurt her, but something deeper inside her knew better. He reached out a hand towards her and he wasn't smiling any more.

Suddenly Sarah found herself praying. Not with words. She wasn't calm enough to put what she needed into words; besides she couldn't think of the right things to say, she hadn't prayed for years. She sent up an arrow of pure desperation, certain for the first time in her life that someone was there to hear it, that He'd understand, and do something to save her. After all, if there was evil, there had to be good.

David put his hand on her arm, and she tried to pull away from him, but his grip was strong. He brought his face close to hers, preparing for the kiss, and the stench of putrefaction almost overwhelmed her. She felt so faint that her knees buckled under her of their own accord, and his lips barely brushed against her hair. He pulled her back up towards him and she screamed *"Let go of me!"* Underneath the fear she could feel disappointment. Why hadn't somebody done something to save her? Now it was too late.

Just then the door to the chapel crashed open. Flint and Bex stood there. They felt a little foolish. Listening outside the door all they'd heard was David trying to comfort a sobbing Sarah, but she'd sounded so frightened they had to burst in and make sure she was all right.

The four of them stood there, in silence, uncertain what to do next. It was David who made the first move. He released Sarah's arm gently, then turned to Bex and Flint. "It's all right," he said smoothly. "There's nothing to worry about. Sarah's getting a bit hysterical, that's all. I was just trying to calm her down."

"Sarah, are you all right?" asked Bex.

"Did he do anything to you?" said Flint, "Because if he did ..."

"No," whispered Sarah, "I'm all right. He just ... I probably got the wrong end of the stick, that's all." She felt a fool for getting so upset. He'd only taken her arm, and tried to kiss her, but she couldn't shake off the feeling that he wasn't what he seemed; that there was something nasty underneath his handsome exterior.

David made his excuses and left, cursing silently at missing out on the little pink soul-light that was Sarah. She was stronger than she looked – and she didn't even know it.

"Thanks," she said to Bex and Flint after David had left the chapel. "I can't explain it but I was terrified. There's something … not right about him. I know it sounds silly but I really felt he was going to hurt me somehow." She paused, then admitted, "Actually, I thought he was going to kill me. I was so scared I was even … praying for help. Then you two burst in." She smiled at them gratefully.

"Don't look at *me* like that," said Flint, sharply. "I'm not the answer to anybody's prayers. We were following David because we thought he might be the cause of what's been going on round here. We thought he might be the … the thing that spoke to us at the party."

"I think you're right," said Sarah. "In fact, I'm sure of it."

"But how do we prove it?" asked Bex.

"We can't," said Flint. "That's the problem. We can't go to the police with a story like this. They'd never believe us."

# Chapter 27

Bex and Flint walked Sarah back to the library, and joined Tim and Nesta, filling them in on everything that had just happened. They were still discussing their suspicions about David when Flint glanced at his watch, swore and stood up.

"I'm late for rehearsal," he announced. "I'd better be off."

"Rehearsals?" said Tim. "At a time like this?"

"I've got to go. Bex, do you want me to walk you home? It's on my way."

"All right," said Bex. "If you're sure you don't mind?"

"Who's going to walk *you* home, Flint?" said Tim, only half-joking. "Seriously, you need to be careful on your way back."

"I will," said Flint. "Come on, Bex."

Bex was pleased to have company on the way to the cathedral, and an excuse to get there quickly. She knew they couldn't tell the police what they suspected, but she could tell Thren and Tor. Perhaps, if they knew how the thing had disguised itself, they'd be able to stop him. And at least Flint wouldn't be hanging around at her place that evening. Not that she minded his company, but she didn't want him finding out about the angels and going all funny on her. She was just thinking about Flint, and how much easier he'd been to get along with lately, when he turned to her and said, "I thought Sarah had more sense ... imagine thinking that we were an answer to prayer."

"Perhaps we were," replied Bex.

"Oh, no. I'm not going along with that," said Flint. "We were outside the chapel all the time, we didn't suddenly appear because Sarah 'wished' us there. We were following David because he's the obvious suspect in all this. Prayer had nothing to do with it."

"How do you know?"

"Because I don't believe in prayer. It's a waste of time. It's not like anyone ever answers. You can pray all you like but the same rotten things keep on happening."

"What things?" asked Bex.

Flint just shrugged and kept on walking. Bex was struggling to keep up with him. She glanced sideways at his face. It was tense and miserable.

"What are you rehearsing?" she asked, trying to change the subject.

"I'm not telling you," he said. "You'll only laugh."

"No, I won't. Come on, Flint, I thought we were friends – or at least starting to be."

He shook his head.

"Don't kid yourself, Bex," he said, bitterly. "I don't do friends. I'm looking out for you because I feel responsible for what happened at the party. I don't want any more deaths on my conscience, that's all. I've got enough to deal with already."

"What do you mean?" asked Bex.

"Nothing," said Flint, and didn't say another word until they reached the archway that led to the abbey green. "See you tomorrow," he said, and walked away.

Bex stared after him, puzzled. He obviously felt guilty about something, and she was sure it wasn't only what had happened at the party. She felt hurt too, at the way he'd denied that they were friends.

Still, there was no time to worry about it right then. She had to find the angels. She fetched Dudley's keys from the house and let herself into the cathedral. She searched everywhere, even climbing the stairs all the way up to the roof, but there was no sign of them.

"Thren! Tor!" she called out, but they couldn't hear her.

The invisibles were making sure of that, by keeping the angels busy on the other side of the city. The creatures were terrifying people by making strange noises in their houses and throwing the furniture around. Thren and Tor had had to go and respond to the situation, to protect the people whose homes were being infested. Besides, the angels hoped that the demon that they were looking for was responsible, so that they could deal with him before he attacked any more of the students.

"Where are you?" called Bex. "I need to tell you something," but the angels still couldn't hear her – which was fair after all. Balance and counter-balance, that's how it worked. Thren had allowed Bex to see him, build up a relationship with him, so Dross had had the chance to come through to the physical world. Tor, too, had broken the rules, by mentioning soul-lights, so some of the lesser invisibles had had a chance to stir up trouble. The angels were dealing with the creatures, and driving them back to where they belonged, but in the process they were missing the chance to talk to Bex, and find out her suspicions about David. Advantage Dross.

Bex wandered down the stairs and back into the main body of the cathedral. It was still empty.

Well, if she couldn't speak to Thren and Tor about the situation, she was going to have to speak to her father. He might know what to do, if she could find him. He hadn't been at home when she fetched the keys. She was about to leave the cathedral when she heard voices coming from the refectory. She walked cautiously through the cloisters, not sure what to expect. Suddenly she heard screams and shouts and she panicked. She ran the last few steps and burst into the room. Everyone turned to look at her. There was total silence. Flint, roped on to a large wooden cross, met her eyes and then looked away in embarrassment. A few people in the room said hello to Bex and then turned back to what they were doing.

"Come along, everybody," said the director. "Concentrate! Now take it from the point where the cross has been raised up. Guards ... where have the guards got to? They're not missing *again*, are they?" The rehearsal continued.

Bex grinned at Flint, trying hard not to giggle. Flint was playing Christ in the Mystery Plays! No wonder he hadn't wanted to tell her. The medieval cycle of plays were performed in Chester every five years. They were a major event; thousands of people came to see them. The plays covered the main stories in the Bible, from Creation to the Last Judgement, and the full cycle was usually performed over two or three evenings, repeated several times over a few weeks of the summer. Bex had been in them herself when she was younger, starting out as a droplet of water in the flood, and moving on to various speaking parts as she got older. She'd nearly got involved in this production, and then thought better of it, in case it interfered with her uni work.

She stood and watched the rehearsal for a few minutes. Flint was very good in the part, but then, he was a drama student. She could see why he'd want to get involved in the production, but could also imagine his embarrassment at landing the part of Jesus, given his scornful attitude towards Christianity. She waved at him, putting him off completely, so that he forgot his lines.

"All right, all right," said the director patiently. He was a pleasant looking middle-aged man, with cropped fair hair and a broad, friendly smile. "Let's take a break, since everyone has stopped concentrating. Flint, climb down from there. Your arms must be getting stiff. Five minutes, everyone."

Then he wandered away with his nose in the script, wondering how to direct the next scene with several members of the cast missing, which was a constant problem, and his lead player, Flint, being distracted by a friend dropping into the rehearsal. Of course, the director knew Bex too, she had practically grown up in the cathedral, and he had been a bedesman there when she was younger. In fact he had given a terrific performance as Pontius Pilate in the first Mystery Plays that Bex had been involved in. Still, fond of her though he was, he couldn't afford to lose too much rehearsal time.

Flint climbed down off the cross, flexing his aching arms, and shuffled towards Bex.

"If you tell anyone about this …" he began.

"Everyone's going to know in a few months anyway," said Bex. "It's not the kind of thing you can keep secret. Besides, it just means you're a good actor."

"Please," said Flint. "Don't tell the others. Not at the moment, anyway."

"Oh, all right," said Bex. "Not that I owe you anything." His remark about not being friends still rankled.

As if he could read her mind, he said, "I'm sorry about before. I didn't mean … I'm just a bit edgy, that's all."

"Me, too," she said. "I can't tell you what I thought was going on in here when I heard all the screaming."

Flint grinned at her, and suddenly they were both laughing. It was the first time they'd relaxed for days. They stopped, feeling guilty, and the grins faded on their faces. How could they laugh in the middle of a crisis?

"Maybe this is what those texts were about?" suggested Bex, "Somebody's found out what part you're playing and they're trying to wind you up."

"If only it was that simple," said Flint, gloomily, "I could handle that, just about."

"Come on, everybody," called the director. "Back to work."

# Chapter 28

Thren and Tor were exhausted. They'd been battling the lesser invisibles for hours. First they'd had to drive them out of people's houses, before the little imps could do too much damage. Then the angels tried to deal with the creatures one by one as they ran through the streets, knocking over pedestrians and causing as much chaos as they could. Of course, humans couldn't see the imps but they could hear their shrill little squeals and feel their pinching fingers.

One of the creatures dived into a litter bin, and threw all the rubbish up into the air, so that it splattered into the face of a child who was in the middle of dropping his lolly stick into the bin. Another got into a department store window and started moving the window display around, and dancing about in the apparently empty clothes, causing a crowd of shoppers to gather on the pavement wondering what new, mechanised technique was being used. One inventive little imp, called Snig, managed to steal some flaming torches off a juggler who was busking in Eastgate Street. To everyone's surprise, including the juggler's, the torches started to jerk about by themselves, thrusting towards people's faces, or sign-writing in the air. Snig's spelling wasn't particularly good so his attempt to write 'Apocalypse', and terrify people, came out as 'A pogo lisps' which simply confused them. However, the fact that the torches were obviously moving of their own accord was frightening enough, and soon the crowd that had collected around the juggler was scattering in all directions, and taking shelter in the shops.

Some of the imps moved out into the non-pedestrianised parts of the city, clinging to cars and making strange popping and squealing sounds. This so unnerved the drivers that they thought their cars had developed faults, and pulled off the road. When they got out to try and discover what was causing the problem they were pelted with soggy, rotting leaves the imps had scooped up from the gutter.

Thren and Tor were kept busy trying to round the creatures up and limit the damage. They could defeat the imps with prayer, by ejecting them bodily from the physical realm, or by sprinkling them with holy water. However, there were so many of the lesser invisibles that it seemed to take forever. Tiring of dealing with each imp individually, the angels eventually managed to herd the remaining creatures into an empty warehouse on the outskirts of the city. Tor added the last of the holy water she was carrying to the sprinkler system. Thren set it off by activating the fire alarm, and the imps, howling with rage, fizzled out of existence in this world, and disappeared back to their own.

**\*\*\***

"That's it," said Thren, as the last of them evaporated, "I've had enough. I'm not lifting another feather tonight. I have had it with these guys. I mean, how did they get through in the first place?"

"I thought we'd established that some time ago," said Tor, primly. "*You* gave them the opportunity."

"Do you really think those little monsters were responsible for what's happening to the students?"

"Don't you?" asked Tor.

"I'm not so sure. I mean, they were tough cookies to get rid of, but don't you think they seemed a bit ... lightweight?

I mean, throwing people's furniture around – causing a bit of a panic – it's not in the same league as killing, is it?"

"There can't be two sets of invisibles loose in the city," said Tor, firmly. "We only broke the rules once."

Thren tried to interrupt her. He had a niggling feeling that the rules had been broken on a second occasion, but he couldn't remember when. Tor didn't give him a chance to speak. "At least now we've dealt with them, we can stop worrying about the students," she said.

Thren felt that worrying about the students was still part of his brief, but he was just too tired to argue.

"Can we call it a night now?" he asked. "We've been wrestling with those guys for hours, and I could really do with some time off."

"Angels don't have time off!" Tor made it sound like an order.

"Well, this is one angel who does," said Thren. "I'm for some R & R. I've not had a moment's peace since I got here, and if the students really are safe now, I can take a break. See ya!"

Thren took off, sailing high over the city. Tor glanced up at him and shook her head disapprovingly. How was she supposed to work with an angel who didn't obey the rules? Tor took off herself, and headed for the cathedral. She could see Bex's soul-light in the house on the abbey green, so with nothing to worry about she decided she could have some rest herself. Tor lay down on the cathedral roof, closed her eyes and slept.

***

An imp crept out of the shadows and sniggered at her. So the angels thought they'd dealt with them all, did they? Big mistake. They'd missed one. Snig, the imp who'd caused such chaos with the flaming torches. He might only be an imp, but even an imp can be trouble – and trouble was what the angels were in, if they thought their problems were over. The diversion had worked, if the angels really believed that they'd defeated the evil that was threatening the students, but that was one battle that hadn't even started yet. The imp set to work. A few minutes later it stepped back to look at its handy work and grinned. Then it scuttled off to find a safe hiding place before morning.

***

Thren was circling lazily over the city, wondering where to go to relax, when he noticed Dudley's soul-light. It wasn't in any trouble or anything, but Thren felt like some company so he decided to check it out. He landed beside the hostel and went inside to find Dudley in the office, talking to Janet.

"I just don't know what to do about him," she was saying to Dudley. "He says he's sixteen, but I'm sure he's younger ... and he won't even tell me his name. He's terrified I'm going to tell the police that he's here – that they'll send him home."

"Are you going to?" asked Dudley.

"I don't know," said Janet. "If he is under sixteen I have to, but I can't prove how old he is, either way. And what if they do take him back where he belongs? The boy's terrified. According to the night staff he's been having bad dreams, talking in his sleep ... I can't just send him home and pretend everything's all right."

"So what do you want me to do?" asked Dudley.

"Talk to him, see what you can find out. After all, he trusts you – you're the one that brought him here."

"And I don't want to betray that trust," said Dudley. "I can't get the boy to talk to me and then pass it all straight on to you."

"It'll be your decision. Just tell me what you think I ought to know." She smiled at him. "After all, I trust you too."

A few minutes later Dudley was sitting next to a boy Thren had seen before: the boy Dudley had found in a shop doorway and brought to the hostel a couple of days before. The boy smiled nervously at Dudley and twisted his hands as he spoke.

"Thanks for bringing me here," he began awkwardly.

"Don't mention it," said Dudley. "But you do seem to be presenting them with a bit of a problem, young man."

The boy shot him a troubled glance, then looked away hurriedly.

"I gather they don't know what to call you," said Dudley, gently. "And Boy does seem a little ... impersonal. Surely it couldn't hurt to tell us your Christian name?"

The boy hesitated. He was scared of being sent home, but he didn't want to lie either. Especially to the person who'd first helped him. Surely it couldn't hurt just to give his first name, or at least *a* first name. He was about to make one up when he caught Dudley's eye. He knew that the old man could guess what he was thinking, so he took a deep breath and gave his real name.

"I'm called Luke," he said. "And that's all I'm telling you."

Thren had a feeling he'd heard the name before, but he couldn't think where. Still, he gave the boy a closer look.

Luke was thin, almost scrawny, with untidy blond hair. He was wearing grubby jeans that looked a bit short in the leg and his bony wrists stuck out a good couple of inches from the sleeves of his battered checked shirt.

'Sure looks like you've been growing lately,' thought Thren. 'What have your folks been doing, standing you in compost?'

The boy looked in Thren's direction, and the angel was startled to see how blue his eyes were. 'Sky-coloured,' thought Thren, with a rush of homesickness that was almost a physical pain. 'And that soul-light looks kinda like sunshine.' It was a fiery yellow-orange, with occasional flickers of red. 'I sure wish I could figure out where you fit in.'

Dudley was still trying to find out more about the boy, but all he'd say was that his name was Luke and he was sixteen. At last Dudley stood up, said goodnight to the boy, had a few words with Janet and set off for home. Thren decided to stay with Luke and see what else he could find out.

**\*\*\***

When Dudley let himself into the house he found Bex waiting for him. She'd cooked supper for them both, and had meant to wait until her father had finished eating before telling him what was on her mind, but before he'd taken more than a couple of forkfuls Dudley said, "Come on, what is it? There's obviously something worrying you."

So Bex told him. She found it difficult at first. She'd already told her father about Thren the night she met him, but explaining what had happened at the party, and that she'd been involved in it, that was harder. She stared at her plate as she talked, not daring to look him in the eye.

He listened in silence, and she was grateful for it. It was hard enough to explain without having to cope with interruptions. She went on to tell him about Marty and Graham, and what she and the others suspected about David. She almost didn't tell him about Tor. Believing in one angel seemed difficult enough, it was a bit much expecting anyone to cope with the idea of two. But in the end she told him about her too. Bex could see her father would need all the information she had, if he was going to be able to give them any useful advice. When she finished speaking she glanced nervously at Dudley.

"If you're waiting for a lecture," he said, "you're not going to get one off me. You know what you did was foolish, but you're hardly going to make the same mistake twice. What matters now is how we deal with this."

Bex smiled. It was such a relief to hear her father say 'we' not 'you'. She was sure that if he was willing to help them, advise them, they'd find a way to stop the ... thing before it did any more damage. She actually had a lot more confidence in him than she did in the angels, but even he wasn't going to be able to put right the damage that was already done.

"Even if we manage to stop this ... creature, it won't help Graham or Marty. We don't know if either of them are going to be all right, and it's all my fault."

"No, Becky," said Dudley gently. "It wasn't you who attacked Graham, or poisoned Marty. Don't take on more guilt than you really deserve. If you'd known the consequences in advance, you wouldn't have played the game, would you?"

"Of course not, none of us would."

"The thing that's doing this is evil. More evil than any of you could have imagined when you gave it a chance to come in."

"Flint says he knew it was bad when he invited it to appear. He feels terrible about it."

"I'm not surprised, but I doubt if even he would willingly have let this happen. Flint's not a bad young man – he's just very ... troubled. I get the impression he was unhappy long before all this started."

"You're probably right," said Bex, "but he's not really the problem right now. The question is, how do we stop anything else happening?"

They talked for hours, and by the end of the evening were no nearer to finding an easy solution, but Dudley did make one suggestion.

"You can't tell the police what you really think is going on," he said, consideringly. "Flint's right about that. They wouldn't believe you – but there's nothing to stop you suggesting that they take a closer look at David. There may be some evidence that could connect him to the crimes."

"Would that help?" asked Bex.

"It might," he said. "If they locked him up it would give

us more time to find a way to send him back to … wherever he came from, before he does any more damage."

"But what if we're wrong?" asked Bex. "What if he's just an ordinary student, like the rest of us? I wouldn't want to get him into trouble."

"If he's innocent the police will just investigate him, and then eliminate him from their enquiries," said her father.

"I suppose it can't do any harm," said Bex. "The police are supposed to be interviewing us tomorrow, anyway. They started this afternoon, but there are so many students they couldn't talk to us all in one day."

"Are they coming here?" asked Dudley.

"No, they've asked all of us to go to the campus."

"But it's Saturday."

"I know, but it can't be helped. Nobody's objecting anyway. They're all too shaken up by what's happened."

"Then it's time you went to bed," said Dudley.

"But there's still so much I don't understand," protested Bex. "About Tor and Thren and … all of it."

"We'll talk about that another time," said her father. "At the moment, you need some sleep. You look exhausted."

"But what about the creature – David? What if he attacks someone else?"

"He won't, not tonight. You're all suspicious of him now. That should make it harder for him. He'll have to plan some other way to get to each of you."

Bex looked at her father as she stood up to leave the room. He looked so stern, so serious. She'd never seen him like that before. She felt that she'd let him down, badly, that he was disappointed with her, and she couldn't bear it. They'd always been so close, and now he seemed like a stranger.

"Goodnight, then," said Bex from the doorway.

"Goodnight, my dear, and God bless."

"Oh, Dad," said Bex, crumbling. Dudley quickly crossed the room and put his arm round his daughter as she sobbed on his shoulder. When she finally finished weeping, he dried her eyes with his hankie and sent her up to bed. A few minutes later he took her up a mug of hot chocolate, and sat on the edge of her bed as she drank it, and settled down to sleep. He tucked the duvet tightly round her, something he hadn't done for years, and stayed to keep her company until she fell asleep.

He sat for some time, watching his sleeping daughter. He knew she thought he was angry with her, but he wasn't. It wasn't anger he was feeling – not towards her anyway. It was fear. Something evil was out there, and it was trying to destroy Bex and her friends. However reassuring he might have been to Bex, he *was* frightened. He couldn't bear the idea of her being in danger. The thought of losing her terrified him.

Once he was sure that Bex was asleep he fetched a book and blanket from his room and made himself comfortable in the chair in her room. He didn't think the 'thing' would try anything that night, but he wasn't taking any chances. He was going to watch over his daughter until morning, and make sure she was safe.

*** 

Across the city, in the hostel for the homeless, Thren was watching over a sleeper too. He was observing Luke as the boy tossed and turned, muttering in his sleep. Thren knelt by the bed, trying to make out what the boy was saying, and thought he caught the name 'Amy'.

'Well, what da ya know?' thought Thren, satisfied. 'Now we're getting somewhere.'

***

David was also trying to get close to someone who was asleep – or rather unconscious. Determined to capture Graham's soul-light now that the boy was unable to put up a fight, David made his way to the hospital. He knew that the angels were being distracted by the invasion of lesser invisibles, and he expected it would be easy to walk into the hospital and finish Graham off. He'd come so close to collecting the boy's soul-light the night before that he was desperate to complete the task. He could almost imagine the taste of it, as he walked along the hospital corridor to the room where Graham was lying.

"Excuse me, sir," said a uniformed policeman, raising from the chair on which he had been sitting, "but I'm afraid no visitors are allowed, except for direct family. Are you related to the young man, by any chance?" David considered lying, and claiming to be Graham's brother, but what was the point, he thought. He could hardly kill the boy and harvest his soul-light under the watchful eye of a policeman.

"No," David replied, "just a friend. I'll come back another time." David walked away down the corridor consumed by frustration and rage.

# Chapter 29

Thren looked down at Tor, trying not to laugh. He hadn't noticed the state she was in when he'd returned to the cathedral late on the previous night, but now the sun was up and he could see her properly.

Her long, golden hair was spread out around her head, but instead of looking immaculate, it was full of knots. The glistening white feathers of her wings looked dull and matted. On closer inspection Thren could see they were covered in some kind of glue or paste, and scrawled across the white of her gown were the words 'Angles go hoome' in large, untidy letters.

'Maybe this ain't so funny,' he thought.

"Hey, Tor. Wake up, rise and shine. We gotta get you cleaned up."

Tor stirred, and her eyes slowly opened. It took her a minute or two to recognise Thren, and when she did she glared at him.

"I'm not asleep," she said, "I'm just resting my eyes."

"Well, I reckon you were out cold all night, otherwise you wouldn't have let this happen to you."

"What?" said Tor, attempting to sit up. She found she couldn't because her feathers were not only stuck to each other but to the cathedral roof. "What's going on? What have you done?"

"Hey, don't blame me, lady," said Thren. "This is not my idea of a joke. Not that you don't look pretty funny like that. You remind me of a fly trapped in a spider's web."

"Kindly skip the natural history lesson and help me up," she demanded.

"No can do," said Thren. "If I pull you up, half your feathers will stay right where they are. We gotta find a way to dissolve this stuff before you try to move."

"What's going on?" said Tor, miserably.

"Search me!" said Thren. "Look, I'll go and see if I can find anything to unglue your feathers. Stay right there."

"Well, I can hardly go anywhere, can I?" said Tor, infuriated.

"It's okay," he said, trying to calm her down. "I won't be long."

"You'd better not be," said Tor, crossly.

"Any more of that and I'll leave you there all day," said Thren. "That way I might get a moment's peace."

Thren took off from the roof. He had no intention of leaving Tor for any longer than he had to. She was far too vulnerable, stuck to the roof like that. Whatever had done that to her might come back, and she was in no state to defend herself. But where do you go for help to try and unglue an angel's wings?

As he hovered over the cathedral he saw Bex and her father leave the house and set off towards the campus.

'Well, she seems okay,' he thought. 'That's one less thing to worry about – not that there's any danger, now we've dealt with the invisibles.'

Seeing Bex had given him an idea. He let himself into the house, went up to her room and began his search.

'Sure is a good thing she's a Biology student,' he thought to himself as he pulled the textbooks off the shelves and rifled through the pages. 'There's gotta be something in here to give me a clue, there's just gotta.'

At last he found an article in a wildlife magazine. It was about some seabirds that had got caught up in an oil slick and how they'd been treated to get the feathers cleaned up.

"That's as near as I'll get, I guess," said Thren, scanning the article.

He went down to the kitchen and collected some washing up liquid and a bowl of water, then carried them carefully up on to the cathedral roof. He'd just had to pick a moment when he thought nobody was looking and hope for the best. If anybody'd seen the items apparently floating up to the roof all by themselves there would have been trouble. Thren put the things down next to Tor, and started cleaning her feathers with the soapy water.

"You're hurting me," she said irritably. "Try to be more careful."

"I *am* trying," said Thren, "But you gotta be patient."

"I don't feel patient," snapped Tor, and she didn't. She was uncomfortable and annoyed, and to be honest, a little frightened, and she didn't really like having to depend on Thren to help her. Rather to her surprise, Thren seemed to be aware of how she was feeling. He stopped cracking jokes and just worked quietly on her feathers, giving her an occasional, reassuring smile.

After a few minutes, Tor said quietly, "Perhaps I was wrong about you."

"What do you mean?" said Thren, not looking up from his task.

"I rather wrote you off from the beginning, I'm afraid," Tor looked shamefaced, "otherwise there were some things I should have told you."

"What things?" questioned Thren, leaning back on his heels.

"It's hard to know where to start. You seem to have got the wrong end of the stick about so many things. The High Council told me to explain some of them to you, but ... well ... I didn't think there was any point. I was wrong. Sorry."

"Am I hearing this right?" asked Thren, grinning. "Did

you just apologise to me?" Tor turned her head away, unwilling to look him in the face. "And you've been keeping me in the dark?"

Tor nodded, guiltily.

"Okay, lady, spill the beans. What is you haven't told me?"

"Why you're here, for a start."

"I know that. I goofed about in guardianship classes and insulted the sheep a few times. Said I didn't know why He bothered with them, right? So I got sent here as a punishment."

"It's not as simple as that. It's not a punishment, it's a test." Seeing Thren still looked confused, she added, "It's so the High Council can make a decision about you."

"I don't get it."

"They have doubts about you, the High Council ... about whether you're in the right place."

"Of course I'm not," Thren protested, "they've sent me *here*! I sure as heck don't belong in this place. That's why I want to go Home."

Tor hesitated. This was much harder than she'd expected. Thren looked at her expectantly. He had no idea what was coming next. "They're not sure you belong there, either."

"Are you out of your tree? There's only Home and here to choose from ... not that I get much choice at the moment."

Tor stayed silent, waiting for the penny to drop. After a moment a horrified look crept across Thren's face. "You mean they think I should be in The Darkness?"

Tor nodded. "I'm sorry Thren, but some of them think you made the wrong choice."

"That is *so* not fair. I made my decision back at the beginning and I've stuck to it."

"Have you? You're constantly rebellious, always causing trouble, never willing to face your responsibilities. You don't even *try* to understand how much He loves people, or why He wants us to help them. You insult them the whole time, and in a way that means you insult Him. After all, He loved them enough to die for them."

"I never did understand that," said Thren quietly.

"Exactly. On top of that, you don't even get on with other angels. The only close friend you ever made, Temporalus, chose The Darkness."

"I didn't go with him."

"But you thought about it."

"We all did! We all had to make a choice, and I made mine. I stayed at Home, with Him. That was my decision."

"And some of the High Council think you made a mistake. Chose the wrong side. They think you should be ... reassigned."

Thren's head was spinning. His whole world was falling apart. They wanted to send him into The Darkness, and he hadn't even known about it. His throat was so dry he could hardly get the words out, "Doesn't *anyone* have any faith in me?"

"Him. That's why you're here. He insisted that you got a chance to prove yourself."

A glimmer of hope stirred inside Thren's heart. If He still believed in him ... "So He trusted me enough to give me a whole city to look after, to prove them wrong. Wow! He must really think a lot of me, otherwise I'd have just started off with a single human, right?" Tor was silent. She was kicking herself for not telling him all of this earlier. The hope on Thren's face faded. "I've gotten it wrong again, haven't I?"

"I'm afraid so. You see, every guardian angel starts with a whole city. That's fine to begin with. You do the best you can for as many people as possible, but after a while, as you get more involved, your failures really begin to get to you. Eventually, you crack up under the strain, and you have to leave that post and take responsibility for fewer people, and so it goes on until at last you're only protecting one person."

"So you really do outrank me?"

Tor smiled apologetically, "I'm afraid so."

"But why don't they just give each human their own angel to begin with?"

"There aren't enough of us to go round."

Silently, Thren returned to cleaning Tor's feathers. He thought about what she'd said, and everything that had happened since he Came Down. "Thanks for telling me, Tor, but it's a bit late now, isn't it? I've already blown it."

***

At the campus, Bex and the others were gathered in one of the lecture rooms, along with dozens of other students, waiting to be interviewed by the police. Her father had insisted on seeing her safely there, which had made her feel about six, but she could see his point.

She was sitting with Tim and Nesta, when Flint drifted in. He'd obviously been home overnight. He was wearing clean clothes, and was carrying a bulging rucksack.

"Why the luggage?" asked Tim, as Flint came over to join them.

"Seemed like a good idea," said Flint. "If we're going to try and stick together, it won't be that easy for me to get home at night ... besides, I don't want to ..." he paused. "There are enough problems at home already."

"You mean you don't want whatever it is following you there?" asked Nesta.

"Something like that," said Flint. "Where are the others?"

"Debbie's still at the hospital with Marty," said Tim, "And Mark and Sam don't need to be here – the police already spoke to them yesterday – but we have warned them to be careful, about David, I mean."

Flint nodded and sat down beside him. Just then Sarah and Paul walked in, looked round and saw the others and waved. Bex beckoned them over.

"Hi, Sarah," she said. "Are you all right?"

"I'm fine," said Sarah, though they could tell from how red her eyes were that she'd spent a lot of the night in tears. "Just a bit jumpy, after what happened in the chapel, but I probably over-reacted yesterday. It's not like David was doing anything wrong."

"I don't think we should take any chances," said Bex.

"That's why I walked her over here," said Paul. "Though, to be fair, I don't really want to be on my own either."

"Any news about Graham?" Bex asked.

Sarah shook her head. "I went to the hospital, but they wouldn't let me in to see him. I'm not family, you see – I'm not even his girl-friend." Struggling to pull herself together she added, "They say he's stable … that's good, isn't it?"

"It's better than critical, anyway," said Flint, trying to sound reassuring. "At least if the police won't let anyone in, then … whatever it is … won't be able to attack him again. He's probably safer than any of us."

"Look, there's Cath," said Sarah, as her friend walked in through the door. "We're over here, Cath." Cath ignored them, and chose to sit by herself.

"You'd better go and ask her over, Sarah," said Flint. "She shouldn't be by herself."

"David's hardly going to do anything to her in a room full of people," said Nesta.

"I know," said Flint. "It's just, well, safety in numbers and all that – besides, we need to decide what to do."

Sarah walked over to Cath, who looked pale and slightly crumpled. "Cath, are you all right?" asked her friend. "You don't look very well."

"I'm fine," said Cath, not really looking at Sarah. Her eyes stared into the distance, as if they were trying to focus on something a long way away.

"Don't you want to join us?" asked Sarah.

"Not really," said Cath. Her voice sounded strange,

almost disconnected.

"Cath, what's wrong?"

"Nothing."

"Something *must* be wrong. Won't you at least talk to me about it?"

"No," said Cath. "Now leave me alone." She stood up and moved away from where Sarah was standing, putting as much distance as possible between herself and her friends. Sarah, troubled, returned to the others.

"Something's wrong," she said, "But Cath won't talk to me about it. She's ... she's not herself at all."

"Maybe she's in shock," suggested Nesta. "She does have a bit of a soft spot for Graham."

Seeing Sarah start to get emotional again at the mention of Graham's name, Paul put a comforting hand on her shoulder, then embarrassed, snatched it away again.

"Perhaps Cath just needs time to come to terms with what's happening," said Paul. "I think we ought to keep an eye on her anyway, even if she doesn't want to hang around with us at the moment."

The others agreed, and went on to talk about what to say to the police. Bex told them what her father had suggested – that they point the police towards David, without explaining their real suspicions.

"We can't all do that," said Tim. "It'll look like a conspiracy."

"It is, in a way," admitted Flint. "But does anyone have a better idea?"

Nobody did, so they agreed that Bex, Flint and Sarah would be the ones to mention him to the police. Flint was just about to go into more detail about what they should say, when Bex kicked him on the ankle. David had walked up to the group and was standing there, smiling. His skin had begun to look grey, and his hair was lank. The scent of his after-shave was overpowering. He'd had to use rather a lot of it, to cover up other nastier smells.

"Morning all," he said, sitting beside them uninvited. He surveyed the group carefully. They all looked guilty, awkward, uncomfortable – and very united. It was going to be hard to pick them off one by one if they insisted on sticking together like that. The only person on her own was Cath, and she didn't interest him. He'd already got what he wanted from her. Of course, all he had to do was wait, and he'd be bound to find opportunities to deal with the others eventually, but he couldn't help realising he was running out of time. If he didn't get a chance to split them up soon, he'd have to find a new body.

# Chapter 30

David hadn't liked the way the police had questioned him. Someone had tipped them off, he was sure of it. Not about what he was, of course, but about the fact that he might be connected with what had happened to Graham and Marty. He'd bluffed his way out of it, naturally. After all, the police didn't have any evidence against him, but it increased his feeling that time was running out. Still, at least the angels weren't on to him yet. It looked like his diversion had worked – using the lesser invisibles to distract them, put them off the scent. If he was going to take advantage of the time that had bought him, he'd have to act fast.

He saw Mark walking past the halls of residence and sauntered over to join him. "Fancy a drink?" asked David. "I'm buying."

Mark hesitated for a moment. After all, Tim and Nesta had warned him that David was dangerous, but Mark just couldn't see it. He'd pretty much managed to convince himself that the business at the party was just a stupid joke, that one of the gang had been playing a trick on the rest of them, and wasn't prepared to admit it. He was sure that what had happened to Marty and Graham were just a couple of unconnected accidents – nasty ones, admittedly, but accidents all the same. It seemed hard to blame David for all of it, when he hadn't even been around for the party. Mark decided to give the guy a break, after all it must be pretty rough to have everyone avoiding you, when you haven't done anything wrong. It seemed to be getting to him too, he was looking really ill – all grey and greasy. Besides, Mark felt he could protect himself if it came to it. He accepted David's offer and the two of them headed into town.

Three hours later David steered a drunken Mark back to the campus. David suggested that the two of them go back to his own room in the halls of residence, claiming to have a bottle of something in there.

Unfortunately for Mark, the bottle was full of chloroform, and in Mark's uncoordinated state, he wasn't able to push David away when he found a moistened cloth held against his face. He realised hazily what was happening, and tried to twist his face away, but David just took a firmer grip on the back of Mark's head with his free hand, and held the cloth more tightly against his face.

"Now, now," said David, "mustn't struggle. Don't want to damage my nice new body do you?" Above the cloth Mark's eyes widened in horror. "Yes, that's right, I'm going to be using *your* body next. This one's pretty much had it. What? Don't you like the idea? Well I'm afraid I don't need your permission, so you'll just have to get used to it." Mark's eyes began to close as the chloroform took effect. "Sleep tight," whispered David, in his ear, "pleasant dreams." Mark went limp, and David laid him gently down on the bed. After all, he would be wearing the shell of the boy soon, so he might as well look after it.

David smiled down at the unconscious student. This was perfect. He was going to have a fresh, undamaged body to move into, a body belonging to someone the rest of the group accepted. That should throw everybody off the scent.

He picked up a pillow and held it over Mark's face, suffocating him. He watched with pleasure as a dark green soul-light prepared to leave the body. It had barely broken away from its owner when David caught and swallowed it, savouring its energy, its state of shock.

As soon as he'd absorbed the soul-light, David removed the pillow from Mark's face. He stared down at the open brown eyes, now staring blankly at the ceiling, and smiled. "Three."

He'd have to wait a couple of hours, of course. If he took the body over now, with the boy's own soul-light still warm inside him, there was a faint chance that Mark might revive and find himself sharing his body with Dross.

Three hours later, David stood over Mark's body. He gathered his energies together, trapping the three stolen soul-lights, and transferred into Mark's body.

The body Dross had been wearing for the last few days crumpled to the floor, dead and rotting. Mark eased himself off the bed and let himself out of the room, locking the door behind him.

# Chapter 31

"Wake up," said Tor, crossly. She prodded Thren with her feet. "You know you don't need to sleep."

"Maybe not," said Thren stirring, "But it sure is nice to have a chance to rest up."

He opened his eyes and looked at Tor. She definitely looked different. He'd managed to clean the gunk off her wings – it had taken all day – but her hair couldn't be salvaged. In the end he'd fetched Bex's scissors and chopped out the tangles. Now Tor's hair stuck out from her head in spikes, like a hedgehog. She'd cried while he cut her long, golden tresses, and when he'd pointed out that angels weren't meant to be vain, she'd kicked him on the shin. Now she was dressed in some clothes he'd borrowed from Bex's wardrobe. Black jeans and a T-shirt, with an old denim jacket. They'd had to cut holes in the clothes for her wings, but Thren didn't think Bex would mind. Actually, he'd forgotten to ask her, he'd been so busy trying to disentangle Tor, and when she was free, they'd spent the night hunting for the imp that had done that to her, though they hadn't found it. Bex had got back from uni to find that her room looked like it had been burgled. Clothes were missing, books were all over the floor. She and Dudley were quite frightened by it all, but they'd cleaned up the mess and tried to get on with things as usual.

\*\*\*

It was Sunday morning, and Dudley was preaching in the cathedral. His text was the letter to the Hebrews and the verses he'd chosen to preach on were about – angels. He was talking about their role as ministering spirits when Tor and Thren floated down to listen. Despite how depressed Thren was feeling about his situation, hearing Dudley preach lifted his spirits.

"That's kinda flattering, don't you think?" he whispered to Tor. "I guess we've made some kind of an impact."

"We're not supposed to," hissed Tor. "We're supposed to be invisible."

"Aw, lighten up," said Thren. "I think it's kinda nice."

Dudley continued to speak about angels, and the unacknowledged help they gave people, to the point where Thren found himself blushing. "Gee, this is embarrassing," he murmured. "We're not *that* good."

"Well, *you* certainly aren't," snapped Tor, "So don't let it go to your head."

But Thren couldn't help being pleased. If there was one human he rated it was Dudley, and to hear the old man preaching about him and Tor made him feel really appreciated. Dudley finished his sermon by reminding people to show hospitality to strangers "… for by doing so, some people have entertained angels unawares."

"Terrific," said Thren, when the service was over. "It's about time people admitted we exist. I'm sick of being spoken about like some kinda extinct species."

Tor turned and stomped away, exasperated. Thren started to drift through the congregation, to see what they'd thought of Dudley's sermon. Quite a few people were talking about it, not just because it was an unusual topic, but because Dudley had sounded as if he, personally, believed in angels: a remarkable admission for a modern clergyman.

Thren found himself next to Pearson and Poole, who were whispering excitedly about what they'd just heard.

"This is perfect," said Pearson, delightedly. "The old fool actually believes in angels. Well, if that's not a sign of senility I don't know what is."

"But angels are biblical," protested Poole gently. "We're all supposed to believe in them."

"Yes, *in the Bible*, where they belong," said Pearson, "But not in real life. Anyone who believes in them in real life is just asking to be locked up."

"You're not going to do that, are you?" asked Poole, looking worried. "You wouldn't want to get him locked up?"

"Of course not," said Pearson. "But this certainly makes it easier to get rid of him. Everybody's bound to agree that it's time he retired after this – and if the angels don't do the trick, I've got some other information that might. You know that hostel he's so involved in?"

"The homeless shelter? What about it?"

"Well, I've been keeping my ear to the ground and I gather the woman who runs the place is being highly irre-sponsible. She's allowing under-age children to stay there, without informing the police. If we play our cards right we should be able to get a nice little scandal out of this."

"What's the point in creating a scandal about the hostel?" asked Poole. "It's not as if he runs the place."

"No, but he's giving it his support. That shows poor judgement, you see; more proof that he's past it."

Poole wanted to ask if Pearson felt his own judgement was quite fair, but as usual he was too cowardly to object to his friend's outrageous statements.

Thren stormed away from the two of them before he did something violent. He had a nasty feeling angels were not supposed to beat up clergymen in a cathedral, which was what he wanted to do right then.

The two men separated, Pearson going off to 'network' as he put it, while Poole went into the vestry to take off his clerical robes. Glancing at himself in the mirror before he did so, Poole felt a pang of guilt. He wasn't at all sure that how he looked on the outside – all pious and holy – was really matched by what was going on in his head. Did he and Pearson really have the right to discredit Dudley Collins? Who gave them the authority to judge the old man and deprive him of his office? He wondered if he should try and get Pearson to drop the idea – but how could he? Pearson never really took much notice of anything Poole said to him, unless it was to offer his wholehearted agreement.

Sometimes Poole wondered why he was friends with Pearson at all, but although he didn't like admitting it to himself, the answer was obvious. Pearson was dynamic, an eloquent speaker, a 'mover and shaker', a person who got things done. People admired him, and listened to what he had to say, and as his friend, some of that respect rubbed off on Poole as well. Without Pearson, Poole would just be a bumbling little man, without any ideas of his own. He'd try to do his job and make wise decisions, but without any overview, without any concept of what the church should be doing today. For that he relied on Pearson.

Ruefully, he admitted to himself that life had been simpler *without* an overview. Sometimes he missed the days – the pre-Pearson days – when he'd just gone about his work, relying on his sense of duty, or even his heart, to guide him. But if he argued with Pearson, if he lost his friendship, who was he to rely on for ideas, for guidance? He'd be on his own – the idea was unthinkable.

\*\*\*

Thren saw Bex standing by herself in the nave and hurried over to join her. He wanted to pour out all his frustrations about Pearson and Poole, but decided she looked worried enough already.

"Hi, Bex, what's up?" he asked.

"Everything," she said simply. "So why are you looking so cheerful?"

"Well, we've dealt with the invisibles that were giving you all such trouble. That's something to feel cheerful about, isn't it?"

"You mean you've found a way to stop David?" asked Bex. "That's wonderful."

"David?" queried Thren. "Who the heck is David?"

So Bex explained what she and the others suspected, and how they were trying to stop David from getting any of them on their own.

"You mean, this guy was still around yesterday?" Thren asked. "Damn. That means we haven't solved the problem after all. And I haven't been keeping a close eye on you all – I thought we'd cracked it."

"Well, you were wrong," said Bex. "He even broke into the house yesterday and turned my room upside down."

Thren suddenly looked embarrassed. "Actually, I meant to talk to you about that, Bex. It wasn't exactly a break in yesterday. It was … it was me."

# Chapter 32

Thren found Tor and told her what Bex had said about David. Within a few moments the angels were hovering over the campus, wondering where to start. Thren saw Flint talking to some students, then watched as the young man turned and ran back into the halls of residence, knocking on various doors, and shouting to his friends to meet him in the canteen.

A few minutes later most of the group of students had caught up with him. Flint had bought a round of coffee, thankful that the police had allowed the canteen to reopen.

He waited until they were all seated, then looked round the group. Tim and Nesta were there, along with Sarah, Sam and Paul.

"Where's Mark?" asked Flint anxiously.

"In bed," replied Sam. "I knocked on his door but he said he had a bad head, and wasn't getting up yet."

"Well, we can't wait for him," said Flint. "Apparently Joanna's disappeared. No one's seen her for two days." There was silence.

"Maybe she's just gone home?" suggested Sarah. "David said she was going home, didn't he?"

"We can't take *his* word for it, can we?" queried Flint. "Does anyone have Joanna's parents' number?" Sarah nodded. "You'd better phone them, make sure she's all right."

Sarah took her mobile outside to get better reception, and made the call. A few minutes later she came back, a worried look on her face. Seeing the concern on their faces she said quickly, "Don't worry, Joanna's all right, she's at home with her parents – but guess who frightened her into leaving?"

"David," said the others in unison. Sarah nodded. "Apparently he turned up in her room, and tried to kiss her. When she wouldn't let him, he got violent. She got away, but didn't want to stick around in case it happened again, so she went home."

"Why didn't she tell us?" asked Tim.

"She thought we'd think she was being silly. She didn't know anything about what had happened to Marty or Graham, or she would have told us.'

"That settles it," said Flint abruptly, "We can't just sit around any longer waiting to be picked off one by one. We've got to do something."

"What do you suggest?" asked Tim.

"I think we should go and see David, front up to him. If we go together he won't be able to do anything to us, but we've got to settle it."

Nobody was sure if this was such a good idea, but none of them wanted to be the one to say it. Besides, no one had a better suggestion, and it was obvious that David would try to get at each one of them in the end, if they let him. They stood up to go.

"Shouldn't Nesta stay here?" asked Sam. "After all, she is …" His voice petered out as the others looked at him.

"I'm part of this too," said Nesta, wheeling herself towards the door. "Come on."

The group headed for David's room, closely followed by the angels. When they reached the door Flint hammered on it threateningly, but there was no reply.

"What do you think?" asked Flint. "Should we break it down?"

"We can't do that," said Sarah, nervously. "We'll get into trouble."

"What do you think we're in now?" asked Tim.

Flint drew back, about to throw himself against the door, just as Thren put his hand against the lock, and it clicked open. The door swung wide as Flint charged, so that he suddenly found himself in David's room. He tried to skid to a halt, but tripped over something on the floor, and fell on top of it.

'It' was David – what was left of him. The stench of rotting flesh was horrible, and Flint could feel it clinging to him as he lifted himself off the corpse, and stood up.

"He looks as if he's been dead for days," said Nesta.

"But we saw him yesterday," protested Sarah. "He was talking to us."

"We'd better fetch the police," said Tim, tearing his eyes away from the body. "I'll go." He set off along the corridor as Flint dived towards the washbasin in the corner of the room and threw up.

"Do you think this means it's all over now?" said Sarah, shaking with shock.

"I hope so," said Paul, who was clinging to the door-frame desperately trying to stay upright. "I really hope so." There was a groan behind them, and Paul and Nesta turned round to see Sam slump to the floor in a dead faint.

*** 

Thren and Tor looked at each other across David's body. They hoped it was over too, but they weren't quite so sure. They kept an eye on the students for the rest of the day, but nothing sinister occurred. Flint was sent to tell Bex what had happened to Joanna and to David, and Tor watched as her charge turned white and sank into a chair.

"The police have taken his body away," said Flint. "They seem to think it had been dead for a while – but as they questioned him yesterday, they're as confused as we are."

"Another death?" said Bex shakily, when he'd finished. "I was hoping it was over."

"It might be now," said Flint, trying to sound reassuring. "With David dead, perhaps it'll stop."

# Chapter 33

The next morning Tor watched over the students, while Thren attended to some other business. He'd heard Dudley and Janet arrange to visit the council offices again, and he wanted to try and help.

Thren caught up with them outside Mr Simpson's office. It was still early; the building had only just opened. Janet was clutching some folders. They'd decided on a new approach – to show Mr Simpson the case studies of some of the individuals the hostel was trying to help. Perhaps if he saw their work in terms of real people he'd change his mind.

Thren perched on top of a bookcase as Janet and Dudley talked to Mr Simpson, and tried to show him the case notes, but he didn't want to know.

'Aw, this just ain't right,' thought Thren. 'He's gotta at least listen.'

Janet placed the folders on Mr Simpson's desk, but he was steadfastly refusing to open them.

"My position on the matter hasn't changed," he was saying. "I still can't help you, and bringing individual cases to my attention changes nothing."

Thren moved forward and knocked the folders off the desk, so they landed on the floor by Mr Simpson's feet. The council official had to bend down to pick them up, since he was the nearest to them, and as he did so Thren blew some of the folders open, so that the photos were visible.

"Look at them," he whispered in Simpson's ear. "Won't you at least look at them? These are real people, not statistics. Don't you even care?"

Mr Simpson found himself looking at the pictures. One of the faces struck a chord. It looked a little like his son, Max. It wasn't, he knew. It couldn't be. His son was miles away, happily married with children of his own, and a good job. And yet ... Mr Simpson remembered a time when his son was younger, a time when they'd quarrelled, and Max had run away. Only for one night, but it had been the longest night of Mr Simpson's life.

Thren whispered in his ear again. "Don't you wanna help? How can you look at these and not care?"

Mr Simpson placed the folders back on his desk, but he left the one that had caught his eye open, and scanned through the notes. Then he looked up at Janet and Dudley.

"Do you really feel the hostel can help these people? Encourage them to make a new start?"

"Sometimes," said Janet, honestly. "We can't work miracles. For some people we are just a bed for the night, but for others, who want to rebuild their lives, or their relationships, who want to get off the streets, we can be a real source of help."

"I can't work miracles either," said Mr Simpson, "but I will take your request to the Housing Committee meeting tomorrow morning." He paused. "I'll ... I'll make the best case I can in your favour."

He stood up, handed the files back to Janet, and showed her and Dudley to the door. As Thren followed them out he whispered in Mr Simpson's ear, "I take it back, mister. You're not a scumbag after all."

Outside Dudley and Janet were discussing the meeting. Janet was feeling confused. "What made him change his mind, I wonder?" she was asking.

"Who knows?" replied Dudley. "Something obviously

got through to him and that was more than we expected. All we can do now is leave it to Mr Simpson and trust him to put our case to the Housing Committee."

Thren smiled to himself. He knew what had got through to Mr Simpson. *He* had. He'd finally managed to influence someone. Of course, the photograph had helped. Mr Simpson obviously had a connection with somebody who looked like the young man in the photo – but more than that, Thren had found the right approach this time. He hadn't appealed to the man's pride or sense of importance, like the last time. He'd spoken to his heart, his better nature, and it had worked. He'd encouraged the guy to *want* to help, and Mr Simpson had responded – and how!

Thren fluttered his wings in a self-congratulatory manner, and took off. He headed for the campus, and found Tor standing outside one of the tutor's rooms with her ear to the door.

"Why don't you just go inside?" he asked, creeping up behind her and making her jump.

"I don't want to intrude," she whispered. "Nesta is asking to transfer back to the Biology course."

"Are they gonna let her?"

"I think so," said Tor. "They weren't very happy about it at first, but when she explained why she felt pushed into changing course in the first place, I think they understood."

***

Just then the door opened and Nesta and Tim came out, smiling. Thren raised his eyebrows at Tor, questioningly.

"I think he's giving her moral support," said Tor, in answer to his unspoken question.

"I think he's crazy," said Thren, disapprovingly. "Encouraging her like that. It's not like he's serious about her. He's dating some chick back home."

"He's just being friendly," said Tor.

"Are you sure she knows that?" he muttered.

"Yes," said Tor. "If anyone's confused at the moment it's Tim not Nesta. Now, can we get down to business? The biologists are about to go on a field trip. Someone ought to watch over them."

"Maybe, but we can't leave the others unattended either," said Thren.

"You stay with them," said Tor firmly, "While I go to the zoo."

"The zoo?" protested Thren, "But *I* like the zoo, I wanna go."

"Don't be such a baby. Bex is a biologist. I'm her guardian, so I get to go."

"It's not fair," growled Thren rebelliously.

"Do you want me to ground you again?" threatened Tor. Thren shut up, and went to check on the English students, leaving Tor to follow the minibus that was taking the Biology students to the zoo.

At the last minute Nesta was included in the trip too, so Tor was keeping an eye on her and Tim, as well as Sam, Mark and, of course, Bex. There were seven other students on the trip, but Tor didn't feel so responsible for them.

Tor watched her group closely as they climbed out of the minibus when it reached the zoo. Bex's soul-light was burning steadily; it was just a nuisance that Tor couldn't see anybody else's to monitor them. It was even more of a nuisance since she couldn't see that Mark wasn't showing a soul-light at all.

Tim and Bex were trying to fill Nesta in on which bits of the course she'd missed, while Sam and Mark sauntered on ahead of the group. Sam turned round and took a picture of the rest of the students coming towards him, then noticed the lion enclosure. He moved closer to it, trying to get a good picture of the lions.

"It's no good," he grumbled to Mark. "However I set it I'm just going to get the mesh spoiling the shot." Sam was leaning on a handrail, about three foot high, which surrounded the lion enclosure, and was set a couple of feet back from it, to keep people away from the mesh.

"Just climb on the rail, and lean against the cage," suggested Mark, casually. "The camera lens will fit between the mesh, you'll get a much better picture."

"What, you want me to get ripped to shreds?" joked Sam.

"Of course not," lied Mark. "You'll still be outside the cage, and the lions are on the far side. They'll never reach you in the time it takes to snap a photo." Sam still hesitated.

"What's the matter, Sam? Scared?" goaded Mark.

"Course not," said Sam. He was determined to prove how tough he could be, especially after fainting in front of everyone the day before.

The sound system above their heads crackled into life, and the voice of a presenter could be heard, telling the public about the lions, and the feeding time people were about to witness. Sam climbed onto the rail, then looked back nervously at Mark.

"Go on," said Mark. "You heard what she said. It's lunch-time – they won't be interested in you."

Sam let his weight fall forward, so his upper body was pressed against the mesh, while his feet balanced on the handrail. He squeezed his camera lens between the mesh and prepared to take a picture. Mark smiled in satisfaction. This was almost too easy. He hadn't even had to get Sam drunk, the young man was gullible enough sober.

Tor looked up to see one of the lions racing across the grass towards the place where Sam was spread-eagled against the bars. Sam was fiddling with his camera settings, unaware of the danger, and too awkwardly placed to do much about it even if he had seen what was coming. Tor leapt into the air and landed in front of the lion just as it started its leap towards Sam. She shoved the creature's chest as it rose up towards her, throwing it off balance, and giving Sam, alerted by the other students, a chance to fall back out of range. Tor made a hasty exit from the enclosure, before the lion came to see what had hit him. She never had liked facing up to those animals. Not that she'd had to for years. Not since Daniel's time, anyway.

'Lions' dens and angels,' she thought. 'History does have a habit of repeating itself.'

Outside the cage she leaned on the handrail, getting her breath back, while the other students fussed around Sam.

Just then the presenter, who'd been giving the lion talk, came running up. She was a tall, athletic-looking young woman with short, brown hair, and a pleasant expression, although it was hard to tell at that moment. She was torn between concern and anger. Sam stood up as she arrived, and seeing that he appeared to be unhurt, she decided to give anger first go.

"Do you realise how dangerous that was?" she said, as she reached him. "The rail is there to keep people back from the bars, to keep you safe. You could have been badly hurt." Sam just looked at her silently. He was suffering from the reaction that follows a near accident, and was torn between guilt at causing a fuss, and defiance at anyone who had the nerve to tell him off. The combination on his usually cheerful face made him look about ten years old. The presenter, who'd had a nasty shock herself, watching a near-accident that she knew could have been fatal, proceeded more gently.

"Sorry, I didn't mean to startle you, but it is serious. As far as the lions are concerned, the handrail marks the boundary of their territory, not the mesh. By leaning against the bars, you invaded that territory. One of them was bound to go for you."

"Don't worry," said Sam, finding his voice at last. "I won't try that again."

"Good," said the presenter, relaxing a little. "Are you

all right?" She signalled to a grey-haired woman keeper who was passing them on a bicycle. "This is one of our first- aiders, she'll take a look at you if you like."

"I'm fine," said Sam, as the keeper dismounted. "Just a bit bruised where I landed, but my camera's had it."

"If you're sure," said the keeper, "but if you start feeling bad later, go and see a doctor," and she pedalled away. Mark smiled furtively. By the time he'd finished with Sam there'd be nothing a doctor could do for him.

Sam had just picked up the broken camera when the Biology tutor caught up with the group.

"Is everything all right?" he asked, looking round the group. "Has there been some kind of trouble?"

Sam looked pleadingly at the presenter, who turned to the tutor and said, "No, it's all right. One of the students has just broken his camera, that's all." She turned back to Sam. "I think they might sell the disposable ones in the shop, if you need one for today." Sam smiled at her grate-fully, then the tutor led the students away.

The presenter watched the group walk off, and shook her head. However safe the zoo tried to make the place there were always people who'd ignore the rules, and get themselves into trouble. Unless you made every cage like a fortress, in which case nobody'd see the animals, you just had to rely on people having the common sense to accept the safety barriers, and most people did. The difficulty lay with the ones who obviously hadn't been around when common sense was dished out.

She turned to inspect the lion. It was one of the young males that was pacing up and down in a puzzled kind of way, but appeared to be unhurt. She decided she'd better tell the head keeper on that section about the incident, so he could keep an eye on the animal, and make sure it hadn't hurt itself when it fell. There was something very odd about that fall, now she came to think about it. The lion had seemed to lose his balance in mid-air, just when she was certain he was about to land against the mesh where the boy was hanging. She didn't even want to think about what the consequences of that would have been.

As the presenter walked away, Tor leaned over the hand-rail and whispered to the lion, "I'm sorry, but what was I supposed to do? Let you get your claws into him?"

The lion twitched his head. He could hear the voice, and smell the creature he'd collided with, but he couldn't see it. Then he heard the satisfying thud of a large chunk of meat landing in the enclosure, and loped off to collect his share.

Tor turned and followed the students. She was beginning to wish that she'd let Thren come on this trip after all. She could have had a nice restful day on campus.

# Chapter 34

Thren was getting bored. Nothing was happening on the campus. Well, nothing except classes, which in his view didn't count.

'Dullsville,' thought Thren, as he listened to yet another English lecture. Sarah was amongst the students, scribbling notes, but there was no sign of Cath, and Debbie was probably still at the hospital with Marty. He decided to check out Debbie first. He reckoned that most of his students were safely stuck in lectures for a while, so he soared over to the intensive care unit.

Debbie was there, sitting beside Marty's bed. Sometimes she talked to him, trying to say the things she hadn't said when she had the chance. Sometimes she was silent, hoping that just being there was enough; that Marty would sense her presence. She didn't look so glamorous now. The fashion clothes had given way to jeans and a sweater, and there was no trace of make-up on her face. Somehow none of that seemed important now.

Thren thought she looked beautiful. He figured Marty would think so too, if the poor guy ever got to wake up and see her. Every so often Debbie would go and stare out of the window or open the door to check the corridor. She was determined to protect Marty from anything else that might happen.

'She's tougher than she looks,' thought Thren. 'And braver. I'd never have had her down as the devoted type.

Guess I was wrong – again!'

He stared guiltily down at Marty, and felt terrible. All this was his fault. Some guardian angel he turned out to be – Marty in a coma, Graham seriously injured, Joanna frightened into dropping her course, and they were no nearer getting Marty's soul-light back.

He left as Marty's parents arrived to take their turn at sitting with their son, and went to check on Graham. The police were still standing guard over him, which was reassuring, in a way, but the boy hadn't regained consciousness. His broken limbs and damaged lung had been treated, but his soul-light still fluttered weakly within him, and the doctors were concerned about the possibility of brain damage, if he did wake up.

"I'm sorry," whispered Thren, looking down at the boy, "I'm real sorry. I never meant for this to happen."

Miserably Thren flew back to the campus. Looking in on Flint, he found the drama students doing some vocal work that seemed to include a lot of shouting and screaming. Since no one could hear him, he decided to join in.

'Gee, that feels better,' thought Thren, half an hour later, having yelled some of his frustration out of his system. 'I sure needed that. Maybe I should try it the next time Tor hacks me off.'

\*\*\*

Tor was feeling pretty hacked off herself, trailing round the zoo after the students. The tutor had split the group into two, accompanying six students to the rhino section, and sending the other six to spend the afternoon with primates.

'Still, at least all mine are together,' thought Tor as she followed them to the monkey house.

There the senior keeper for the primates met them. He was a tall man, with short dark hair, slightly greying at the temples, and a no-nonsense approach.

'At least they won't get into any trouble with him,' thought Tor, satisfied. They were shown around the monkey house and the chimp complex without incident. Mark was quieter than usual, frustrated by the failure of his plan, but the others were fascinated by what the keeper was telling them as he showed them around.

Then he led them to the ape house to see the orangutans. Having decided that they seemed a sensible, interested bunch of students, he took them behind the scenes to see one of the orangs close to. The students were overawed as they stood only a foot or two away from the bars, and the orang inspected them with gentle eyes.

'She's beautiful,' thought Tor, going soppy over an animal for the first time in her life. The ape looked at the angel, and Tor could have sworn she smiled, then the animal caught sight of Mark and started to kick up a fuss, so the keeper led them away.

At the far end of the corridor below the ape house they came to a pile of waders.

"To finish your tour of the section I'm going to take some of you over to Lemur Island," said the keeper. He looked apologetically at Nesta. "I'm sorry, but you won't be able to come with us, the only way onto the island is to wade across."

"That's all right," said Nesta, trying not to show her disappointment. "I'll watch from the edge of the water."

The others donned waders and were handed buckets of chopped banana. Bex whispered to Nesta, "Do you want me to keep you company?"

"No, you go," her friend replied. "It's too good a chance to miss."

Then the keeper led them to the edge of the water. Nesta watched as they waded awkwardly across. She noticed that Emily, another Biology student, seemed to be clinging to Tim's arm far more tightly than was necessary to cross over to the island. She was annoyed with herself for feeling jealous about such a silly little thing. She wasn't even going out with Tim. She never would be. That was the problem. He was still trying to keep things going with Nicola, his girlfriend back home. Even if he wasn't, there was no reason to think he'd ever be interested in Nesta, except as a friend.

She felt frustrated too, at not being able to go over to Lemur Island. Perhaps it *had* been a mistake, transferring back to the Biology course. After all, Mark and the others had been right. She couldn't do everything on the course. She couldn't wade through water, for a start. She watched enviously as Mark followed Sam into the water. Then Mark appeared to slip, reached out and grabbed hold of Sam to regain his balance, and pulled both of them under the water. The keeper was there and pulled Mark upright even before Tor reached them. Somehow Mark had managed to land on top of Sam, trapping his friend under the water. Sam struggled for air as he surfaced. For a horrible moment he'd had a feeling Mark was holding him under the water – trying to drown him, but then Sam decided he must have imagined it. After all, Mark was his best friend, wasn't he?

"Sorry, Sam," said Mark, smiling ruefully.

"It's all right," said Sam. "No harm done."

The keeper checked that they were both all right, and then led them onto the island. "Now you know why this section isn't open to the public! Try to be more careful on the way back."

They all nodded, and then started to feed the ring-tailed lemurs with bits of banana from the buckets they'd brought over. The animals came towards them cautiously, then gained confidence and approached more closely to accept their favourite fruit. Soon one was sitting on Tim's shoulder, taking pieces of banana out of his hand, while another was letting Bex stroke its stomach. A few minutes later the keeper led them back through the water. Nesta noticed that Sam deliberately put some distance between himself and Mark as they crossed, though he seemed a little embarrassed about it.

Once everyone had taken off their waders and put their own shoes back on the keeper turned to Nesta and said, "Sorry you had to miss out on that, but there's someone you might like to meet on the way to join up with the other students." A few minutes later Nesta was introduced to a hand-tame red-ruffed lemur which seemed quite happy to sit on her lap and accept little pieces of fruit, while the rest of the group asked the keeper questions about the animals they'd seen that day.

Tor was glad the trip was nearly over. Sam and Mark were both soaking wet, and it was freezing. She felt like ordering them both to go straight home and change their clothes, not that they were her problem. The only trouble they'd run into all day had been of their own making, so she could hardly blame the invisibles for it – *if* any of them were still around.

They met up with the other half dozen students who were being led across the zoo by one of the rhino team. The big, bearded keeper, although a little shy, was talking enthusiastically to the group about his charges. He introduced them to a bespectacled male presenter, who despite the weather, was wearing shorts and brightly coloured socks. The presenter led all the students off for their last activity of the day. This was a talk about coatimundi, which the jolly presenter rather theatrically described as 'stretched out racoons', but the students could see what he meant. The coatis themselves ran along the ropes strung up across their enclosure like tightrope walkers. Most of the students watched them in delight, and Tor was fascinated by them.

She decided it was just as well that Thren hadn't supervised the trip. He'd have been up on the ropes doing gymnastics with the animals instead of watching over the students. The tutor was busy chatting to a tall man with curly brown hair, who was wearing a suit, rather than a keeper's uniform. This was the Curator of Mammals, and the tutor wanted to make a good impression on him, hoping that some of his students might have the opportunity to do projects there.

Nesta, who was close enough to hear the conversation, wondered if she had any chance of being chosen. As if he knew what she was thinking the curator turned round and smiled at her, saying, "I don't see why we can't find suitable projects for *all* your students. We're doing a lot of work on environmental enrichment, and it's always helpful to have people recording the animals reactions to anything new we add to their enclosures." Nesta smiled back at the curator. For the first time that day she was *sure* she'd made the right decision, switching back onto the Biology course. She was determined to make a go of it.

It was the curator who noticed that Sam was beginning to shake with cold, and pointed it out to the tutor. Seeing that two of his students were wet through, he decided that it was time to leave. He shepherded them back to the minibus, and drove them back to the campus. Tor followed slowly behind, wondering why she'd bothered. She'd wasted the whole day, and nothing had happened – apart from a fractious lion. Not an invisible in sight ... in a manner of speaking.

***

Thren's day hadn't felt too constructive either. He'd had to sit through lectures on English Literature, Drama and, worst of all in his opinion, Art History. Then he'd got a nasty shock when he'd found Paul in the library searching through a book full of paintings of angels.

"Does this guy know something he shouldn't?" he wondered.

Thren looked at the pictures over Paul's shoulder. Paul

froze for a moment then carried on studying the paintings. "Some of those images are way too cute," muttered Thren, looking at the rounded faces of assorted cherubs. "And even the ones which are halfway accurate look kinda … detached. You'd think they didn't care about the people they're talking to at all." He ignored the fact he'd been pretty detached himself only a few days ago. Even now he was struggling to care about more than a handful of people at once.

Thren glanced at Paul's notebook. The heading definitely said 'Angels'. Thren just hoped the notes the boy was taking were to do with an essay or something, 'Otherwise we're in *big* trouble,' he thought. Thren moved to the other side of the table to study Paul more intently. 'Well, he doesn't look suspicious, and he sure couldn't *guess* that we were around. Not unless somebody told him, and Bex wouldn't do that.'

Thren moved away and Paul breathed a sigh of relief. He couldn't exactly see when they were around, but he was catching vague glimpses of them, reflected in his glasses when they were behind him – and he could sort of … sense them. Of course, he couldn't tell anyone – they'd think he'd gone mad; and he was sure the figures he was seeing weren't … whatever had been at the party. They felt safe, protective. All the same, they made him feel a little uncomfortable. He didn't believe in that sort of thing. Paul corrected himself – he *hadn't* believed in that sort of thing. If you could call an angel a thing – and there wasn't really anyone he could talk to about it. His gran would have understood, but she'd died a year ago.

Paul had been wondering why he could see the angels when no one else could. The only conclusion he could come to was that it had something to do with his eyes. He'd had several eye operations as a child to correct his faulty vision, but he still had a slightly distorted view of the world. The doctors said it was because he had an extra layer of cells on his retina, like a piece of coloured cling-film, which couldn't be removed. It was a condition that ran in their family, and his gran had always called it her 'inner eye' and joked that it was 'for seeing fairies with, my lovely'. Now he was beginning to doubt if it had been just a joke, or whether she'd seen things she couldn't explain too.

***

Thren was looking for Cath. She was the one student he hadn't seen all day. He'd kept meaning to go and check on her but then had been distracted by the others. If he was honest, he wasn't as worried about Cath as he was about the others. He couldn't find a connection with her somehow. 'Besides, she's so efficient she's scary,' thought Thren. 'Nothing would dare attack *her*.' Unfortunately he was just about to find out how wrong he was.

He spotted Cath crossing the campus, heading towards the halls of residence. She seemed to be wandering a little, instead of walking in her usual determined manner – and, he realised, he hadn't seen her in any of the English lectures. Something must be wrong!

Thren watched her for a couple of minutes before he realised what it was. Her soul-light was missing! When had that happened? And how was she walking around without it? This was getting too weird for him. He moved closer to Cath and stared into her eyes. They were blank – unfocused – and full of tears. Thren felt overwhelmed by a tidal wave of guilt. 'How did we let this happen?'

# Chapter 35

"I guess David's death didn't solve our problems after all," Thren was explaining. "I mean, if it did, the soul-lights would have been released, right? Marty would have woken up from his coma, and Cath wouldn't be wandering around like a zombie."

"All right," said Tor defensively, "we were wrong, but I don't know what you expect me to do about it. We're back to square one. We've still no idea what we're looking for."

"A demon – I figure that much is clear."

"Yes, but in what form?"

"I guess he's taken another body."

"And until we know which one, there's very little we can do."

"I still don't get it," said Thren, thoughtfully. "How come Cath's still wandering around when Marty's in a coma?"

"I explained before," Tor answered tiredly. "It all depends on *how* a soul is taken. The demon succeeded in killing Marty, but the poison's been flushed out of his system, and the life support equipment is sustaining him. If he woke up now, he'd be in the same state as Cath, but *because* he's in that state he won't wake up. Not without his soul-light. Cath must have had the soul-light taken out of her without her body being damaged. That's why she's still walking around, but she's like an empty shell. She'll gradually shut down, go into a coma, like Marty."

"But how could the demon take her soul-light without hurting her body?"

"By kissing her."

Thren turned away, revolted at the very thought of it. He'd seen David's rotting body when the students broke into his room. The thought of Cath being kissed, having her soul-light sucked out of her – by that! He couldn't bear to think about it ... and *he'd* let it happen. Perhaps the High Council was right, perhaps he did deserve to be reassigned. He'd never liked humans, never seen the point of them really, and if he was honest, he'd always been a bit jealous of them. Thren had never been able to understand why He had created them at all, when He already had the angels for company. Weren't they good enough for Him? One of the reasons Thren had never got on with other angels that well was because they all seemed to share His obsession with humans. Now he was beginning to understand why. Humans were so fragile, so vulnerable, there were bound to be times when even the toughest of them needed protection.

Temporalus had been Thren's only close friend, and a lot of what they had had in common was a dislike of humans and a total disregard for responsibility. When Lucifer led his rebellious angels out into The Darkness Temporalus had tried to persuade Thren to go with them. He *had* been tempted, he had to admit it, but something had held him back. Now it looked like he was going to be joining his friend after all, and the thought made him shudder. He'd failed the test he'd been set before he'd even realised it *was* a test. Worst of all, his failure had cost two people their souls.

He wondered how much longer it would be before the High Council reassigned him. He hoped he'd have a chance to deal with the demon first, and protect the remaining students. Thren was determined not to let any more of them slip through his fingers. He turned back to Tor. To his surprise she was watching him sympathetically. He straightened himself up, "Well," he demanded, "what's the plan, Wonderwings?"

Nettled, Tor admitted that there wasn't a plan. She had no idea what to do next. Thren and Tor continued arguing in circles all evening, glancing over the city from the cathedral roof every so often, to make sure nothing dangerous was happening. Unfortunately, the more they argued, the less efficiently they kept watch. After the first hour the imp felt it was safe enough to crawl out of hiding and look for something to do.

Snig mooched around the city for a while, but it was too early to start any real trouble, so it wandered towards the racecourse. Then it heard a voice, shouting, inside one of the houses. 'Anger,' thought the imp. 'This should be fun.' It glanced in through the window to see a big, untidy man shouting at a small girl in a muddy school uniform.

"It's your own fault," he was saying. "You should have stuck up for yourself."

"But they pushed me over," said the girl. "I couldn't stop them."

"Well, you can just go to school like that tomorrow. I don't see why I should get you cleaned up. You're not my problem."

"But there isn't anyone else to help," wailed the girl. "Not since Luke ..."

"Mention his name one more time ..." said the man, raising his hand threateningly.

'Violence,' thought the imp. 'Even better!' The creature watched excitedly, but instead of hitting the child the man turned away.

"Go to your room, and stay there," he said.

"But I'm supposed to ..."

The man interrupted her shouting, "Go to your room now!" and the little girl went upstairs.

The man went into the sitting-room and flung himself in an armchair, then used a remote control to switch the television on. The imp, attracted by the emotional state the man was in, crept into the house, and started to cause trouble.

Snig started by playing with the television aerial, so that the picture became a mass of snow-like dots. When the man moved forward to adjust the set, the imp turned his armchair through one hundred and eighty degrees, so it was facing the wall. While the human stared at the chair in confusion the imp, invisible to the human eye, swept everything off the mantelpiece, sending ornaments crashing to the floor, and causing a handful of stray photographs to flutter around the man's feet.

He went pale, staring at the photograph that had landed nearest to him. It was of a woman and two children, a boy and a girl, all smiling happily up at the man. Seeing his reaction the imp grabbed the photograph and started waving it around, flapping it in the man's face and carrying it round the room so that it appeared to swirl around the man's head.

"No, Maggie, no!" said the man. "It wasn't my fault!' Then he ran out of the room, through the front door and down the street.

Inside the house, the Snig decided not to give chase. There was still fun to be had indoors. It crept up the stairs to the little girl's room. It could hear her sobbing on the other side of the door. 'Sorrow,' it thought. 'Not as good as anger, but I can have some fun with it.' It searched the other rooms and found a small rucksack, which it flung outside the child's door. Looking in the airing cupboard it found a T-shirt – a bit big but it would do – and a small pair of jeans. It threw them on top of the rucksack and flung the door open. The girl looked up from the bed she'd been lying on.

She saw the things on the landing and wondered what

they were doing there. Perhaps Harry had put them out for her. Perhaps this was his way of telling her to go. He'd made it plain enough he didn't want her there.

"Harry?" she called out. "Harry?" There was no reply. She picked up the clothes and bag. Then she changed out of her school uniform and shoved a few things into the rucksack. "Harry?" she called, as she walked down the stairs. On the floor in the hall she found the photo of her mother, with herself and Luke. She slipped it into the rucksack and headed for the open front door. When she reached it she turned and called, "Goodbye, Harry." There was no reply. "I'm going to look for Luke," she added, but the house remained silent. Amy turned and walked up the street, heading into the city. Snig rubbed his hands – well, claws – and followed her. This was going to be fun.

# Chapter 36

Mark stood outside Sam's room and knocked. "I thought I'd take you for a drink," he said, when Sam opened the door. "I owe you one, for giving you a soaking this afternoon."

"Thanks," said Sam, "but I don't fancy going out tonight."

"Okay," said Mark, "I'll get some cans and we can have a drink here."

"No," said Sam quickly, starting to close the door. "I'm a bit tired, and there's some work I want to catch up on. I haven't got much done the last few days."

Mark considered pushing his way into Sam's room, but he could feel the boy's tension already. Sam didn't trust him. He must have realised that Mark really had been trying to hold him down under the water that afternoon. In which case, how much more had he guessed?

"Oh – and Mark," said Sam, still holding the door half-shut, "I think it's time we stopped winding Flint up, don't you? There's too much stuff going on, nobody needs any more hassle."

Mark didn't know what Sam was talking about, "Winding Flint up?"

"Yeah, the text messages, you know. It's time to give it a rest."

"The text messages," echoed Mark, trying to sound like he knew what Sam was talking about. "Yeah, right. Time to give it a rest. See you tomorrow." Mark turned away.

He heard Sam's door shut firmly behind him, and the key turn in the lock.

It was going to be important to get rid of Sam quickly, but he couldn't risk an outright attack. Sam was suspicious now, he'd fight back, and it would attract attention. No, better to be casual about it, act normally, and let Sam think he'd imagined the whole thing. In a day or two the boy would relax again, and then Mark would take the first chance he got to finish him off.

**\*\*\***

Behind his locked door Sam heaved a sigh of relief. He was sure Mark hadn't known what he was talking about when he mentioned the texts they'd been sending Flint. Which was weird, given that the wind-up had been Mark's idea. Which meant that Mark wasn't exactly Mark any more. Which made sense of what had happened at the zoo that day. Sam reached for his mobile to phone the others. It wasn't working. He remembered that it had been in his pocket during the zoo trip. Either the fall or the wetting it had received had ruined it.

Sam wasn't sure what to do next. He wanted to warn the others, but he didn't dare leave his room. It was obvious that Mark had chosen him as his – its – next victim. Sam sat down on the bed suddenly, as the full implication of what was going on hit him. He looked over at his pinboard. It was covered with pictures of him and Mark messing around on campus, or at parties, with their arms round the girls they were seeing that week. There was one of Mark, covered in paint splatters, after Sam had chased him round the halls with a paintball gun. They'd got into a lot of trouble over that.

Tears began to roll down Sam's cheeks. Whatever it was that had just knocked on his door, however much it looked like Mark, it wasn't. Which meant that Mark was dead. He had to be. Either that or it was the best wind-up ever …

or the worst. "Shit," whispered Sam, his face crumpling, "shit, shit, shit."

Mark walked down the corridor. He looked calm enough, but inside he was furious. Perhaps this body hadn't been such a good choice after all. He'd forgotten when he decided to take it over, that although Mark was part of the group, and accepted by them, that also meant he was already in a specific relationship with each of them. He was expected to know things about them without being told, like that stuff about text messages. He thought he'd bluffed his way out of it all right, but he wasn't sure.

There were other problems too. He couldn't just start kissing girls that Mark had never made a pass at before; they'd get suspicious. Even the boys were being harder to deal with than he'd expected. Tim, Flint and Paul weren't particular friends of Mark, so it was going to be hard to get any of them on their own. Sam no longer trusted him, but Mark was hoping the boy wasn't sure enough about what had happened that day to say anything about it. After all, Mark was his closest friend.

He went looking for the others. They were in Nesta's room, arguing. He could hear them from outside the door. Mark smiled to himself as he listened. He couldn't help but find the discussion funny.

"I'll walk Bex home," Flint was saying.

"Do you mind? You're making me sound like a pet poodle. I don't need walking."

"Yes, you do," said Flint firmly.

Bex wanted to say that she was the one person there who didn't need protecting, she had her own guardian angel to look after her – but she could imagine how the others would react to that, Flint especially. Besides, Thren and Tor weren't exactly inspiring her with confidence. She knew they were *trying* to protect everyone, but it was pretty obvious they weren't succeeding.

"All right," she sighed. "You can walk me home if

you're really bothered."

"And where's Flint going to stay?" asked Tim. "He can't go home alone. And I'm not joking, we do need to stick together, for safety. Where are you planning to crash tonight, Flint?"

Flint shrugged.

"You can sleep on my floor, if you like?" Tim offered.

"If you're going to walk me home, you might as well stay at our place again, Flint," said Bex. "Dad won't mind, and our sofa is more comfortable than Tim's floor anyway."

"All right," said Flint, ungraciously. "I suppose I might as well – but I'd be just as happy to walk back on my own, and crash at Tim's."

"No," said everyone else simultaneously.

"I can look after myself, you know," said Flint loudly.

"I expect that's what Graham thought too," said Sarah quietly. No one said anything for a few moments. Paul patted her hand reassuringly, then moved his own hand away quickly, embarrassed at being so demonstrative.

"We may be worrying about nothing," said Flint, trying to sound positive. "After all, David's dead."

"He was dead already," Nesta pointed out. "So I don't find that a very comforting thought."

"Come on," said Paul, standing up to leave. "What are we doing?"

"Why don't you walk Sarah back to her room?" said Flint. "And I'll walk Bex back to the cathedral."

Then they all said their goodnights, and Paul and Sarah left.

"Come on, Bex," said Flint. "Walkies!"

"Woof," said Bex, and stood up. Flint patted her on the head.

"That's a good girl. Now come along. Walk to heel, and if you're a good dog you can have a biscuit when you get home."

"Careful," said Bex, threateningly. "I might bite."

They left, bickering amicably, and Tim turned to say goodnight to Nesta.

"You will lock your door, after I've gone, won't you?" he said.

"Actually, I thought I'd leave it wide open, with a sign on it saying 'Killer come in,'" she replied sarcastically.

"All right, it was a stupid question," agreed Tim. "Night, Nesta."

He went out of the room, shutting her door behind him. Nesta wheeled herself forward and locked the door. Then she went to the window to see if that was properly shut too. As she opened the curtains to check the window catch she saw Tim crossing the quad. It occurred to her that he'd been left to walk home alone, after all his concern about everyone else's safety. Still, it was only a couple of minutes to his room.

She saw Mark step out of the shadows and talk to him, and she felt quite relieved. Now he wouldn't be walking back alone. Mark seemed agitated. He appeared to be trying to get Tim to go with him. Tim looked reluctant, but eventually they turned, and set off towards the main road.

Nesta felt troubled. Mark was one of them; he couldn't be a threat, not really. And yet so many strange things had happened ...

She thought about the trip to the zoo that afternoon. It was Mark who'd encouraged Sam to lean against the mesh on the lion cage to try and get a better picture. It was Mark who'd pulled Sam under the water. And since then Sam had been avoiding him. He must be suspicious too.

Nesta tried to remember everything Mark had done and said that day. Come to think of it, he wasn't acting like himself at all. Usually he and Sam were like a double act, cracking jokes and annoying people. Today he'd been really quiet. What was more, he hadn't made any pointed remarks about Nesta re-joining the Biology course. He hadn't even made any cracks about her wheelchair when she couldn't get over to Lemur Island. She'd have expected him to really rub that in – and if he wasn't himself … who was he?

Nesta unlocked her door, and set off after Tim and Mark. By the time she caught sight of them they were walking under the arch of the Northgate. A few yards further on, Mark led Tim into one of the old inns that lined that side of the road. They were obviously going for a drink.

Nesta would have followed them inside but the stone steps up into the pub prevented her. She'd just have to wait outside until they finished. She moved away from the door, and took shelter under the overhang. It kept the rain off her, but couldn't keep out the cold. It was freezing, and she hadn't even grabbed a coat when she set off after Tim and Mark. She hoped they weren't going to be long.

Inside Mark had sat Tim down in a dimly lit corner. Then he'd gone to the bar to fetch some drinks. Tim had made it pretty clear that he was only going to stay for one pint, so getting him drunk wasn't going to work. As Mark carried the drinks back to Tim, he slipped some tablets into one of the glasses, then put it down on the table in front of Tim.

"There you go," said Mark cheerfully.

"Look, what did you want to talk to me about?" asked Tim. "I'm not really in the mood for a late night, so let's get to the point."

"Okay," said Mark, trying to think of something to talk about. He just needed to occupy Tim long enough for him to finish his pint and give the drugs a chance to kick in. "It's Nesta. Did you encourage her to re-join the Biology course?"

"Of course I did," said Tim.

"Well, you shouldn't have. You know it's a waste of time. Look at what happened today – she couldn't even get across to the island."

"You didn't get across that well yourself," said Tim.

"You went under and took Sam with you."

"I missed my footing, that's all," replied Mark. "But Nesta couldn't get over there at all. And there's going to be loads of things like that over the next three years. It's pointless her being on the course at all.

"It's people like you saying things like that that made her ditch the course in the first place," said Tim, getting annoyed. "You've no right to decide what she should and shouldn't do."

"Why not?" said Mark. "It affects me. It affects all of us. I expect they'll try and arrange the course to make it easier for her – more accessible. Well, who says that's in our best interests? And they'll probably want us to help her keep up with the bits she can't do."

"Don't worry, Mark, nobody in his right mind would expect *you* to help her. Your work isn't up to it – and if she needs any help *I'll* be there for her."

"Oooh, lucky Nesta," sneered Mark. "Her very own knight in shining armour. I wonder what your girlfriend thinks about this ... Nicola, isn't it? Perhaps someone should write and tell her."

"There's nothing to tell," said Tim defensively. "Nesta and I are just friends, that's all."

"You don't really believe that, do you?" goaded Mark. "You're not the saint you think you are. You fancy her really – Nicola or no Nicola – and everyone knows she's soft on you."

"It's not true," protested Tim, beginning to feel very strange. "We're just friends."

"Oh, right, yeah, and we all believe that! You're no better than anyone else. You just want to get a sordid little thing going with Nesta in term-time, and then go back to the lovely Nicola in the holidays. How pathetic is that?"

"It's not true!' said Tim, standing up.

"What are you going to do about it?" said Mark. "Fight me? Make me eat my words?"

"All right," said Tim. "Why not? Come on, fight me." Tim was dimly aware that he was acting oddly. He never got into fights. He didn't think they solved anything – and now he seemed to have challenged Mark, and couldn't think of a way out of it.

"You're on," said Mark triumphantly. "But not here, outside." Mark led Tim out of the pub and turned back towards the Northgate. "Not out in the street either. Don't want the police coming along and busting it up. Up there on the walls." And he led the dazed Tim up the steps and on to the Roman city walls. Tim turned to him.

"If we're going to fight, let's get it over with. Come on, hit me," said Tim, trying to keep his balance as the world spun around him. Mark didn't hit him. He lunged forward instead and caught him by the throat, trying to choke the life out of him. Tim felt too weak and disorientated to fight back; he couldn't seem to find the energy. He began to lose consciousness. Then he thought he heard Nesta's voice calling out.

"*Stop it!* Leave him alone."

She was at the bottom of the Northgate steps, looking up at Mark and Tim. Mark swung round, surprised, releasing his grip on Tim's throat for a moment. Tim took the opportunity to pull back, aware that he had to get away from Mark. He leapt over the far side of the wall, and landed on the roof of the building beside it. Desperate to get away, he scrambled up to the apex of the roof and down the other side. Mark raced after him, catching up quickly, and once he'd climbed over the rooftop he aimed a kick down at Tim, who was clinging to the roof below him. Tim lost his grip and fell. Mark smiled. There was an almost sheer drop of forty feet into the canal from there. The building Tim had been clinging to was built on top of the steep walls of the canal, with just a narrow shelf a few inches wide at floor level, to break his fall, before the long drop into the canal. Mark heard a scream then a thud. He peered down, to see Tim lying at an awkward angle, half draped over a tiny bridge that crossed the canal from the building they were on to the old Bluecoat hospital. The Bridge of Sighs. Just Mark's luck. Now he'd have to go down there and push the boy off.

Nesta was watching the whole thing, horrified. She wanted to climb up there and stop Mark. She wanted to get over to the bridge and help Tim. She couldn't do either, stuck in her wheelchair. Then she remembered her mobile. She pulled it out of her pocket and started to punch in Bex's number.

By now Mark had realised what Nesta was doing. Leaving Tim clinging to the narrow bridge he pulled himself back over the roof, and jumped across to the city walls. He ran down the steps, grabbed the phone out of Nesta's hand and tossed it away. Then he hauled her out of her chair. She was small and light, easier to lift than he'd expected. He tried to swing her over the iron railings that were there to stop people falling from the pavement down into the canal, but Nesta fought back, lashing out at him, and clinging onto the railings from the street side. Mark made a final effort and lifted Nesta above the railings, then let go, expecting her to fall all the way down into the canal. She managed to grab hold of the railings from the other side, and hung there over the water.

Her arms were strong, from manoeuvring her chair, but they weren't used to supporting her full weight like that and her fingers began to lose their grip on the rusty iron. A chunk of loose paint came away in her hand and one arm dropped to her side. She felt her other hand slipping and panic washed over her. Inside her head she was screaming for help, willing someone, anyone, to come to their rescue, but the words wouldn't come out of her mouth. Mark leaned forward, grinning, and began to prise her remaining fingers loose.

**\*\*\***

Bex and Flint were sitting on the sofa in Bex's house. After a uneventful walk home they were beginning to feel that perhaps, with David dead, they were in the clear after all.

"Have you had any more texts?" Bex asked. Flint shook his head. "Then maybe they *were* connected to everything else that's going on … and now it's over."

"I'd like to think so," said Flint gloomily, "but I doubt it. I told you, the first one arrived just before all this started, and besides, it doesn't *feel* like the same thing." He reached over and picked up another chocolate biscuit.

**\*\*\***

Up on the cathedral roof Thren and Tor were still arguing about what to do next.

"We can't just hang around until it attacks again. We gotta do something. We gotta strike the first blow."

"That's all very well," said Tor, wearily, "but we don't know where to strike."

Suddenly Thren swayed, and clutched at his chest, looking bewildered. "Hey! what's going on?"

"What is it?" asked Tor. "Are you in pain?" Thren nodded. "Then one of them is in trouble," she said firmly, "look for the soul-lights."

Thren turned and stared out over the city. Not far away he could see Nesta's yellow soul-light blue-rimmed with fear, while Tim's green one appeared to hover in mid-air. He took off immediately, desperate to reach them before it was too late.

**\*\*\***

Flint turned to Bex, a half-eaten biscuit in his mouth. He was tempted to tell her the truth, explain what the texts were about. After all, she'd been a pretty good friend to him since all this started. Perhaps she'd be okay about it, perhaps she'd be the one person who'd understand that it had been an accident. That he hadn't meant it to happen. He had to talk to somebody, he'd been bottling it all up for too long. He swallowed the biscuit and started to speak, "Bex, there's something I need to tell –"

The phone in the hall started to ring. Bex jumped up to answer it, reaching it just as her father hurried out of the kitchen, but when she lifted the receiver no one spoke. She could just hear a scuffling sound in the distance. She slammed the phone down and dialled 1471, and the tinny BT voice recited a mobile number. Recognising it as Nesta's, Bex called "Come on, Flint. We need to get to the halls. I think Nesta's in trouble."

Followed by Dudley, Bex and Flint ran out of the house, under the archway, and headed towards the looming shadow of the Northgate, on their way to the campus.

*****

While Mark prised the fingers of one of Nesta's hands off the railing, she managed to reach back up with her other arm, scrabbling to get a hold on the brickwork the railings were fixed in. Mark brought his foot down hard on her fingertips, where they protruded onto his side of the ironwork, and she lost her grip. Her body began to spin downwards towards the dark, glistening canal. Above her she could catch glimpses of Tim, still balanced precariously on the bridge. She closed her eyes and braced herself for the impact she knew was coming …. but instead of plunging into the canal, she suddenly shot back up in the air, as if a strong wind had lifted her. She opened her eyes, then shut them again quickly. Now Tim was *below* her on the bridge. What was going on?

*****

To Thren's horror, as he flew upwards carrying Nesta, Tim began to slide off the bridge. Thren dropped down again, reaching out a hand to catch the boy, but he couldn't support both of them at once. Nesta was struggling in his other arm, so he twisted round until she was level with the railings. She reached out and grabbed onto them. Thren positioned himself below her, trying to support her weight on his outstretched legs, while his arms reached across attempting to stop Tim slipping off the bridge. He really needed some help, but he knew that Tor had set off after Mark, who had started to run as soon as the angels approached. She was determined to catch him before he attacked anyone else.

He heard footsteps running towards them then Bex's voice calling out "Nesta, hold on, we're coming." Bex reached forward and grabbed hold of Nesta's wrists. Finding her friend lighter than she expected Bex peered down towards the canal. She could see Thren, struggling to help Nesta and Tim at the same time. "I sure am glad to see you," Thren gasped, "I can't stay like this forever."

Flint started to chase after Mark, then realised it would be more useful to help Bex with Nesta. By the time Flint ran back to them Tim was starting to stir. He lay across the bridge, which was only a foot or so wide, and groaned. His left arm dangled uselessly over the water.

"Don't move, Tim. Stay where you are," called Flint.

"Get some help," said Bex, still hanging on to Nesta's wrists. She didn't dare let go, even though she knew Thren was taking some of her friend's weight. She was afraid Nesta would overbalance and fall anyway if she lost her grip on the railings.

"Use Nesta's mobile," said Bex. "It's over there."

Flint picked the phone up off the pavement and dialled 999.

"Where's Tor?" whispered Bex down to Thren.

"She's gone after Mark – figured one of us oughta."

"Will she be all right?"

"I sure hope so, but now ain't the moment to go after her. I'm kinda busy myself."

Tim groaned again, and tried to roll over.

"Stay still," called Flint, but Tim barely heard him. Between the drugs Mark had slipped into his drink, and the pain he was in from the fall, he couldn't make sense of what was happening at all. He could see water a long way below him, and thought, 'Water, that would cool me down. My arm's burning up.' He began to wriggle along the bridge, which unfortunately put him out of Thren's reach, but there didn't seem to be a way off. The tiny bridge didn't go anywhere any more. Both ends had been sealed off. It had once been used by condemned prisoners going from the city gaol in the old Northgate to the chapel in the Bluecoat Hospital to receive the last rites before their execution. Now the bridge led from nowhere to nowhere. Tim was completely cut off. 'I'll have to go down there then,' reasoned Tim to himself, his thinking blurred. 'Down, down, down.' He moved his weight forward so he could roll off the bridge and fall into the cool, dark water below, but just before he fell he felt hands grabbing at his shirt, pulling him back.

"Oh no, you don't," said Flint, who'd climbed over the railings and along the ledge to get to him. "You're not going anywhere. Let's just wait for the fire brigade shall we?"

By this time Dudley had caught up with Bex and Flint, and was surprised to see Flint straddling the bridge, holding on to Tim, who was thrashing about, trying to throw himself into the canal below.

"You know what Mark said?" slurred Tim loudly. "He said I fancied Nesta. That's why we had a fight. 'Cept it wasn't a fight ... it was a strung ... strang ... strangulation. You don't think I fancy Nesta, do you?"

"Why?" said Flint. "Are you going to fight me too?"

"No," smiled Tim dreamily. "It wasn't just what he said, it was how he said it. Horrible … insulting. Couldn't let him get away with it. Couldn't let him insult Nesta. Not lovely little Nesta … Did I tell you he said I fancied her?"

"You did just mention it," said Flint. "And he's probably right, but now is not the time to discuss it."

"Can I help?" asked Dudley, standing beside Bex and taking hold of one of Nesta's wrists. He, too, noticed that she wasn't as heavy as he expected her to be and he looked down through the railings, then turned to look sharply at Bex. "Is that …?"

"Thren? Yes. Can you see him?"

"Sort of. Bit of a blurred outline, anyway."

Thren, hearing the whispered conversation, adjusted his wing-beats so as to be invisible. Like he didn't have enough to do without worrying about being seen. Now that Flint was hanging onto Tim, Thren could change his position and get a better grip on Nesta. He hoped Flint hadn't caught a glimpse of him too. He'd been getting much better lately, about setting his wings to the 'invisible' frequency so humans couldn't see him. Now he'd blown it again. He'd let Dudley see him, which would probably cause even more trouble. 'I am *so* not cut out for this job,' he thought. He wished the fire brigade would arrive. He wanted to go after Tor, make sure she wasn't in trouble, but he didn't dare let go of Nesta's legs. Then there was a screeching of sirens, and the emergency services arrived. All three of them.

The fire brigade soon got Nesta into a safety harness and lifted her over the railings. Then they used a more complicated system of ropes, pulleys and harnesses to get Tim and Flint safely off the bridge. Flint protested that he didn't need a harness, he'd got himself there all right, but the firemen insisted. When Flint glanced down at the canal below him, he didn't really mind wearing a safety harness. It was a long way down.

Once Tim and Nesta were on the pavement the ambulance team checked them over, and the police began asking questions. It was Nesta who had to do most of the explaining – Tim was still out of it. She explained what Mark had tried to do to them both, and that he had probably drugged Tim. He certainly hadn't got into that state on one pint of beer, and they hadn't been in the pub long enough to drink more than that. The ambulance carried Tim and Nesta off to hospital to be examined properly. Tim's left arm had been broken, and they wanted to make sure there was no other damage.

**\*\*\***

In the ambulance Tim turned and looked at Nesta. "Mark said I fancied you … did you know that?"

Nesta nodded. "I heard you telling Flint."

"No," said Tim. "I mean – did you know I fancy you? I do, you know. I think he was right about that. I just didn't realise it."

Nesta was embarrassed. Not that she didn't want Tim to be in love with her, but it was complicated. There was Nicola, for a start. "Don't, Tim. Don't talk about it now. You're … you're not yourself at the moment. You might say something you don't mean."

"He said you were soft on me."

"Did he?"

"Yes – was he right about that too?" Tim reached out and took Nesta's hand. She didn't answer. She didn't dare look at him, or he'd know how she felt about him. "He was wrong about one thing," Tim continued. "He said I was your knight in shining armour, but I'm not. You rescued me tonight – does that make me a damsel in distress? I hope not, I'd look silly in a dress." Tim drifted into silence.

Nesta turned and looked at him. He was asleep. She tried to draw her hand away from his, but he clung on to it tightly, so she left it there. She'd have to sort things out with him in the morning. Make sure he realised that a relation-ship with her wasn't going to happen. If he remembered anything at all about it. He'd probably have forgotten the whole conversation in the morning. Nesta's eyes pricked with tears, which slowly began to trickle down her cheeks, as she sat holding Tim's hand, probably for the only time.

"You all right, love?" asked the ambulance man.

Nesta nodded. "Just a bit shaky, that's all."

"Shock, I expect," said the ambulance man. "Don't worry, we'll be there soon. Things will be better once you get to hospital."

Nesta nodded. There was no point in disagreeing with him, but she was sure things wouldn't be better. Not for her or any of the others. Not until this was over.

# Chapter 37

Dudley stood next to Bex and Flint, watching the ambulance and police car drive away. "Come along," he said, putting an arm round each of their shoulders, "Let's go home." The old man tried to keep a straight face, but he couldn't help smiling. He'd seen an angel, well, sort of seen it, which was more than he'd ever expected. He guided the others back to the house. It was only a few minutes walk from the cathedral green to the Bridge of Sighs, though it had seemed much further when they'd run there.

"Time for some hot chocolate, I think," said Dudley when they reached the house. "Would you like some, Flint?"

Flint nodded tiredly. Reaction was setting in, now that the danger was past. Bex looked exhausted too. Dudley told them to go and sit down, while he made the drinks, but by the time he came back into the room, carrying a tray of steaming mugs, they were both asleep. Bex's head was resting on Flint's shoulder, while he was leaning against the arm of the sofa. Dudley shook his head as he looked at them. 'They *have* got themselves into a mess,' he thought. 'So how are we going to get them out of it?'

*** 

Meanwhile, Thren, having seen them safely home, set off to look for Tor. He'd last seen her when she flew away down the road, chasing Mark, or whatever Mark had become.

'I sure hope she's okay,' thought Thren as he circled the city. 'She shouldn't oughta tackle him on her own.' He shivered, as rain began to fall, soaking into his feathers. He scanned the streets again, and saw a familiar little soul-light moving hesitantly along one of them. He flew down to investigate and found Amy trudging towards the cathedral. A small rucksack was on her back and tears were rolling down her face, mixing with the rain, which was getting heavier. She was stopping to look in every doorway, and calling out, "Luke ... Luke, where are you?"

Thren could have kicked himself. He knew where Luke was, had known for a couple of days, in fact, and hadn't done anything about it. 'What am I like?' he complained to himself. 'Leaving the little kid worrying like that.' Just then he saw a figure move out of the shadows. It grabbed the straps of Amy's rucksack, and swung her round and round, giggling, while she screamed in panic.

"I guess we missed one," said Thren, and landed on the creature heavily from above.

There was a satisfying crunch, then a cracked little voice said, "Oh-oh!"

Thren grabbed an arm that was waving about helplessly, the rest of the creature being hidden by Thren's feet, which had it trapped against the cobbles. He hoisted the imp up in the air as he stepped off it, and Snig hung there, thrashing about powerlessly.

"Let me go," cried the imp indignantly.

"No way, Jose," said Thren. "The only place I'm letting you go is back where you belong."

"But I've been having fun here."

"I can figure out how, too. Was it you who glued all Tor's feathers together?"

"Good joke," sniggered the imp. "Made me laugh."

"Well, Tor didn't think it was so funny. I hadda cut all her hair off."

"Bald angel – nice one," said Snig. "Like the new look."

"Well, how's this for a look?" said Thren taking the imp and thrusting its rubbery face against the nearest shop window.

"Verici netmgo," muttered the imp, unintelligibly.

"I'll let you go when you've told me what you know about the demon." Thren peeled the creature off the glass.

"He's called Dross … He's clever," gasped Snig, "Strong … cruel … too tough for you."

"Wanna bet?" said Thren. "Now how did you and the other imps get through?"

"Tor's fault. She told girl about soul-lights. Broke rule, got trouble."

"It's only a little rule," protested Thren.

"So she only got small imps. You gonna let me go now?"

"I'm gonna let you go home."

"Don't want to."

"Tough. We can do this the easy way or we can do it the hard way! Which is it to be?"

"What's the options again?" asked the imp.

"I can kick you back to where you belong, I can pray over you, or I can find a font and dunk you in holy water."

"Don't I have any nice options? Anything involving mess, and trouble and annoying people?"

"No."

"Oh, all right, spoilsport, kick me back. I hate prayers, and holy water brings me out in blisters."

Thren drew back his foot and kicked the little creature up into the air. It shot up into the sky, shouting defiantly, "My name's Snig. Remember it, I'll be back." There was a pop, and it disappeared back into its own dimension.

Thren turned to look at Amy. She'd fallen to the ground when Thren attacked the imp, and although she'd picked herself up she was limping. Thren reached out and took the little girl's hand. She looked surprised. She could feel someone leading her along, but she couldn't see anyone. Still, the hand holding hers felt warm, and since she didn't know where to go next she was happy enough to be led.

Fifteen minutes later they were standing outside the hostel. Thren knocked on the door. One of the night staff opened it, and saw the child standing there alone.

"What are you doing here?" the woman asked.

"Looking for Luke. He's my brother," answered Amy.

"You'd better come in then."

Thren let go of Amy's hand and she stepped forward into the hostel. Thren sighed with relief as the door closed behind her. "Well, that's one problem sorted, for tonight anyway. What was Harry thinking of, letting her wander off like that?"

Thren flew to Harry's house, and got there just as the man returned from a long session at the pub.

"Amy? Amy? You here? Why's the door open?"

Harry stuck his head in the sitting-room. The armchair was still facing the wall, the television screen was still snowy and the things from the mantelpiece were lying on the rug. Harry searched for the photograph of Maggie and the kids. There was no sign of it. He lumbered clumsily upstairs and looked in Amy's room. Her muddy school uniform was on the floor, but there was no sign of the girl. Guiltily, Harry picked up the uniform and carried it downstairs to put in the washing machine.

"Amy, come out, it's all right. I'm not angry ... Look, I'm washing your school things." Harry shoved the clothes in the machine, put far too much powder in the tray, and started the washing cycle.

"Amy, I'm sorry. Please come out now ... Amy? She's gone. Even she's left me. Thinks I killed her mother ... I didn't ... I didn't ... Why won't anyone believe me?"

Thren watched as the man smashed his fist against the wall time after time to the rhythm of the words, "I didn't do it, I didn't do it, I didn't do it."

Thren crept miserably out of the house. "How do you help someone like that? Why even bother? And yet ... the guy's in such a state. Something real bad must have happened to make him feel like that."

# Chapter 38

"I lost him," said Tor, crossly. "And once I'd lost sight of him I couldn't find him again. I searched everywhere, but there was no sign. You might have come to help me."

"I tried," said Thren, "Honest I did, but first I had to stop Nesta and Tim falling into the canal, then I had to deal with an imp, and take Amy, the little girl I told you about, somewhere safe. After that I went to check out a guy called Harry, and by the time I'd done all that I saw you flying back towards the cathedral, so here I am."

Tor sank down on to a parapet tiredly. "What are we going to do?" she asked. "He's winning, isn't he? The most we're managing to do is react to each attack, and half the time we don't succeed at that."

"We did tonight," said Thren, sitting down beside her. "We saved Tim and Nesta."

"You did," said Tor miserably. "All I did was let the demon escape."

"Can you explain something to me, Tor? How come I got a pain in my chest for a moment when Nesta and Tim were in trouble? That ain't never happened to me before."

"If you must know," replied Tor, "it means you're getting better at the job, that you're beginning to connect with people."

"Grrreat. All this hassle and pain too. Terrific! Just when I thought I'd reached rock bottom." So he was getting better at the job. Big Deal. What did it matter anyway?

He'd already made a complete mess of things.

There was a long silence, then Thren said quietly, "He was using Mark's body."

"So that's another one gone," Tor agreed, "And we're no nearer finding a way to stop it, and get the missing soul-lights back."

"It's too late for Mark even if we do," said Thren guiltily. "I feel totally awful. This whole thing is my fault. I'm supposed to be protecting these guys, and they're dropping like flies."

"I've just realised," said Tor suddenly, "If the demon's been using Mark's body all day, then the things that happened at the zoo weren't accidents either. He was trying to kill Sam."

"Hello," said a voice quietly from the doorway that led onto the roof.

"Bex, what are you doing here?" said Thren. "You oughta be in bed."

"I couldn't sleep … and I wanted to make sure Tor was all right. You said she went after Mark … you seemed worried about her."

"I was," Thren admitted.

"Were you?" said Tor, surprised.

"Yeah, but she's okay," Thren smiled.

"Is she here?" asked Bex shyly.

Tor glowed with pleasure at Bex's concern, and made herself visible. "Hello, Bex."

"Wow, you look … different," said Bex, taking in the short hair and denim outfit – the stuff Thren had borrowed from her room.

"Oh, dear," said Tor, embarrassed. "Sorry about the clothes, but my robe got ruined; some horrid imp played a joke on me, but it wasn't very funny."

"But what happened to your beautiful hair?" asked Bex.

"The imp tangled it all up, and glued my feathers to the

roof. Thren got the feathers unglued, but the hair had to go," said Tor, sadly.

"I'm sorry," said Bex. "Still, the new look suits you – makes you look much less...' Bex stopped. She'd been going to say prissy, but it wouldn't have sounded very kind, and Tor looked so vulnerable standing there in her borrowed clothing, with her hair roughly shorn off. "It makes you look ... younger." She decided that sounded all right, and it was true. An angel with long, golden locks and a flowing robe had a timeless quality, whereas Tor's new look was very – now.

"I ought to give you the clothes back," said Tor guiltily.

"You keep them, they're not much use to me with ... wing holes in and, anyway, they look better on you."

Tor smiled and Bex smiled back at her.

"Actually," said Thren feeling left out, "I dealt with the imp that did you over. Name of Snig, apparently. And I found out why the lesser invisibles were here ... And guess what? It was nothing to do with me. They were down to you, lady. You were the one who dropped the words 'soul-light' into the conversation when you first met Bex."

"Oh," said Tor forlornly, "I'd forgotten about that."

"Never mind," said Bex, surprised to find herself wanting to cheer Tor up. "I was thinking – about the zoo. Was it you that stopped that lion getting Sam?" Tor nodded. "I didn't realise at the time, and then later I thought ... it must have been one of you, turning the lion in mid-air like that."

"You're not supposed to realise," said Tor, starting to sound like her old self again. "People aren't supposed to know we're there at all."

"Well, Dad realises. He ... sort of saw Thren tonight."

"What?" said Tor menacingly.

"Don't start," said Thren, "I was trying to rescue Nesta at the time. I just got the frequency of my wing-beats wrong."

"It's all right. Dad knows about you two anyway – and I think he's always believed in angels."

"Is that who you think you're talking to?" said a sneering voice from the doorway.

"Flint," said Bex, turning round. "What are you doing here?"

"Keeping an eye on you. I heard you sneaking out and I wondered where you were going to in the middle of the night – besides, I thought you might get attacked by that … by Mark – so I came after you. Oddly enough, I didn't expect to find you up on the cathedral roof talking to imaginary angels."

"They're not imaginary," she protested.

"Oh, yeah," said Flint.

"They're not. You could see them if they let you." She turned and looked hopefully at Tor and Thren. "Please."

"Sorry, Bex, but we're in enough trouble already," said Tor.

"Look what happened when I let you see me," said Thren.

"But you didn't *let* me see you – I can see you all the time."

"What's up?" said Flint. "Don't your imaginary friends want to play any more?"

"They're not imaginary."

"Look, Bex," said Flint more gently. "I know we're all going through a difficult time at the moment, but it won't help anybody if you crack up, will it? Come on, let's get you back to the house."

"I'm not cracking up," said Bex indignantly. "Stop talking to me as if I'm going mad."

"Of course you're not mad … you're just under a lot of strain, that's all. We all are, but there's no need to go round imagining angels. They won't be able to make anything better," and Flint started to lead Bex towards the stairs.

"Thren, do something, *please*," she called from the

doorway.

"Gee, I'm sorry, Bex, but I daren't break the rules again, not just to prove a point like that."

"Traitor," she called back, as Flint followed her down the stairs and shut the door behind them.

"Oh dear," said Tor.

"Now she's mad at me," said Thren. "I thought she liked me."

"She does," said Tor. "I think she likes both of us – but I have a horrible feeling she likes Flint too. I can understand her not wanting to look bad in his eyes. Perhaps it's a good thing, if he thinks she's a bit strange. I don't want them getting too close."

"Why not?" asked Thren.

"I can't imagine Flint being the right person for her … she can do much better."

"You're starting to sound like a nanny again."

***

A few minutes later Bex was back in her bedroom, and Flint was trying to sleep on the sofa downstairs. "Angels," he was muttering to himself. "Huh!"

He was glad he hadn't told Bex his secret earlier. She was obviously cracking up, so it wouldn't have done any good trying to talk to her about his problems. Anyway, he doubted if she would have understood, she'd just have condemned him, like everyone else did. He rolled over and drifted off into a fitful sleep. At first his dreams were filled with what had happened on the bridge, and the sense of menace hanging over them all. Then his dream changed. He was driving. It was icy. He couldn't keep the car on the road. The tree was rushing towards them. Flint woke up, sweating. He hated that dream.

Upstairs there was a soft tapping on Bex's bedroom window. She crawled out of bed and pulled back the curtains. Thren was hovering outside.

"Can I come in?" he was mouthing.

Bex opened the window, letting in a blast of icy air and an angel.

"What are you doing here?" she said, grumpily.

"I just came to see if you were still mad at me."

"I am," said Bex.

"Aw, I'm sorry, Bex. I didn't mean to let you down, but I daren't just break the rules like that. Look at the mess I've gotten us all into already. I sure don't want to make things worse."

"What about Dad seeing you? Is that going to cause trouble?"

"Tor doesn't think so, under the circumstances. It wasn't on purpose; he just caught a glimpse of me trying to rescue Nesta. I guess that kinda thing happens sometimes."

"Good," said Bex. "In a way, I'm glad he saw you."

"Me too," said Thren. "I really like your old man. Well, I'd better go." He walked over to the window, then turned back to her. "No hard feelings? About tonight?"

"No," said Bex. "Not really."

"Good," said Thren smiling. "I'd hate to fall out with you. Now come and close this window behind me – and make sure you lock it."

Thren climbed out of the window and heard Bex close it behind him. He flew up to the cathedral roof, wondering what was happening to him. He'd just gone to make his peace with a *human*. He'd told her he liked her father, and he'd meant it. 'I gotta get outta here before it's too late,' he thought, but he had a nasty suspicion it was too late already. He was getting involved. Thren, the angel who never got involved with anyone or anything was getting roped into this ridiculous human world full of hopes and fears and emotions. '*Emotions*. Ugh! I *really* need to sort myself out.' Then he remembered what the High Council had planned for him. 'Guess I'll be outta here soon enough anyway.'

# Chapter 39

Thren was pacing up and down inside the cathedral. The weather that morning was too disgusting to stay up on the roof. He'd checked on all the students three times already but it seemed that the demon was keeping a low profile for a while. 'Maybe the fact that he didn't manage to destroy Tim and Nesta last night has put him off his stride,' thought Thren. 'Things aren't going all his own way.'

Thren passed the Chapter House. The clergy appeared to be having some kind of meeting in there. Dudley, Pearson and Poole were present, amongst others, but the meeting was obviously just finishing. Everyone was standing up, collecting their papers and coats. The phone rang, and someone beckoned Dudley over to it. Thren saw Pearson slide after him, trying to be inconspicuous while getting near enough to hear what was said. Thren listened in too. He heard Janet, on the other end of the line, telling Dudley about Amy's arrival at the hostel the night before, and the fact that she seemed to be Luke's little sister. Dudley said he'd join her at the hostel immediately, and put the phone down. Thren watched as the old clergyman collected his coat and set off for the hostel.

One by one the other people who had been at the meeting left the Chapter House, till Pearson and Poole were on their own. "This is our chance," Pearson was saying. "Apparently there's a little girl at the hostel Dudley's involved with. Far too young to be there. The woman who runs the place should have called the police at once, but she hasn't."

"Isn't that rather irresponsible?" asked Poole.

"Exactly," said Pearson, excitedly.

"What are you going to do?" asked Poole. "Are you going to phone the police about the little girl?"

"No," said Pearson, with a smug sort of smile. "I'm going to phone the local paper."

Thren was furious. *He'd* been the one to take Amy to the hostel, and he hadn't meant to cause trouble for anyone. He just wanted to get Luke and Amy back together. He decided he'd better hurry to the hostel, and try to warn Janet and Dudley somehow. The last thing they needed was some sleazy reporter snooping around, trying to make a story out of other people's problems.

***

He caught up with Dudley just as he reached the hostel, and Janet opened the door to him.

"Good morning, Dudley. I am glad you're here," she said, showing the old man into her office. "I've spoken to the children and it seems they're both frightened of the man they're living with. He's their mother's boyfriend, or he was. The mother's dead and it appears the children think that this man, Harry, killed her."

"Oh dear," said Dudley. "No wonder they're afraid of him."

"Luke finally gave me the phone number. I rang the man this morning and he's coming to see me ... I was going to phone the police, but he seemed in such a dreadful state, Dudley, that I didn't want to do anything too quickly. He said he'd been up most of the night, searching for Amy. He sounded so relieved that she was safe. I didn't want to make any trouble for him without even knowing the whole story."

"That sounds fair," said Dudley. "Do you want me to

stay with you while you talk to him?"

"I was hoping you would," said Janet, smiling.

A few minutes later Harry was shown into the office. Thren noticed he'd made a bit of an effort to clean himself up. He'd showered and shaved and put on some fairly clean clothes, but he still looked wrecked. His eyes were red and his voice a bit hoarse. He really had been out most of the night calling Amy's name, trying to find her.

"Is she all right?" he asked, as soon as he entered the office. "I couldn't bear it if anything had happened to her."

"She's quite safe," said Janet. "But we do need to get to the bottom of what's been going on. Are you the children's only guardian?"

"Yeah," said Harry, "I suppose you could say that. They're not my kids, see, either of them. Their mother and I ... well ... she moved in with me and the kids came too. Got on all right, Maggie and I did, to begin with. Even got on all right with the kids. Then Maggie and I started falling out ... I drink a bit, you see. Maggie didn't like it. We used to row ... I ... I hit her once or twice. I think she'd have moved out, but she didn't have anywhere to go. She gave up her flat when she moved in with me."

"I see," said Janet, trying not to sound judgmental. She wanted to give Harry a chance to tell his side of the story, and she knew he'd clam up if she started criticising him. "What happened then?"

"Well, one night, when I was drunk, I hit her. I'm not proud of it," he added defiantly, "But it happened, and I can't change that. She was bleeding from her head where she fell against a table. I took her to the hospital and they insisted on a brain scan. Turned out Maggie had a brain tumour, just there," said Harry, pointing to the back of his skull. "Said they'd have to operate at once. Said it was a good thing she'd had a fall and I'd taken her in ... that's what we told them, you see, that she'd had a fall. Said if they hadn't found the tumour right then, it would have been too late to operate – but it was too late anyway. She died on the operating table the next day." He looked up at Janet and Dudley, trying to look them squarely in the eye. "I know I shouldn't have hit her, but it wasn't my fault she died. I told the kids what had happened, but they never quite believed me. They thought it was my fault Maggie was dead. I tried to do my best for them – well, they didn't have anyone else, did they? But it didn't work. They hate me. I took to drinking more. Luke and I kept arguing, and eventually I hit him. That's when he ran away ... I've hit Amy too, once or twice ... but I never wanted anything bad to happen to her ... to either of them. They're good kids ... we used to get on all right, when Maggie first moved in ... I just..."

He stopped, unable to speak any more. It was the first time he'd put what was happening into words. It had taken all the courage he had, and now he felt drained. Thren noticed that his soul-light seemed a little softer. It was beginning to lose its angry red glow.

"You can't cope," finished Janet, sympathetically.

"No, I can't," admitted Harry. "I have tried, but it's not working. So what do we do now?"

"Well, I honestly think the best thing for the children would be for them to go into care. We'll ask Social Services to place them with a foster family that can give them the support they need."

Harry nodded. He'd failed and he knew it. There was nothing to be gained by sending the children back to him. "Can I see them?" he asked.

"Of course," said Janet. She paused awkwardly. "One of our staff will have to supervise you." She could hardly leave the children alone with him, when he'd admitted that he'd hit them.

"I understand," said Harry, and stood up. Janet introduced him to a member of staff, who took him to see Luke and Amy. In the office, Janet picked up the phone and called Social Services.

"Are you going to phone the police?" asked Dudley when she'd finished the call.

"I don't know. I suppose I'll have to," said Janet. "The main thing is to get the children away from him, so that he can't hurt them in the future, and he's agreed to that. It seems a shame to punish him any more, when he's been through so much already."

"I think he needs help himself," said Dudley. "Perhaps we should encourage him to ask for it."

Janet's phone rang. She listened in silence for a few minutes, then said, "Well, thank you for trying anyway Mr Simpson. We really do appreciate it." She put the phone down, and looked over at Dudley. She felt completely defeated.

"Let me guess," said Dudley, gently, "the Housing Committee aren't going to help us find another building."

"Mr Simpson did try, but they just weren't interested'

Thren could feel their disappointment. The Housing Committee had been their only chance. If they weren't prepared to offer them an alternative building for the hostel, then what?

"Well, what happens next?" asked Dudley.

"I suppose we'll have to close. There's nothing else we can do. We'll never find another suitable building with rent this low, and we don't have the funds to pay more."

Thren shared their sense of failure. He, too, had done his best to keep the hostel open, influencing Mr Simpson into supporting their cause, but it hadn't been enough. He was beginning to feel as if he'd never succeed at anything.

Leaving Dudley and Janet in the office, Thren went upstairs to find Harry and the children. The man was explaining to them, as calmly and clearly as he could, exactly what had happened to their mother, and for the first time, the children were starting to believe him.

"They're going to put you into care," said Harry at last. "It'll be better for you. A nice foster home. Better than living with a drunk like me." He smiled at them nervously. "I hope they find you somewhere decent. I'm sorry things didn't work out between us. I did mean them to. I really did. I shouldn't have hit you ... either of you. I'm sorry." He stood up to leave. "I'll pack all your things. I expect Social Services will come round to collect them for you."

He hesitated at the door. "You're good kids, both of you. Don't blame yourselves."

Amy suddenly pulled away from Luke and ran over to give Harry a hug. "Goodbye, Harry."

"Goodbye, Amy ... Luke. If you want to ... to keep in touch ... you know where I am," and he turned and left the room.

Thren followed him down the stairs. Harry was genuinely upset at saying goodbye to the children. He knew he'd failed them, but they were all the family he had, and, in a strange sort of way, he was going to miss them.

Not long after Harry had left, Social Services came to collect the children. They'd found a suitable foster home, and were going to take the children directly there. It was only a temporary arrangement, but it was a start.

Thren listened, as the social worker explained the situation to the children.

"You see, you'll only be able to stay at this foster home for a week, because the couple we're placing you with are about to go away, to visit their own children who are grown up now. In the meantime we'll try to find somewhere else for you. Somewhere you can stay for longer."

Luke and Amy were sitting together on Luke's bed. He put his arm protectively round his little sister. "We will be together, won't we?" asked Luke.

"For this week certainly," the woman replied. "After that we'll have to see."

"But we've only just found each other again," whispered

Amy, clinging to her brother.

"I'm sorry, we'll do our best to keep you together, of course, but it's very difficult to find foster homes who'll accept two children, instead of one."

"I've abandoned Amy once," said Luke, firmly. "I thought if I ran away, if I wasn't there to make Harry angry, that he'd look after Amy properly. I was wrong. I'm not leaving her again."

"We'll do our best, that's all I can promise."

Thren was horrified. He'd only just got the children back together, and Social Services were talking about splitting them up again. It seemed like nothing was ever simple. He'd have to keep looking out for the kids, wherever they were taken. Except he wouldn't get the chance, not once he was reassigned. He wondered if another angel would take over, and look after them for him. 'I sure hope so,' thought Thren.

As Luke and Amy were being shepherded into the car, Pearson and Poole turned up, with a reporter from the local paper. Since Social Services were already involved it was obvious that Pearson's exposé of the hostel was a non-starter. Pearson was livid. He'd been convinced that this was his chance to get rid of Dudley. Leaving the reporter chatting to Janet and Dudley, Pearson pulled Poole to one side.

"The story about sheltering under-age children obviously isn't going to work," said Pearson. "Do you think we could find some kind of sleazy connection between Dudley and the woman who runs this place?"

"Start a scandal, you mean?" asked Poole.

"Exactly," said Pearson. "Nothing too tacky, but just enough to make people wonder if there's no smoke without fire." He glanced over at Janet. "She's not a bad looking woman, after all, and Dudley's not that old."

"But there isn't anything going on between them, is there?" asked Poole.

"Of course not," said Pearson, patiently. "We'd have to invent it, tell it to the reporter, and hope he prints it. I wonder if he's going to take one or two pictures while he's here? '

Poole looked down at the ground, covered in puddles after the rain the night before. He could just about see his reflection in one of them, distorted by some pebbles that were breaking through the surface of the water. He felt distorted inside, too. Twisted around and hauled out of shape by Pearson's scheming. If he went along with this, if he helped to blacken Dudley's name just to suit his friend, he doubted he'd ever be able to look at himself in a mirror again. Not with a clear conscience. Was Pearson's friendship really worth it?

Poole tore his eyes away from the puddle, looked at Pearson consideringly and said, "I'm beginning to suspect that you're not a very nice person. I can't think how I got involved with you, but since I am and I know what you're up to, it's my job to stop it."

'Way to go,' thought Thren delightedly. 'You tell him, buster. It's good to see the worm turn at last.'

Pearson was staring at Poole in amazement. His friend never answered him back.

"If you make up some horrid scandal," Poole continued, "I'll deny it. I'll say you invented it to get rid of Dudley. I'll even ..." he took a deep breath, "I'll even tell the Bishop, if I have to."

# Chapter 40

"He's ignoring me," said Nesta to Bex, as they drank their coffee in the canteen when lectures were over for the day. "He won't even look me in the eye."

"I know the feeling," said Bex, glancing towards where Tim and Flint were sitting on the far side of the cafeteria.

"I thought you and Flint were getting on really well at the moment."

"We were ... well, I thought we were," replied Bex, "but I don't think he likes anyone to get too close to him."

"But sitting on the other side of the room's a bit extreme, isn't it?" Nesta continued. "There must be more to it than that."

"We ... we fell out over something last night."

"What?" asked Nesta.

"Oh, nothing much," said Bex, who wasn't about to start explaining about the angels. "We're just all a bit stressed at the moment."

"Which is hardly surprising," said Nesta gloomily. "I can't believe what happened last night. It was all so ... strange."

"Well, at least you and Tim survived!"

"I know, and I am thankful, but look at us! Tim's got a broken arm *and* he's not talking to me. We were such good friends before."

"You will be again," said Bex, optimistically. "He's just a bit embarrassed about what he said last night."

"He doesn't have to avoid me," said Nesta. "I know he didn't mean what he said. It was just the state he was in, and the way Mark ...or whatever it was ... was winding him up. If he'd just talk to me I could tell him that I didn't take it seriously."

"He said something about going to see Nicola at the weekend," said Bex. "I ... er ... I thought you should know."

"It's none of my business," said Nesta. "He can see anyone he wants to. I know he'll never see me as a ... a ... well, a girlfriend, but I don't want to lose him as a friend."

"He means a lot to you, doesn't he?" asked Bex.

"Everything," said Nesta simply. "Last night, when I saw Mark attacking him, I just wanted to climb on to the roof and protect him, but there was nothing I could do. I felt so helpless."

"You called us," said Bex. "If you hadn't tried to get help, Mark would have finished you both off." She couldn't add that they'd had more than one kind of help, that if Thren hadn't got there in time then nothing she and Flint could have done would have helped.

"Except that it wasn't Mark really," said Nesta. "It's strange to think that whatever that thing is – it's taken over ... one of us. It makes you wonder who you can trust."

"You can trust me, for a start," said Bex, "And you can trust Tim. He'll be all right in a few days."

"I hope so," said Nesta.

Paul and Sarah walked into the cafeteria, and paused, unsure what to do. Usually everyone sat together. After a moment Sarah went over to join Bex and Nesta, and Paul found himself sitting next to Flint.

"What's going on?" he asked, puzzled. "Boys versus girls?"

"Something like that," said Flint. "You heard about what happened last night?"

"About Mark attacking Tim and Nesta? Yes, Sarah told me," said Paul. "I suppose that means Mark's dead?"

"I think so," said Flint. "I think it needs a dead body to inhabit, and if it can't find one ... it makes one."

"But how come none of us noticed?" asked Tim.

"Well, it couldn't have taken over Mark that long ago, could it?" said Flint. "It was walking around as David until Saturday night."

"Where are the others?" asked Paul.

"Sam said he'd keep an eye on Cath," said Tim. "She's getting weirder and weirder. She seems to have gone to pieces completely. Not eating, not looking after herself. She hardly leaves her room now."

"Perhaps we should call a doctor?" suggested Paul. "It sounds like she needs proper help."

"You could be right," said Flint. "I'm beginning to wonder if the ... thing hasn't done something to her already, but for the life of me I can't figure out what. Paul ... Paul, are you all right?"

"Yes," said Paul, who'd just seen the figures of Thren and Tor reflected in his glasses as they entered the canteen and stood behind him. He took his glasses off and placed them on the table. "Sorry, just a bit distracted, that's all." He glanced round nervously. "What were you saying?"

"I think the ... thing has done something to Cath. I think that might be what's wrong with her." Flint paused. "I think Bex is going a bit strange too."

"What do you mean?" asked Tim. "She seems fine."

"Oh, she's just ... starting to imagine things, that's all."

"What kind of things?" asked Paul.

"Angels!" said Flint, and immediately wished he hadn't.

"Angels?" laughed Tim, leaning back in his chair.

"Angels?" said Paul, more urgently. "Are you sure about that?" He glanced round again, but without his glasses he couldn't see Thren and Tor exchanging nervous glances.

"I mighta known he couldn't keep his mouth shut," muttered Thren.

"I doubt if anyone will believe him," said Tor, "Or at least, they won't believe in us. They'll just tease Bex about it for a while."

"Terrific," said Thren. "Like she *really* needs people giving her a hard time right now," and he wandered over to the girls' table where Sarah was talking to Bex and Nesta. Her usually cheerful face was serious, and her fuzzy pink soul-light tinged with grey.

"I can't believe what that thing's done to Mark," she was saying. "What happened to Marty and ... and Graham was bad enough. I still haven't got my head round the idea of Joanna being frightened into running away and none of us realising ... and now this. Well, it has to be worse, doesn't it? Being taken over by that ... whatever it is. Just being touched by him gave me the creeps. Imagine having him ... ugh."

"We think Mark must have been dead for it to be able to take him over," said Bex.

"I hope so," said Sarah. The others looked at her slightly shocked. "I know that sounds terrible, but that thing, whatever it is, is evil, pure evil. Being dead has to be better than being controlled by it, knowing what it's doing, but not being able to stop it."

"I suppose so," said Bex. "It just sounds so ... harsh, putting it into words."

"I did like him, you know," said Sarah defensively. "We all did."

Nesta felt guilty. Mark had been one of the main people to put her down, make her feel she shouldn't be on the Biology course. She just couldn't feel the same way about his death as she did about what had happened to the others. Especially after last night, when it had been Mark – well, his body, that was trying to kill Tim and drop her down into the canal. Still, she didn't wish him any harm, and she knew Sarah didn't either.

"I suppose," said Nesta, thinking it through, "there are worse things than being dead."

"That's what I meant," said Sarah, gratefully.

Over at the boys' table, Tim was trying to get Flint to tell him more about Bex's imaginary angels.

"She's not serious, is she?" asked Tim. "Not about believing in something like that?" Flint didn't reply.

"It's not that weird," said Paul, hesitantly. "We all believe there's something ... bad that's trying to get each of us. It's even succeeding. So why shouldn't there be something good?"

"But angels?" joked Tim. "With wings and robes and halos – it's a bit much, isn't it?"

Paul nearly said that they didn't seem to have halos, but he didn't want the others teasing him, the way they were obviously going to tease Bex, so he shut up.

"Christians do believe in some strange things," said Flint.

"Not *that* strange, surely?" said Tim, leaning forward. There was a crunching sound, as the plaster cast on his arm crushed Paul's glasses, breaking one of the lenses.

"Oh, sorry Paul," said Tim, apologetically, "I didn't see them. What were they doing on the table anyway? You usually keep them on."

"Just got a bit of a headache, that's all," lied Paul, twisting his now useless glasses in his hands. "I'd better go and fetch my spare pair, I can't see a thing without them."

He stood up and walked out of the canteen. It was dark outside, and bitterly cold. A few flakes of snow were falling, though they were melting as soon as they touched the ground.

Paul headed for his room in the halls of residence, squinting into the darkness to try and find his way. The world was very blurred without his glasses, it would be a relief to get back to his room and find his other pair.

The campus seemed unusually empty, considering it was only half-past five, but the weather had driven everybody indoors. Paul was wondering if he dared talk to Bex about the angels Flint said she was imagining. Perhaps they could compare notes; work out what was going on – but that would mean admitting that *he* was seeing things too. Flint would really go to town about that if he found out. It had taken Paul a long time to find a group of people to fit in with at uni. Not that he did 'fit in' exactly. He knew they all thought he was a bit of a geek, and that the subject he was studying was pretty irrelevant. Still, they let him hang around with them anyway, and he was grateful for that. At school he'd always been a bit of a loner, ignored by the girls and laughed at by the boys. Here he actually felt he'd made some friends, even some girlfriends. Well, not girl-friends exactly, but friends who were girls.

Last term he'd fallen heavily for Joanna, though he knew she'd never give him a second glance. When he got to know the group better, he'd felt attracted to Bex because she seemed genuinely friendly. Not that he'd ever ask her out – she'd probably laugh at him, and besides, he couldn't work out if she and Flint were an item.

It really wasn't the right time to be wandering round alone, thinking about other things. Paul didn't even notice Mark step out of the shadows behind him. The first he knew was when he felt something, like a coat, being flung over his face so he couldn't see. Then a loop of rope was dropped over his head, and used to pin his arms by his side. Anxious to get his victim out of sight, Mark dragged Paul to the building that housed the swimming pool, and thrust him in through the doors. The coat slipped from Paul's head, so that he could see Mark's face, now starting to get the greyish tinge that had characterised David. The face barely looked like Mark now. It was distorted with greed and hatred. Almost three days dead, this body too was starting to smell, and its owner wasn't bothering to cover it up with mints and after-shave, since everyone now knew where the demon had taken up residence.

Paul glanced round. Without his glasses his eyesight was very poor, but he could tell the swimming pool was unoccupied. The building was completely silent and he knew nobody was likely to come to his rescue.

Mark seemed to know what he was thinking. "Don't bother. You're on your own. No one's going to come looking for you. They won't even notice you're missing. It's not like you're really part of the group, they just allow you to hang around with them."

Paul hung his head. Mark – the thing that was in Mark – was right. He didn't belong, not really. Paul felt a tremendous sense of defeat and loneliness sweep through him. He was on his own, and he knew he'd never be able to fight off his attacker without the others to help him. Mark stretched the stiffening skin of his face into a sickening grin. It was even more disgusting than his previous look of hatred. He could feel the fight draining out of Paul as he taunted him, and was filled with expectation. The boy's soul-light was going to taste delicious – so much misery – almost as satisfying as guilt. Mark reached out and flicked the light switch, bathing the pool with light – he wanted to see the distress he was causing, enjoy the fear he could generate, before he devoured the boy's soul-light. He thrust his face close to his prisoner's and Paul almost passed out.

His blurred vision hadn't allowed him to see Mark's face properly before. Now it was only inches from his own it was brought sharply into focus. The signs of decay were unmistakable. It seemed to Paul that Mark's eyeballs were beginning to dry out, so that the surfaces were dry and ridged, and the skin round the edges of them was split from rubbing against the uneven tissue, exposing raw flesh. A blackened tongue protruded through his teeth and blood-speckled drool oozed from the corner of his mouth. The stench he was breathing into Paul's face was indescribable.

It reminded him of a rat he'd had to dissect once, in a school Biology class. The freezer where the dead rats had been stored had broken down, and the specimens had started to decay, but the teacher had insisted that they dissected the creatures anyway. Obediently, they had done so, running out of the room every few minutes to throw up. The smell had stayed with them for days, and Paul had dropped Biology the following term. He had thought there couldn't be a worse smell in the whole world. Now he knew differently. Compared to Mark's breath, the rats were nothing. Even David's rotting corpse hadn't been this bad. Its 'owner' had looked after it until he found another.

Now the pretence was over, the demon wasn't wasting any of the energy from the soul-lights it had stolen to reduce the rate at which Mark's body decayed. The evil that was inside seemed to infect every part of it, including its breath.

Paul stepped backwards towards the pool, deciding he'd rather drown than suffocate in that nauseating miasma.

Mark continued to taunt him, taking pleasure in the despair he could induce.

"I wonder how many days it will be before anyone realises what's happened to you? When they do they won't be that bothered. You'll be just another corpse. They're past caring now. They just want to save their own skins – not that they'll be able to. I'll get them all in the end."

His arrogance sparked a glimmer of defiance in Paul, who suddenly realised what Mark was trying to do to him. He was trying to stop him fighting back. Well Paul wasn't going to be manipulated like that.

"They do care! All of them." Paul suddenly remembered the images he'd been glimpsing, "And not just them. You won't be allowed to have it all your own way."

Furious, Mark lunged at him, intending to shove him into the pool. With the rope still binding Paul's arms to his sides, he'd be unable to swim. Mark was looking forward to a quick death by drowning, and then a tasty soul-light.

Paul took a deep breath, and yelled as loudly as he could. "*Help!* If you're there, angels, help me!"

He would have added 'please' but Mark had charged at him before he finished calling for help, and thrown him into the pool.

Over in the cafeteria, Thren felt a slight pain in his chest. He listened carefully and thought he could hear something. Someone was calling for an angel, shouting desperately for help. He glanced up and scanned the campus. It took him less than a second to pinpoint Paul's soul-light, ice-blue with fear, in the swimming pool.

"Tor, get moving, we're needed," yelled Thren, making Bex, who hadn't noticed he was behind her, jump out of her skin. The two angels shot out of the building, and headed for the swimming pool. Bex stood up and moved swiftly over to where Tim and Flint were sitting.

"Where are the others?" she asked urgently.

"Sam's keeping an eye on Cath," said Tim, "and Paul's gone to get some glasses. I broke these ones." He held up the shattered pair Paul had left on the table.

"On his own?" asked Bex. "You let him go on his own?"

"What's up?" said Flint, standing.

"I don't know," said Bex, "But I think he's in trouble." She ran out of the cafeteria, followed by the others.

When Thren and Tor reached the swimming pool Paul was in real trouble. He was struggling to free his arms, but he couldn't loosen the rope, and his efforts to free himself just seemed to make him sink below the surface, and take in more water. He was starting to choke, and convinced that each breath would be his last. At any moment he was expecting to see images of his past, rather ordinary, life flashing before his eyes.

Thren dived into the pool and swam under Paul, taking the boy's weight and lifting him up to the surface, so he could get some air. Coughing and spluttering, Paul twisted his head and glanced down into the water to see who was supporting him. With so much light reflecting off the water little was visible except a blurred shape, but when he reached down with his fingertips he was sure he could feel feathers – wet feathers, just below him, and he could feel the warmth of Thren's body holding him up so he could breathe.

"I don't know who you are," gasped Paul, when he got his breath back, "But thanks a lot."

Mark had been standing at the side of the pool, watching Paul drown, waiting to catch the boy's soul-light, but when the angels burst in he turned to confront them. He didn't move quickly enough to stop Thren from diving in to rescue Paul, but he stepped forward to face Tor, taking up a fighting stance.

"Well," he sneered. "Do you think you can tackle me one to one, or are you a bit out of your league?"

Tor had to admit to herself that she didn't like what she saw. The creature that was inhabiting Mark's body seemed to be almost bursting out of it, making it look bloated. Tor readied herself for a battle that she wasn't at all sure she could win on her own, and took a flying lunge at Mark, who side-stepped neatly so she landed in the pool. Paul was hit by a wave for no apparent reason, and he knew that whatever – whoever – Mark had been taunting had just fallen in the water.

"Is that the best you can do?" the demon was hissing. "How pathetic – and you're supposed to help people. You can't even help yourselves."

Tor was climbing out of the pool, getting ready to fight back, but her wet clothes and sodden wings were making movement difficult. Thren wanted to help her, but he was fully occupied with keeping Paul afloat. He was struggling to move his wings under water, the weight of it slowed him down, making it impossible to beat his wings at the right frequency to remain invisible, and he couldn't raise Paul out of the pool. Thren wanted to lift him up and roll him onto the side of the pool but he couldn't find a way to do it from beneath the boy's body.

"This is going to be fun," said Mark, advancing on Tor as she crouched at the edge of the pool. He grabbed hold of her shoulders, and was swinging her round to smash her head down on to the tiles beside the pool when the doors opened and the students piled in. Sarah already had her mobile phone out, and dialled 999 as soon as she saw Mark. Bex couldn't see Thren, hidden beneath Paul in the water, or Tor, but it was obvious Mark was struggling with one of them. She ran towards him, then stopped, unsure what to do next.

Mark dropped Tor, so quickly that her head bounced off the tiles, and turned to face the students. "I suppose you think you're *so* clever, don't you? Well, you're not. I'll get you in the end. I'll get all of you, just like I got your friends." He glared at Bex and at Flint, who was just behind her, adding, "And you two will be next!'

Then he glanced round, calculatingly, knowing he couldn't deal with all of them, and the angels, before the police arrived to cart his body away. The students braced themselves in the doorway, expecting him to make a bolt for it. Instead he turned and leapt against one of the plate glass windows that lined the other side of the building. There was a crash as the glass shattered, and Mark disappeared into the night.

"Are you all right?" called Bex, hoping to hear one of the angels answer her, but all she heard was Paul saying, "Get me out of here quickly, please."

He knew that he wasn't going to drown. He'd known as soon as someone had lifted him to the surface – but he was concerned for whoever was supporting him. If they were underwater, how were they breathing? If they needed to.

The others hauled Paul out of the water, and untied the

rope. As soon as Paul's weight was lifted off him, Thren made a tremendous effort to adjust his wingbeats and burst up to the surface, desperate for air. He could manage longer without it than a human, but it had been a very uncomfortable experience. A physical body did seem to have basic physical needs, like breathing.

'Who's bright idea was that? I gotta get back where I belong,' thought Thren as he climbed awkwardly out of the pool. 'That was *gross*. Nobody said I'd have to get myself half-drowned when I took this job. Totally not part of the deal.'

By now the police had arrived and were starting to question the students about what had happened. Bex moved away from the group a little and whispered to Thren, "Where's Tor? Is she all right?"

Thren turned and saw Tor, still lying in a soggy heap beside the pool. Hitting her head on the floor tiles appeared to have knocked her out, but fortunately the light haze hadn't dispersed around her yet, so she was still invisible to the others. "Tor, are you all right?" said Thren, kneeling beside her. "Wake up, Tor. You gotta wake up! Right now, you hear me?" He shook her roughly, as Bex watched anxiously. "Come on, wake up, don't do this to me." Bex saw the look of relief on his face as Tor began to stir. He smiled at Bex, signalling that Tor was okay, as the police came over to her, asking for her statement about what had happened that night. Bex had to turn away and answer the police questions. She couldn't keep staring at an apparently empty space beside the swimming pool. It was going to be hard enough to explain how she knew Paul was in trouble.

Tor gazed up at Thren blearily. "Is everyone all right?"

"Yeah, they're fine; it's you I'm worried about," Thren replied, realising with a sinking feeling that it was true. 'This just gets better and better,' he thought sarcastically. 'Now I'm worrying about humans *and* other angels. What did I do to deserve this? Whatever it was, I musta paid for it by now. Why can't I just go home? .... Like I'm gonna get the chance.' To Tor he said, "Come on, let's get you back to the cathedral," as he helped her gently onto her feet.

# Chapter 41

"I'm bored," said Tor, the next morning, as she lay on Bex's bed. Her head was still hurting, and she felt thoroughly bad-tempered. Thren had taken her back to the cathedral the night before, but the snow had started to settle on the roof and they were both cold and wet. So in the end Thren had knocked on Bex's bedroom window and asked if they could spend the night in her room, where it was warm.

Bex herself had been driven back to the house by the police, which had settled the whole 'who's going to walk who home' argument. She was glad about that. She didn't want any more rows with Flint. He'd made his feelings quite plain enough by avoiding her the whole of the day after their quarrel. The last thing she wanted was to have to be grateful to him for protecting her. She didn't need him watching her all the time, either, to see if she was 'talking to angels' again.

"I'm still bored," said Tor, when neither Bex nor Thren had responded to her first comment.

Tor had rather enjoyed being fussed over the night before. Bex had insisted on her having the bed, while Bex herself slept in the chair, and Thren, inevitably, had had to settle for the floor. Even Thren had been nice to her, mused Tor, when she woke up the next morning. 'Perhaps there are some compensations to be beaten up by a demon,' she thought.

"Bored, bored, bored," said Tor, petulantly.

"Aw, shut up," said Thren. "I think I liked it better when you were unconscious."

"That's a horrid thing to say," said Tor. "I was only injured because I was trying to tackle the demon, stop him killing any more students."

"His name's Dross – the demon. That imp, Snig, told me before I sent him back to where he belonged," said Thren, hoping to distract Tor so that she'd stop complaining.

"Dross?" said Tor sarcastically. "How nice to know the name of one's enemy. That makes me feel so much better … I'm still bored."

"Oh, all right," said Bex, who couldn't take any more. "I'll go and see if the paper's arrived yet. Perhaps that will shut you up."

"Well, really," said Tor offended, as Bex pulled on her dressing gown and slippers and huffed out of the room. "After all I've done for that girl."

"You are ladling it on a bit," said Thren. "I mean, you're not at death's door, are you? You just got a bit of a bump on the head, that's all."

"Much you care," sulked Tor.

"Now look, Wonderwings," said Thren firmly, "You can grouch at me all you like, but don't take it out on Bex. She's a good kid, and she's got enough to worry about at the moment."

"Look," said Bex, bursting into the room clutching the local paper, "Look at this! There's a picture of dad, and an article about the hostel closing. He'll be so pleased somebody's taking some notice."

Thren grabbed the paper out of her hands and scanned it quickly.

"Excuse me," said Tor stiffly, "I thought Bex fetched that to entertain *me*."

"This is real cool," said Thren. "It gives your dad and Janet such a good write-up. It's just a shame it's come too late to keep the hostel open."

"Can *I* see the paper now?" whined Tor.

"All right," said Thren, handing it over. "There you are."

"Would you mind giving me some privacy for a few minutes?" said Bex, "I'd like to get dressed and go and show Dad the paper."

"Oh, so that's *it*, is it?" said Tor, offended. "One minute it's 'Come in, Tor; lie down, Tor; do have the bed, Tor,' and now it's 'Please go away. I've got better things to do.'"

"Come on, Tor," said Thren, taking her arm and pulling her off the bed. "You know you're feeling better than you were yesterday. Why don't you give the girl a break?" Reluctantly Tor climbed out over the window sill, and she and Thren flew up to the cathedral roof.

Bex had just finished dressing when her father knocked on the door. "Come in," called Bex.

Dudley stuck his head into the room asking, "Have they gone?"

"How did you know they were here?"

"I heard you talking to them," said her father, smiling. "Well, I heard you talking to someone, and since you're not in the habit of talking to yourself, I thought it must be the angels."

"It was," said Bex, and then, remembering the newspaper article, thrust it at her father saying, "Look at this!'

***

A few hours later there was another meeting in the Chapter House. Thren sent a rather pathetic Tor to keep an eye on the students, while he made sure that Pearson didn't come up with any more devious plans to get rid of Dudley. The clergy had gathered and the meeting was about to begin when the Bishop entered. He was a middle-aged man with a bright golden soul-light that dazzled Thren's eyes, and an air of gentle authority. All the clergy sat up straighter as the Bishop entered the room, and Thren found himself standing to attention.

"Excuse me for interrupting the meeting," said the Bishop, politely, "But there is a matter I need to discuss with you, and this seemed to be the best place to find you all together." He beamed at them. "First of all, I'd like to congratulate Dudley, here, on the excellent work he's been doing at the shelter for the homeless." Everyone smiled and nodded approvingly – except Pearson. "I'm proud of his dedication and commitment to the work, which he maintains despite a certain amount of criticism from his colleagues." There were a few red faces around the table.

"I know he does the work for its own sake, and not for personal gain, but it is nice to see goodness rewarded occasionally." Now people were beginning to look puzzled. "I've just had a phone call from the television company that wants to film here in the cathedral. It seems they saw the rather nice article in this morning's local paper, and they're very impressed with how Dudley comes over. They'd like him to front the programme."

"But I'm supposed to be doing that!" protested Pearson.

"What television company?" asked Dudley, completely in the dark. Everyone quickly filled him in on the proposal to make a television series based on the life of the cathedral and its workers.

"So, you see," said the Bishop jovially, "if you front the programme for them, they'll pay you a handsome fee. You could use it for anything you like. You could even donate it to the work of the hostel. I'm sure the extra money would make it easier to find an alternative building."

"Oh," said Dudley. "Oh dear. It's very tempting, I know, but I really don't think *I* should front the programme. I wouldn't feel comfortable doing all that talking to the camera, putting myself forward like that, but I do think filming here is an excellent idea. Show people what the place is really like ... that we're not a museum, but a real place of worship tackling genuine problems. It would be splendid to get away from the image of being a tourist attraction, and show people that we're a proper church, warts and all."

Pearson listened in amazement. The old man actually *liked* the idea of a film crew following them everywhere, making a programme about the cathedral, which meant ...

"You needn't have tried to get rid of him after all," whispered Poole in his ear. "He wouldn't have stopped them making the series at all. In fact he loves the idea. Good for him!"

The Bishop smiled at Dudley, clapping him warmly on the back. "I thought you might feel like that about it," he said, "so here's what I suggest. *Whoever* fronts the programme, the fee goes to the hostel. That way nobody in the cathedral benefits personally from the filming. It wouldn't be appropriate really, when everyone will be involved, and they do want to film the hostel too, if there's no objection, so it's only fair that it should gain financially from the arrangement. After all, it's doing splendid work, and will need the money to refit its new premises."

"If it gets any," said Dudley cautiously. "It's already been turned down by the Housing Committee."

"It's bound to be possible to relocate it, if we put our minds to it," said the Bishop, confidently. "Think positive. Now the newspaper's interested, you can start a public campaign to keep the place open, and you'll have the full support of the cathedral." He stared pointedly at the clergy seated round the table, making it clear that he expected their cooperation.

"Who *is* going to front the programme?" asked Pearson, tentatively.

"Well, I've given the matter a great deal of thought," said the Bishop, "And since Dudley is reluctant to do it, I suggest that I just pick someone to save any arguments.

The television company has agreed to my proposal. They had to really, if they wanted my consent to the filming."

"So who have you picked?" asked Pearson, preening himself.

"I thought Ernest Poole might be just the man for the job," said the Bishop, smiling encouragingly at Poole.

"But I ... I ... wouldn't know what to do," said Poole, stunned. "I'm not used to public speaking, or anything ... I don't have a ..." He tried to think of the word Pearson had used, "... profile. I don't have a profile. I wouldn't be any good at it."

"Exactly," said the Bishop. "You're a modest man, Ernest. You wouldn't put yourself forward, try to dominate the programme the way somebody with," he smiled, "a 'profile' might. You'll give everyone a chance to have their say, and show what they can do without trying to compete with them, or decide who's more important. I think that will help to create a well-balanced view of the cathedral."

"You really want *me* to do it," said Poole, who couldn't believe the Bishop had so much faith in him. He didn't see himself as important, and wasn't used to other people singling him out. Then he had a guilty thought. "But I thought the Reverend Pearson was going to be fronting the programme. I wouldn't want to disappoint him, and to be honest, I really don't deserve ..."

The Bishop interrupted him, saying, "Very few of us get exactly what we deserve, Ernest – which is just as well for most of us." The Bishop caught and held Pearson's eye. It was Pearson who looked away first.

"By the way, Reverend Pearson," added the Bishop, "I believe we have you to thank, for telling the newspaper about the homeless shelter. Just think, if you hadn't drawn it to their attention, they would never have run that article, and the whole business wouldn't have been settled in such a satisfactory manner."

Thren grinned. The Bishop had outmanoeuvred Pearson, and taken the wind out of his sails completely. He must have got word of what Pearson was up to, and decided to put a stop to it – and in the process made some really inventive decisions about the money going to the hostel, and Poole fronting the programme.

Thren reckoned the Bishop had chosen the right man for the job. Poole was easily led, sure, but he'd shown real courage fronting up to Pearson at the hostel like that. If he could just get out from under his friend's thumb he could be quite a decent guy. And the Bishop was right. Poole wouldn't put himself forward on TV; he'd let other people have some input … just as long as Pearson didn't take too much control behind the scenes, although Thren reckoned the Bishop would know how to deal with that too. Some guy!

'Now,' thought Thren, 'All we gotta do is find a way to outmanoeuvre Dross, the way the Bishop outmanoeuvred Pearson. He didn't just sit around waiting for things to happen, he *made* things happen the way he wanted them to for everybody's sake, and that's what we gotta do. It's time to stop chasing around after Dross. We gotta get him to come to us. We gotta take control!'

# Chapter 42

Thren found Tor and the students in the cafeteria at lunch-time. "All quiet," said Tor, "except for my head, which is throbbing. Can I go and get some rest, now you're here?"

"'Fraid not," said Thren. "We got work to do." He told her about the idea he'd hatched while watching the Bishop in action. "Well, what do you think? Will it work?"

"We'll only find out by trying," said Tor, "And it's better than just waiting around until the next attack, and hoping we get there in time."

They moved nearer to the students who were all sitting together this time, although the conversation was still a bit strained.

"We should have got a doctor for her days ago," said Sarah. "I can't believe we let her get into that state."

"We thought she was just in shock," said Sam, "And we've all been through that in the last week. How were we to know she was really ill?"

"There's no point in worrying about what we *should* have done," said Bex. "The point is they've taken Cath to hospital, and they'll do everything they can for her."

"*If* they can work out what's wrong with her in the first place," said Flint, grimly, "which I *doubt*, because it's not a normal illness. It's something that … thing has done to her."

"We don't *know* that," said Nesta, trying to be positive.

"No," said Tim, "But we can have a pretty good guess."

"It has tried to attack each of us," agreed Paul.

"Except you two," said Tim, looking at Bex and Flint.

"Don't worry," said Flint. "We're obviously next on the list."

"Sorry," said Tim, reddening, "I didn't mean it like that."

There was an awkward silence as everybody tried to avoid looking at everybody else. Flint was tossing his mobile from one hand to the other, glaring at it suspiciously when he thought no one was looking, though he hadn't had any more strange texts lately. "Flint," Sam looked embarrassed, "can I have a word, in private?"

"If this is another of your stupid jokes," groaned Flint, standing up, "I'm not in the mood."

"Nor am I, believe me," Sam dragged him out of earshot of the others, but nearer to Tor, much to her satisfaction.

"Look, Flint," Sam began, "I don't know how to tell you this but it was me and Mark – the real Mark, I mean – who were sending you those texts. We found out about your secret, and thought it would be fun to wind you up for a bit."

"What?" Flint's face froze.

"It was just a joke," Sam spoke quickly, willing Flint to see the funny side. "You were getting so wound up about it, we thought we'd keep it going for a bit … but with everything that's happened, I thought you ought to know, it has nothing to do with everything else that's going on." Sam ground to a halt. "In case you were wondering."

"A joke?" Flint was livid. "How could you possibly joke about something like that?" He felt cold and hot at the same time. Now everybody would know about his past – as if he didn't have enough to deal with right now. Whatever happened next he was about to lose the only friends he had.

"Hey, it's only a name," Sam tried to pacify him. "A stupid one, okay, but only a name."

Flint stared at Sam, feeling relief flood through him. "A name? That's all you meant? You found out I changed my name?"

"I don't blame you," Sam grinned, "I wouldn't want to be called Fabian either."

"Right," Flint tried to grin back at Sam, "Who would? By the way, how did you find out?"

"It wasn't me, it was Mark. He saw your registration file open in the office one day, and happened to glance at it."

"And that's all he saw, about me changing my name?" Flint felt weak with relief.

"What else is there?" asked Sam, casually, heading back to where the others were sitting.

"Why I changed it," said Flint under his breath.

"There," said Tor triumphantly. "I knew he was trouble."

"Give the guy a break," said Thren. He would have said more but he was distracted. All the male students were staring at a young woman who'd just walked into the cafeteria. She was tall and blonde, and absolutely beautiful. She seemed a little younger than the students around her, but her looks gave her a confidence unusual in someone of her age. She glided across the room, fully aware of the admiring glances of the male students, and enjoying the sensation she was causing. Thren noticed that her soul-light was pale lilac, which brightened significantly when she caught sight of Tim.

"Nicola," he called out, "what are you doing here?"

"I came to see how you were. I ran into your mum and she said you'd broken your arm or something."

Thren looked across at Nesta. She seemed to be shrivelling up in front of him, her soul-light visibly dimming. Thren could see her point. In terms of competition the kid could beat her hands down. She was gorgeous, on top of which she had a pair of healthy legs. Not just healthy, but very well shaped, as her short skirt made more than apparent.

"Your mouth is open," said Tor, tartly, in Thren's ear. "You'll catch flies."

"Is that kid built or is that kid built?" said Thren. "She looks more like an angel than you do, Tor. Poor old Nesta doesn't stand a chance."

"Shouldn't you be at school?" Tim was asking Nicola.

"Yes, but I was worried about you, so I bunked off," she replied with a smile so charming that it always got her what she wanted.

"You shouldn't have," said Tim sternly. "I was going to come and see you this weekend anyway."

"I know, but I couldn't wait," said Nicola.

Tim looked uncomfortable, and everyone else at the table suddenly decided they ought to be somewhere else.

"I want to get over to the lab," said Nesta, "get that practical set up." She started to move her chair, but caught it on the table leg.

"I'll give you a hand," said Sam suddenly. He stood up and went to help Nesta manoeuvre her chair out from behind the table. The others looked at him in amazement. He never offered to help Nesta; he was another of the ones who'd tried to put her off the Biology course. "What?" he said, looking at the stunned faces round him. "What's wrong with being helpful? Ready to go, Nesta?"

"Yes please, Sam," she said, looking miserably at Nicola.

Sam bent his head over hers and whispered, "Do you mind if I push your chair? It'll be quicker."

She whispered back, "Go ahead, just get me out of here," and Sam whisked her out of the canteen before the others had stopped staring.

Thren suddenly sensed what Bex was thinking. "Sam? Being helpful *and* tactful at the same time? What's got into him?"

For a moment Thren felt her panic. Maybe 'it' had taken him over. She glanced around nervously and saw Thren. He shook his head reassuringly and said, "Don't worry, Sam's fine. I guess he's just changed a bit in the last week."

Paul saw Bex making eye contact with something he couldn't see. He turned his head so that the place she was looking at would be reflected in the back of his glasses. Yes, there they were. He could see them more clearly now, and they didn't make him nervous any more. He definitely knew which side they were on – but it still seemed a little … weird.

He could see Thren talking to Bex, although he couldn't hear what the angel was saying, but he heard Bex's whispered reply, "Six o'clock, all right." A moment later she whispered, "I'll try, but I don't know if he'll come," and then "the cathedral," and she nodded.

Sarah stood up and said to Paul, "Do you mind walking me over to my next lecture. I don't … there isn't anyone left for me to walk with."

Paul smiled at her and stood up. He knew what she meant. All her friends from the English course were at the hospital. Even Debbie had hardly been seen all week, she was so busy standing guard over Marty.

"Of course," said Paul. "Come on," and he and Sarah left the canteen. He wanted to go to the library anyway. There were some things he needed to look up.

Bex kicked Flint on the shins. He was still staring at Nicola in a bemused male way. "Come on," Bex said, "give them some space." She didn't know why she'd bothered to whisper her replies to Thren. She could have shouted about angels from the rooftops and Flint wouldn't have noticed while Nicola was in the room. "Men!" thought Bex, towing him out of the cafeteria. As they left Thren heard her ask, "Do you mind walking me home tonight, Flint?"

Flint just shrugged and said, "Suppose not."

"That boy definitely lacks charm," said Tor, and followed them out.

Thren had a lot of things to do before the evening. Check out exactly where in the hospital Cath was; make sure they hadn't moved Marty; find a way to get Dudley in position; try and persuade Tor to do him a favour. Instead of which he sat down to watch Tim and Nicola. Somehow Tim didn't seem as happy to see his girlfriend as Thren had expected.

"Aren't you pleased I'm here?" she asked when they were on their own.

"Of course," said Tim.

'He's lying,' Thren realised with surprise. 'I wonder why? I'd be pleased if a chick like that came to see me.'

Tim was talking to Nicola, but he had a slightly hunted look in his eye. "Look," he was saying, "I'm not sure it's such a good idea, you coming to see me like this."

"Why not?" asked Nicola.

"Well, you've bunked off school, for a start."

"So? It's not like you've never done it."

"No, but ... like I say, I was planning to come home and see you this weekend anyway."

"You still can. A whole weekend would be much better than an afternoon – and there's a party at Jenny's on Saturday. It would be great if you could come."

"I'm afraid I can't", said Tim emphatically.

"Why not, if you're coming back for the weekend?"

"Because I was coming back to see you ... to talk to you – not to go to a party."

"That sounds a bit ... heavy," said Nicola, suddenly looking less confident. "What did you want to talk to me about?"

"It's not working, Nicola," said Tim, struggling to find the best way to put it. "You and me, going out, when I'm up here and you're at home. It just doesn't work."

"Yes, it does," she said. "We're halfway through the

first year already, and you know I've applied to come here next year. I know it's hard being apart, but we can make it work, Tim."

"No, we can't," said Tim, "Because … I don't want to. Not any more."

There was a long pause while Nicola absorbed what he'd just said. This wasn't how she'd imagined this visit at all. Tim couldn't dump her. Nobody dumped *her*. She was the person who ended her relationships when *she* was ready to. She felt anger rising inside her.

"Is there someone else?" she asked, almost sure she could guess the answer.

"Yes," said Tim guiltily. "There is."

"How could you?" said Nicola. "Two-timing me, dating somebody else behind my back."

"I haven't been," said Tim, "Nesta and I are just friends … but I've realised I want to be more than that – and it's not fair to you. I needed to see you … finish with you, before I said anything to her."

"How chivalrous," said Nicola sarcastically, then asked, more gently, "is it because I'm still at school? I'm only a year younger than you. That's nothing really. I'll be at university next year. I might even be here."

"No, it's nothing like that," said Tim. "It's just that … I've fallen in love."

"But I thought *we* were in love," said Nicola, sounding like a petulant child.

"So did I," said Tim gently, "But I was wrong."

He felt terrible, but there was nothing he could do to make it easier for her, and he wasn't about to cheat and see Nesta behind her back. Not that Nesta would even consider going out with him while he was still seeing Nicola.

"Look, it was really kind of you to come and see me," said Tim. "I'm just sorry it's turned out this way. Let me get you a coffee, and then I'll walk you to the station – or do you want to look around the campus first?" he added.

It seemed a bit mean to send her back home on the first available train.

"All right," said Nicola, distractedly, "But tell me what she's like first. This person you've met ... *fallen in love with* ... Is she prettier than me?"

"No," said Tim honestly. "Not at all."

"Then what *is* she like?" persisted Nicola. "I want to see her before I go."

"You already have," said Tim. "She was here when you arrived."

Nicola thought about the three girls that had been sitting at the table when she'd walked in. None of them could hold a candle to her. They were all pretty average by comparison.

"Which one?" she asked fiercely, leaning closer to Tim.

"The girl in the wheelchair," said Tim awkwardly.

"You're dumping *me* for *her*?"

"I wouldn't put it like that," said Tim apologetically.

"I would," said Nicola standing up. "Well, you're welcome to her. If you're really stupid enough to prefer someone like *her* to me I'm better off without you." She walked off, leaving Tim alone in the canteen. He stared after Nicola, feeling miserable about hurting her. They'd been going out for over a year. He felt awful, but he didn't know what else he could have done. Once he'd realised how he felt about Nesta, he could see that what he'd felt for Nicola was just infatuation. He'd had to sort things out with her, but that didn't make him feel any better. It was a horrible way to end their relationship.

Tim glanced at his watch, then leapt out of the chair. He was late for his practical. He ran across the campus, and arrived in the lab short of breath, and very nervous. He glanced at Nesta, who didn't dare look at him. All after-noon they worked side by side in the lab without saying a word to each other. Bex and Sam kept staring at them, wondering what was going on. None of them had expected to see Tim at that afternoon's practical – not with Nicola there.

Thren filled Tor in on what had happened, and the two angels stood and watched as Tim and Nesta studiously ignored each other.

"Oh, for heaven's sake," said Tor. "Why doesn't he just get on with it?"

"In the middle of the lab with everyone watching?" said Thren. "The poor guy's gotta wait till the practical's over, and he can talk to her properly."

"That could take another hour," said Tor. "There are things we have to do before tonight."

"I know," said Thren sadly, "I guess we'll just have to leave them to it."

"No way, Jose," said Tor unexpectedly, and waved her hand in the air. All the Bunsen burners flared brightly, the contents of the flasks and beakers bubbled over the top of the containers, splashing onto the benches, and the air began to fill with acrid, purple smoke. The tutor evacuated the lab, and within a couple of minutes everyone was waiting about outside the building. Tim was standing next to Nesta.

There was an awkward pause, then Nesta said, "Nicola seems very ... nice." There was another pause, so she added, "Very beautiful."

"She is," said Tim, "but I'm not going out with her any more."

Nesta stared at him.

"Is ... is that what she came to tell you? I'm sorry," said Nesta sympathetically, trying to mean it.

"No. It was my idea, not hers. I felt really mean after she'd come all this way to see me, but I didn't have any choice. That's why I'd planned to go and see her at the weekend. To tell her it was over." Tim looked at Nesta hopefully, trying to judge how she was taking the news. "Well, aren't you going to say anything?" he asked.

Nesta didn't say a word, in case Tim didn't mean what she hoped he meant, and she ended up making a fool of herself.

"Oh, for heaven's sake," said Tor, "Just kiss her! What's the point of my getting you out of that practical if you're just going to stand around talking?"

Tim stopped talking, leant down and kissed Nesta. The other students, who'd all been giving the impression they weren't watching, turned and stared at them.

"But I thought you didn't like me any more!" said Nesta, when Tim released her. "You've been avoiding me for the last two days."

"Only because I realised how I really felt about you, the night we were attacked," said Tim ruefully. "I knew if I talked to you, I've have told you what I felt, asked you out, and it wouldn't be fair to Nicola – to either of you. I had to sort things out with her before I did this," and he leant down and kissed her again. This time the other students cheered, clapped or catcalled their encouragement, as Nesta kissed him back.

Thren turned to Tor and said, "Happy now? We really oughta get going, you know."

"I know," said Tor, smiling. Thren saw her wipe a tear out of the corner of her eye.

"You old romantic," he teased. "Now come on, we got work to see to do – and I need you to do me a favour."

"What?"

"You gotta go talk to the High Council. There's something I need to know."

# Chapter 43

"Well," asked Thren, "what did they tell you?" Tor was staring straight ahead, stunned. Thren tried again, "Did they answer my question, the High Council? Did they tell you why Bex can see me?" Still Tor gazed into the distance. "Will you snap out of it, lady? I gotta know. Now!" Slowly, Tor turned and looked at Thren, though he still wasn't sure it was really him she was focusing on.

"I've watched over that girl all her life, and they never told me."

"Told you what?"

"Why."

"Gee, this is going to be hard work. Come on, Tor, fill me in. We don't have much time. You know they'll be here soon." Tor started to talk, in a dreamy sort of way.

"You know the legend of Eskarron?"

"The angel who fell in love with a human? Sure, who doesn't? The story's as old as Home itself."

"Except," said Tor, "it isn't a story. Not a made up one, anyway. Apparently Eskarron really did fall in love, with a woman called Phyllida. He loved her so much that he begged to be allowed to put aside his angel status, and live on earth as a human. It seems He granted the angel's request. How could He, who created love, condemn one of his own creation for loving too deeply?"

"Enough with the mush," Thren said, disgusted by the very idea. "What's it got to do with Bex?"

"She has angel blood in her," Tor snapped abruptly. "She's one of Eskarron's descendants. That's why she needs her own guardian angel. And they never told me!"

"Angel blood?"

"Eskarron may have put aside his powers, his position as an angel, but when he married Phyllida, he was still of angel stock. Their children had angel blood in their veins. It's been diluted down the generations, but his descendants are still connected to us. They still have angel blood."

"So that's why some people have their own guardian angels?

"No, there are all sorts of reasons why somebody might be given their own guardian, but it is why Bex has one."

"So Bex can see me because …?"

"Because you're related."

"Then why can't she see *you*?" Thren was having trouble figuring all this out.

"I'm a more distant relation, apparently. Eskarron came from the same flight of angels as you. That's why she can see you."

"Then how come it caused so much trouble, Bex seeing me? It just doesn't seem fair."

"*Seeing* you was one thing. If she'd just seen you, when you crashed into that building, it might not have done too much harm. She wouldn't have been certain you were an angel, and after a while she might have thought she'd imagined the whole thing, but you had to go and chat to her, let her walk you home, taunt her about not being your responsibility, drive her to the point where a demon could make contact with her … need I go on?"

"Okay, okay, I'm sorry. It's all my fault, but what do we do now?" Thren queried. "I thought that knowing why Bex could see me might give us some clues about how to defeat the demon, but it doesn't help at all."

"It does tell us one thing though," Tor answered. "It tells us just *how* important it is to protect Bex from Dross –

because if a demon gets hold of a human with angel blood in them all hell breaks loose. Literally!"

*** 

Flint was walking Bex home. "I can't believe Tim dropped Nicola to go out with Nesta," he was saying.

"I thought you liked Nesta?" said Bex.

"I do. She's great, but you've got to admit Nicola's a real stunner."

"Looks aren't everything," snapped Bex.

"I know that."

"Do you? You were practically drooling all over her in the canteen."

"No, I wasn't."

"Yes, you were, all the boys were."

"Paul wasn't," said Flint. "I think he prefers you ... but then, he is very short-sighted."

Bex swung her bag at him, but he dodged it, and she missed, the momentum swinging her round so that she lost her balance. Flint caught her, and stood her up.

"Thanks," she said stiffly.

"You're welcome," said Flint, equally formal. Then he relaxed a little. "Actually, I'm really glad Tim and Nesta have finally got together. I was just a little surprised, that's all. Now, can we call a truce?"

"Okay, I suppose we'd better." They'd reached the archway leading to the abbey green.

"Are you all right from here?" said Flint, "Or do you want me to see you all the way to the door?"

"I'm not going home," said Bex nervously. "Not yet, anyway. I said I'd meet Dad in the cathedral. Do you mind walking me over?"

"I don't have to walk into some prayer meeting, do I?" said Flint suspiciously, "'Cos you know how I feel about that stuff."

"Not exactly," said Bex. "It'll just be Dad." 'And

a couple of angels,' she thought, 'and later, probably, a demon.' She felt guilty, as if she was leading Flint into a trap, but Thren's plan was the only way to deal with the demon once and for all.

The cathedral loomed black against the night sky as they approached and went through a side door. Dudley was waiting for them both in the nave.

"Dad, you made it," said Bex with relief. "You do know why we're here, don't you?"

"Oh yes," said Dudley. "Thren called round this afternoon and explained it all to me."

"He called round?" queried Bex, confused.

"Apparently he ran out of time to organise a more subtle method of getting me here. Got held up on campus, I gather, so he just dropped in for a cup of tea. Good news about Tim and Nesta, isn't it?"

Flint was looking at the two of them bewildered. "What on earth are you talking about?"

"You don't wanna know," said Thren, stepping forward out of the shadows, completely visible.

"Unfortunately," said Tor, appearing beside him, "you have to know or you won't be ready."

Flint stared at the angels. His brain was trying to battle with the information his eyes were giving him. These *were* angels. They really were. So Bex wasn't mad after all. On the other hand, *he* probably was.

"Ready for what?" he said slowly, turning the question round in his brain. "What won't I be ready for?"

"Me," boomed Mark's voice from the far end of the nave. "I said I'd get the two of you next. Well, here I am, and I'm coming to get you, ready or not."

What remained of Mark advanced up the nave towards them. Once tall and elegant, he now looked like an animated scarecrow. Chunks of skin were hanging off, where the glass had shredded it the day before, revealing the putrid flesh beneath, and the stench was overpowering.

Tor reached for the bottle in her pocket, then realised with horror that she hadn't refilled it with holy water after using it in the sprinkler system to expel the lesser invisibles.

If she had been given to swearing, she would have sworn at that moment. Instead she stepped forward and said, "You really should look after yourself better, that body's a complete disgrace."

"I'm really not that bothered," said the creature, advancing towards her. "I suppose you think you've been clever, luring me into the cathedral, using those two as bait?"

"Bait?" hissed Flint at Bex. "Did you know about this?"

"Well," the thing was saying, "I may be weaker in here than I am out there, but I'm still stronger than all of you put together."

"I wouldn't bet on it," said Thren, taking up his position beside Tor.

The demon had reached the crossing – the point beneath the great tower where the two transepts join the nave to form a cross. The heart of the cathedral. As it got to the spot Dudley began to pray, quietly and calmly. The demon started to curse, and whimper.

"A godly man," it muttered. "Where did you find a godly man?"

The creature appeared to be enfolded in a soft white light, pinning it in position. "Come and fight me, then," it called out to the angels. "If you want to cast me out of the physical world, you'll have to fight me – and I'm still stronger than either of you. My power has increased with every soul-light I've taken."

Dudley's prayers were keeping the demon trapped in one place, but on their own they weren't enough to destroy it. The angels looked at each other, and Thren nodded. Suddenly they both flung themselves on the creature, trying to wrestle it to the floor, but it tossed them both away as if they weighed nothing. Tor was thrown against a pillar, which stunned her briefly. Thren landed in the pews, but was able to pick himself up quickly.

"I still have the right to try and capture their soul-lights," said the creature, pointing to Bex and Flint. "They're the ones responsible."

Bex and Flint found themselves edging backwards until they were just in front of Dudley, who put a protective hand on each of their shoulders, as he continued to pray.

"We kinda need your help," said Thren to Bex. "I think you two have to undo what you did at the party."

Bex took a deep breath and stepped forward until she was just outside the circle of prayer light enclosing the demon. She felt sick when she saw it close to. It seemed to be wearing what was left of Mark's body like torn clothing; the skin itself was bloated and bursting, and the smell of decaying flesh made her want to throw up. It swivelled its eyes to look at her and she heard a rattling sound as the withered eyeballs grated against their dried-out sockets.

"Whatever I did or felt, that allowed you to communicate with us at the party – I renounce it. You're evil, and I want nothing to do with you. None of us do."

The demon seemed to shrivel a little. It opened its mouth to speak but only howls and squeals came out.

Tor got to her feet and looked at Flint, saying, "Your turn."

Flint froze. "I can't do it."

"Yes you can," said Dudley, reassuringly.

"No, you don't understand." Flint was beginning to panic, "How could you? You're all … good. You … you have the right to fight this. I don't … it won't listen to me."

"What do you mean?" asked Dudley gently. "What makes you think it won't listen?" Flint didn't answer.

Battling against the power of Bex's renunciation, the demon forced his ragged lips to shape the words, "Name … to do with … the name … Mark told me … in the pub

... night he died. You changed your name ... he never said why." The creature slavered with greed as it sensed Flint's shame, which seemed to be oozing out of the boy like a sickly yellow vapour. His soul-light was going to be the tastiest the demon had ever eaten. Guilt was always the best flavouring.

"All right," said Flint, defiantly, "You want to know why I changed my name? To make a new start. So people wouldn't know what I'd done."

The others looked at each other uncomfortably. Nobody wanted to be the one to ask. Eventually Thren said, "Sorry, kid, but we gotta know."

"I killed my brother."

There was a shocked silence, broken only by a scratching sound as Dross eagerly licked his lips.

Flint looked at Bex. She seemed surprised, confused, sad, but there was no hatred in her eyes. Slowly Flint turned to look at Dudley and the others, expecting to see anger, fear, rejection. Instead, even though the news had obviously shaken them, they just waited calmly for him to explain.

He took a deep breath "I was joyriding ... I took him with me ... the roads were icy ... I crashed the car." He paused for a moment, then added "That's why that thing won't listen to me, because it should have been me that died, not him. I'm the one who *deserves* to die."

Flint felt Dudley's hand, which was still on his shoulder, urging him gently forward. "You *do* have the right to fight this. Nothing you've done can take that away from you. All you need is the will to stand up to it. The creature has no more claim on you than it has on the others."

Flint was stunned. He'd been dreading the moment when his past caught up with him, when people discovered what he was really like. Now it was here, they weren't reacting the way he'd expected at all. They weren't condemning him, they were telling him to fight the creature that was trying to lay claim to him.

Slowly Flint moved to stand beside Bex on the edge of the circle of light and said, "I'm not sure how to put this … but I … *uninvite* you. Go back to where you belong."

The creature screamed with rage, then lunged forward with its arms outstretched. It grabbed Flint around the throat with one hand, and twisted Bex's neck with the other, trying to kill them speedily, to gain the strength their soul-lights would give it. Thren and Tor dived at the demon again, forcing it back. It had to release Bex and Flint, to defend itself from the angels. This time their attack was more effective. The demon seemed less able to defend itself now that Flint and Bex had withdrawn their invitation.

Flint had dropped to the ground when the demon released him, struggling to breathe. Bex was half-crouched above him, still at the edge of the circle of light. She was rubbing her neck, where the creature's hand had clutched it, surprised that she wasn't more badly hurt.

The demon feigned weakness and the angels drew back, allowing it space to depart. Instead it stood there, staring at Bex, concentrating its energy on regaining control of its speech.

"Interesting … she's different to the others … something about her feels … strange. I wonder why?" Slowly Dross pivoted round to stare at Thren. "Well, Threnody? Aren't you going to tell me? For old times' sake?"

Thren stared at the demon, bewildered. "I changed my name too, when I made *my* 'new start', but I thought you'd recognise me anyway. After all, you were my closest friend."

"Temporalus?" Thren whispered.

"At last," said the demon, with a diabolical grin. "I wondered how long it would take you."

Thren looked at the remains of his friend in horror. *This* was what an angel turned into in The Darkness. He'd known it in his head, but he'd never really understood it before. That's what the demons were – fallen angels.

"What's the matter?" drooled Dross. "Don't you like what you see? You're going to see a lot more when I take you back with me."

"Back?" Thren almost choked on the words.

"Why not? I've heard you're being reassigned, anyway. You might as well come back with me now. You've lost. You've failed the test. If I could take you back with me, it would add to my triumph, wouldn't it? And you want what's best for your friend, don't you? That's what friendship's all about."

"I'm not your friend!' declared Thren, revolted, "I don't understand how I ever was."

"So you refuse my offer? You'll regret it. If you had chosen to come back with me willingly, I could have given you some protection, maybe even a little power. Things could be just the way they would have been if you'd come with me in the beginning. It's too late for that now. The High Council will reassign you. You'll be sent into The Darkness to become one of us ... and I'll make sure your existence is a living nightmare. Believe me, I'll have the power to do it, once I've collected the other soul-lights."

Suddenly Dross leapt at Bex, grabbing her by the throat, dragging her into the circle with him. Dudley panicked and stopped praying. The enclosing circle vanished, and the thing began to drag Bex backwards down the nave, away from the crossing. Much as it wanted to devour her soul-light, she was more use just then as a hostage – at least until they got outside the building.

The angels prepared to attack again, but it was Flint who reached the demon first, kicking and punching the creature in an effort to make it release Bex. It did, but then it promptly wrapped both its hands round Flint's throat, choking the life out of him. As the boy began to pass out Mark pressed what was left of his face against Flint's and kissed him, wrenching the soul-light out of him.

"*No!*" screamed Thren, feeling the pain in his own

chest echoing what was happening to the boy. "Leave him alone!" but it was too late.

"Four," said the demon triumphantly, as it smashed its fist into Flint's face, sending the boy crashing into the side of a pew. He lay there motionless as Bex struggled to reach him, but the demon grasped her neck again, holding her against him like a shield, to stop the angels attacking. She could feel the rancid flesh of his chest pressed against her cheek. There were still some shards of glass sticking out of his skin, and as Dross jerked her back step by step, a piece scratched her face. A thin trickle of blood began to snake down her cheek.

Ignoring the pain in his chest, Thren moved slowly forward. "Let her go, Temporalus. Let her go and … you can take me instead. I'll go with you, willingly."

Inside he was feeling numb. The thought of becoming like Dross repelled him, but he couldn't think of anything else to do. If that was what it took to free Bex, then he'd do it.

"Too late," said Dross, casually, the extra power he had gained from Flint's soul-light giving him confidence. The demon's arm brushed against Bex's bleeding face as he twisted her round.

He froze. "By all the powers of darkness …" He whispered slowly, "Look what I've found … A child of Eskarron. Now *that*'s what I call a power supply." He turned Bex round, looking at her from every angle, as he began to calculate what she was worth to him. "If I can take her back alive, her blood could release us all."

Thren launched himself at the demon, spinning round to attack from the side, so as not to hurt Bex. Catching Dross off guard, Thren managed to knock him to the ground, as Tor swooped in to lift Bex out of the demon's grasp.

Then Thren felt Mark's body clutching at him, pulling him down. The demon twisted, flinging himself on top of Thren, pinning him to the floor. Dross shoved his face into the angel's saying, "I'm taking you with me and then I'm coming back for *her* … and there's nothing you can do to stop me."

"But you *can't* come back," called Tor, horrified, "You don't have the right."

"If I leave the physical realm *by choice* to deliver my prisoner into The Darkness, then I'm free to come back and finish what I started." Thren wrestled with the demon, but he couldn't get a proper grip on the bloated body. "It's too late," the creature hissed malevolently, "you've made the deal. You have to come with me, that's what you agreed."

Through the ripped skin of Mark's back burst black, leathery wings, which spread out above him like a torn umbrella. Dross took a tighter hold on Thren and began to lift him off the ground. The demon was planning to carry Thren into The Darkness, and Thren was powerless to stop him.

Thren stopped fighting. What was the point? One way or the other he was going to end up in The Darkness. At least if he went with Dross – Temporalus – he might be able to find a way to stop him telling the other demons about Bex. Perhaps he could prevent him coming back for her. He wondered if he'd have enough of his own personality left to make those decisions when he got there, or whether he'd automatically go along with whatever plans his 'friend' made.

"I guess it's outta my hands now," he sighed, surprised to find himself filled with a sense of peace. Finally he'd made the right decision.

Despite being in the shadow of Dross's huge wings, Thren suddenly felt as if he was being washed in a stream of light. Dudley had started praying again. Thren could hear Bex's voice joining with her father's. He wanted to tell them not to bother, that he'd found some kind of a solution, but he was too drowsy. Their prayers were starting to work, holding Dross down so that he couldn't lift Thren any higher. The dark wings began to beat faster and faster, battling against the power that was pinning them down. Gradually, Thren felt their bodies leaving the ground.

He was dimly aware of Bex saying "Tor, do something – help him."

"I can't. Thren's given himself willingly, I'm not allowed to interfere." Her voice sounded shaky.

'She's upset,' Thren thought, feeling vaguely surprised, 'That's kinda nice. I guess she doesn't dislike me so much after all. Coo ...' His eyelids closed and he lost consciousness. Above him Dross screeched in triumph, but Thren didn't hear him.

***

A moment later the angel was jerked abruptly awake as the demon let out a howl of agony, and the pair of them crashed back down onto the ground. Thren smelt the stench of burning, blistering flesh, and then the weight was lifted off his chest as Dross raised himself up to see who had attacked him, and with what.

Paul was standing in the shadows holding a big metal cross he'd grabbed from one of the side altars. The demon cringed away from him, snarling "You can't make me release him, he offered himself to me of his own free will."

"You turned him down," said Paul, trying to stop his voice from shaking, "I heard you. When he offered to take Bex's place you refused. You wanted them both. Well, you can't have them."

Tor, staggered, realised that Paul was right – Dross *had* refused Thren's offer – she could still fight on Thren's behalf. Tor threw herself on top of the demon saying "Fight, Thren, fight!" and Thren started to fight back.

With one angel attacking him from below and another kicking and punching him from above, Dross began to weaken. Paul swung the cross down hard on the demon's head, and the creature rolled off Thren and lay gasping on the floor.

Pulling a wooden spike and a hammer out of his pocket Paul leapt on top of the demon and drove the stake into its heart. Dross looked at the object sticking out of his chest in surprise, and Tor whispered, "That's for vampires, dear, this is a demon. Still, ten out of ten for effort."

Paul scrambled hastily to his feet, trying to put some space between himself and the demon.

Dross pulled the spike out of his chest and started to get to his feet. He advanced on Paul menacingly, weighing the stake in his hand, preparing to thrust it into the boy's chest. "Here," said the demon, "Let me return your stick!"

Thren hauled himself up and leaped between Paul and the spike. The pointed wood ripped Thren's robe, and cut into his flesh, before breaking off, leaving Dross empty-handed.

"What do we do now?" asked Paul, panicking, as the demon eyed him malevolently.

Tor picked herself up off the floor and answered "Pray!"

Paul looked uncertain, "But I'm not sure I believe …"

"This would be a real good time to start, kid," suggested Thren.

Quickly they formed a circle around the demon. With the prayers of both angels, Dudley, Bex and Paul surrounding him, the demon began to lose his power. He staggered and dropped to his knees. Dross's strength was already diminished by the atmosphere of the cathedral, and his rejection by Bex and Flint, as well as by the battle he had fought. Now their combined prayers seemed to be draining him of his remaining energy, but still he clung to the shell he'd chosen to inhabit. Mark's ruined body, now burnt and blistered from its contact with the cross, was pitiful, but Dross knew if he was driven out of it, he would lack the strength to find another.

Paul pulled a bottle out of his pocket and offered it to

Thren. "Is this any use? It's holy water from the font. I collected it earlier."

Tor smiled at the young man approvingly, relieved that someone had come prepared.

"You sure have done your homework, kid," said Thren as he grabbed the bottle and twisted off the cap. He began sprinkling it over Mark's body. The demon let out an unearthly scream as the holy water took effect. Dross found himself withdrawing from every area of Mark's body that came in contact with it. Soon the demon was cramped into the very core of what had once been Mark, and the pressure was intolerable. The prayers of those surrounding him were an incessant torment. Dross could feel them prising him loose from his tenuous hold on Mark. At last the demon could stand it no longer. There was a hiss and a splutter, and a dark mist emerged from Mark's body, a reminder of how the whole nightmare had all begun, at the party.

It formed itself into a distorted shape, with a hideous translucent face, and hung above them mouthing obscenities. Dudley stepped forward and said, "In the name of Christ, depart."

The mist twisted and coiled, beginning to spin. It turned faster and faster, forming a vortex, which sucked the remaining darkness into itself before disappearing with a piercing shriek. The sound echoed round the cathedral, bouncing off the ancient stones, then faded away into silence.

Thren scrambled to his feet and got ready to field the soul-lights that were starting to appear above the corpse. He grabbed a dark grey one that was spinning in confusion and tossed it to Tor. Although she couldn't see it, she could feel the warmth of it as it fluttered in her hands. She ran back up the nave and thrust the soul-light into Flint's mouth, who groaned as he started to regain consciousness.

One by one the soul-lights came out. Thren grabbed Marty's amber light, and Cathy's brown one, wrapping his wings around them to prevent their escape. Then he watched as a dark green soul-light spun round and round, circling upwards to the cathedral roof, and passed through it, to shoot up into the sky. Dudley said a prayer as it departed – the soul-light of the boy who had been Mark.

# Chapter 44

"Come on," said Tor. "We have to get those soul-lights back to their bodies quickly, before they escape."

"Yeah, right," said Thren, "And how am I supposed to fly when I'm using my wings to hang on to these?"

"I'll tow you," said Tor, and she grabbed Thren by the scruff of his neck and dragged him out of the cathedral.

They flew across the city to the hospital. Thren could see the soul-lights of Debbie, Tim, Nesta, Sarah and Sam waiting in the hospital. 'That's gotta be a good sign,' thought Thren, 'I guess they took Bex's hint to go and visit.' He'd asked Bex to try and fix it for everyone else to be at the hospital that night, for two reasons: if they'd failed to deal with Dross, and he'd made a break for it, they didn't want the students too spread out, too vulnerable. If they succeeded, Cath and Marty would need their friends there as they came to and tried to adjust to what had happened.

Thren insisted that they go to Cath first. He still felt bad about letting her down; being less bothered about her than the others. He and Tor stood by her bed while Cath stared blankly up at the ceiling. Sam was sitting beside her, looking distressed at the state she was in.

"I'm sorry, Cath," said Thren, reaching into his feathers and pulling out her soul-light. "Real sorry." He placed the soul-light in her mouth, and watched in relief as she swallowed it. After a moment her eyes began to focus. She sat up and stared at her friend, saying, "Sam? What's happening? What am I doing here?"

The angels left them to their explanations and went to find Marty. Debbie was sitting on the edge of the bed holding his hand, while Tim and Nesta were over by the window. Thren placed Marty's soul-light in the boy's mouth, and he began to revive. Even before his eyes opened the life support equipment began to sound different, causing Tim to run out of the room and fetch the nurse. By the time they came back, followed by a doctor, Marty was starting to stir. He opened his eyes and looked straight at Debbie, saying weakly, "Sorry, I guess I passed out for a moment."

She smiled at him, almost too relieved to speak. All she said was, "That's okay. I waited for you to come round."

"Thanks," said Marty taking both of her hands in his. "I knew you would."

Over by the window, Tim and Nesta were smiling so broadly Thren thought their faces would split, while doctors and nurses ran about excitedly disconnecting bits of equipment.

"*Way* too much emotion in here," said Thren. He walked through the hospital to the room where Graham was lying. The boy was still unconscious, but the police had finally withdrawn their protection, since nothing had occurred to suggest he was still at risk. Sarah had been allowed in to see him at last, and was sitting by the bed, crying. It was the first time she'd seen him since his fall, and she was shocked by the extent of his injuries. A doctor was standing beside her, trying to explain how pleased they were with the progress Graham was making. "The scans don't show any sign of brain damage," the doctor was saying, "which is an encouraging sign."

"But he's still unconscious," Sarah protested, "how can you tell?"

"Well, of course, we won't know for certain until he regains consciousness."

"When will that be?" asked Sarah, anxiously. The doctor couldn't answer.

Thren looked hopefully at Tor. "Can't we do something?" he asked.

"Just tell her it's going to be all right," Tor replied.

"But we don't know that!" argued Thren, "How can I give her hope when we don't know what's going to happen?"

"Don't we?" questioned Tor. Suddenly a movement caught Thren's eye. Graham's soul-light was no longer weak and fluttering, but had started to burn a bright, steady yellow.

"How did you know? You can't see his soul-light!'

"You just learn to sense these things." Tor smiled complacently.

"But he's still unconscious," queried Thren, "isn't there anything we can do?"

Tor shook her head. "His injuries are natural, and they have to heal naturally. Just give it time."

"But ..." Thren opened his mouth to argue again, but Tor placed her hand over it to silence him. "You just have to learn to trust, all right?"

"All right, I'll try," Thren agreed, reluctantly, and he whispered reassuringly in Sarah's ear. He wasn't sure he'd convinced her not to worry, but she did seem a little calmer when they left her. As they walked out of the room she was still sitting beside Graham's bed, waiting patiently for him to wake up.

***

Thren flew slowly towards the cathedral. He felt completely drained. Even the pain in his chest, where part of the wooden spike was still embedded, was numbed by exhaustion. He turned his head to look at Tor as she travelled beside him, matching his speed.

"Dross will be back for Bex, won't he?" Thren asked.

"He can't come back unless the rules get broken again."

"We broke them already, didn't we, by letting Dudley and the others see us during the battle?"

"That was different," said Tor reassuringly, "They were already involved, they had a right to be part of the solution. Besides, we needed their help...*and* I got permission off the High Council when I spoke to them earlier."

"But sooner or later the rules are bound to be broken again. I was thinking, when I'm reassigned, maybe I can stop him somehow. I mean, if I can still remember ... if there's enough of me left to care."

"You won't be reassigned."

"You reckon? After all the mistakes I made?"

"You were willing to sacrifice yourself to save someone, someone who isn't even your responsibility."

"What's that got to do with anything?"

"A great deal. I think the High Council will consider that sufficient proof of where you belong. And I'm certain your examiner will submit a very favourable report."

"Examiner?" Thren was so shocked he nearly fell out of the sky. *Hold the phone, lady.* You never mentioned any examiner."

"Of course there's an examiner." Tor smiled complacently. "You can't take a test without someone there to test you."

Thren glared at her as realisation dawned. "It's you, isn't it? Of all the sneaky, low down ...Why didn't you warn me? If I'd known ..."

Tor interrupted him. "I wasn't allowed to tell you."

"That's no excuse. Anyway," he added sadly, "I still don't see how you can say I passed the test when somebody died."

Tor looked at him wonderingly, shaking her head. "You still don't get it, do you? The things that happened weren't the test. He would never have allowed any of that to happen to people just to test you. He cares about them too much. What happened happened because the rules got broken, because people made mistakes. Your test was how you dealt with it. Whether or not you learned to care."

"And I passed?"

"Eventually. It seems He was right to have faith in you after all."

Thren blushed so warmly that even his wings took on a pinkish glow. He was filled with an incredible sense of relief at the thought of not being sent into The Darkness, not having to turn into a demon like Dross – Temporalus. Strange to think that creature had once been his best, his only friend, although sadly Thren realised that he and Temporalus had never really been friends at all. He could see that now he understood what real friendship was. The thought amazed him. Was that what he felt? Not just for Tor but for Dudley, Bex and the others. Surely he couldn't be friends with humans? 'Nah, that can't be right.' Thren pushed the thought away.

***

When the angels returned to the cathedral the others were still in the nave. Watching from the shadows, Thren and Tor paused for a moment before approaching them. "They think it's over, don't they?" Thren whispered to Tor.

"It's never over," she replied. "That's why they need us."

***

Dudley was staring sadly down at Mark's body. It was in a terrible state, so he fetched an altar cloth and laid it gently over the dead boy, before going off to phone the police. What he really wanted was a nice cup of tea, but he supposed it would have to wait until later. He sighed, suddenly feeling very old.

Paul was sitting on the edge of a pew, trying to stop his legs shaking. Now it was all over he was starting to go into shock. He could hardly believe what had happened. *He* had stood up to a demon.

Bex was kneeling on the floor beside Flint, trying to explain what had happened as clearly as she could remember it. There was no point in trying to keep secrets now, but there was so much she didn't understand that it made explanations difficult.

Flint's throat was hurting where Mark had tried to throttle him, and his nose bled from being punched, but apart from that things weren't too bad. Nobody had mentioned anything about his brother yet. He wasn't sure what to make of that, but he was grateful for it. Grateful, too, that they still seemed to be treating him normally.

Of course, there was the small matter of his world turning upside down. He'd managed to accept the idea of a demon – well, something evil, anyway, but now he had to make room in his mind for *angels*. Actual angels with wings and robes – or in Tor's case, jeans and jacket. Weird. Almost as strange was the fact that Paul had turned up out of nowhere and seemed to know what to do to defeat the creature.

They looked at Paul, still sitting on his own, unsure what to do next. Bex waved him over, and he came shyly across to join them.

"How did you know what to do to the demon?" asked Flint, almost accusingly.

"I spent the afternoon in the library," said Paul apologetically.

"The place has its uses after all," joked Flint weakly.

"I just looked up anything I could think of," explained Paul. "Vampires, demons, imps, anything really. I wasn't sure what we were dealing with ... apart from the angels, and they were on our side."

"You knew about them?" asked Flint. "No, don't tell

me. You can see them too?"

"Only a little," said Paul. "But I can sort of sense them."

"Well, you shouldn't be able to," said Tor crossly, appearing beside them. "Nobody should. I don't know what's going on round here." She glared at Thren accusingly. "These things have only started happening since you came down."

"Well, don't look at me. It's not *all* my fault," said Thren, "so quit trying to blame me for everything."

"Do you two ever stop arguing?" said Bex. "You're like a couple of kids."

"Sorry, Bex," said Tor.

"Yeah, me too," nodded Thren sheepishly.

Flint looked at his friend in amazement. Not only did angels exist but Bex was telling them off. The world was a whole lot stranger than he'd ever imagined.

"You can say that again," said Thren, who'd suddenly known what Flint was thinking.

"I didn't say anything," said Flint defensively.

"You didn't have to," said Thren. They stared at each other, aware for a brief moment of what the other was thinking – probably because they were both thinking the same thing.

'What on earth am I doing getting mixed up in all this? I don't *do* friendship. I never wanted to get involved with people.'

"Sorry, Flint," said Thren, "But it's *way* too late to be thinking like that. You already *are* involved, we both are." A horrified look crossed Thren's face. "I don't *believe* I just said that."